SAMVIDA AND THE PURSE OF GOLD

PATERSON LOARN

Samvida and the Purse of Gold is a work of fiction. Names, characters, business, events and incidents are the products of the author's imagination. Any resemblance to actual persons, living or dead, or actual events is purely coincidental.

1

Cascais, Portugal
April 1991

Two children were playing on a private beach. The bronzed four year old boy ran up and down so fast the nanny had trouble keeping up with him. The girl was just old enough to stand up on her own. Every time she flopped down on to the rug she giggled and her blonde curls bobbed up and down. From time to time the boy hunkered down beside the baby and gave her a toy.

'Aren't they sweet together?' Frankie said to Teddy.

The brother and sister sat beside the pool of the Edeldico beach house, sipping cocktails from glasses topped up by a waiter. The patio was decorated with flowers and fairy lights, and parrots chattered from an aviary. Frankie was elegant in the way of women who enjoy unlimited wealth and leisure. Teddy was wiry and tanned from working out of doors in the sun.

When the boy scampered too close to the baby Teddy sprang to his feet. 'Careful, Em! You're kicking sand in Nina's eyes.'

The little boy burst into tears, ran to his father and clasped him around the knees.

'Don't stress, Teddy,' said Frankie. 'There's no harm done. Cheer up, Em.'

Em stopped crying and settled down to build a sand castle. When he'd finished Nina demolished his creation with chubby hands.

Frankie put down her glass. 'You've been a bundle of nerves ever since you got here. What's the matter?'

'I'm worried about Ana. She thinks she's being followed.'

'By whom?'

'Those guys who want to buy Estancia Arcanjo.'

'Don't let her drag you into her mess,' said Frankie. 'She shouldn't have got herself involved with the protests.'

Teddy sighed. 'Sis, that ranch has been in her family for over two hundred years.'

Frankie ran her fingers through her hair. 'Urban says the only way to make money from Estancia Arcanjo is to cut down the trees.'

'Sounds like Urban,' said Teddy grimly.

'Hush,' said Frankie. 'Here's Pedro with the pitcher.'

The waiter refreshed their drinks, then went to fetch the beach umbrella. The maid picked up the baby and carried her indoors. Em helped out by gathering the toys together in the rug and dragging it into the house.

'It must be time for the children's supper,' said Frankie. 'Our dinner will be ready soon. I hope it's lobster. Chef's a genius with lobster.'

'Will Urban be joining us?'

'He had to dash back to London to complete a deal. He should be back in time to say goodbye to you and Em. When are you going back to Brazil?'

'Friday. Ana's arranged a protest rally for the weekend. I want to be there.'

'Don't go,' said Frankie. 'Stay with us. There are so many trees in Brazil, I'm sure nobody will miss a few. And Urban says protesting is dangerous. Apparently people have been killed.'

Em ran on to the deck in his pyjamas. Teddy caught up with him just in time to stop him opening the catch on the aviary door. Frankie pulled Em on to her knee.

'Come to auntie, darling. You like the birdies, don't you?'

When Em replied in Portuguese Teddy looked nervously at Frankie.

'Teddy, are you and Ana living in a hut in the forest?'

'Not all of the time. We're often at our apartment in the city.'

'Then why did your son just tell me that birds like these live in the trees near his house?'

'Hush,' said Teddy. 'Here's Maria.'

The maid was carrying Nina and a bottle. Frankie put Em down and took the baby. Em climbed on to Teddy's knee. While Nina sucked contentedly they played at wrestling.

'We'll miss you two when you're gone,' said Frankie.

'Doesn't it bother you that Urban's away so much?'

'Not at all. He takes care of business. I take care of Nina and our homes. As you can see, we want for nothing.'

A young man in swim trunks strode out of the house with a towel slung over his shoulder. When Teddy stood up to greet the newcomer, Em cowered behind his father.

'Evening Luc,' said Frankie. 'Will you be joining us for dinner?'

'No,' said Luc. 'I'm going for a swim. Where's my uncle?'

'In London.'

'Hi Luc,' said Teddy. 'Good to see you again.'

Ignoring Teddy and Em, Luc bent to kiss his aunt's cheek.

3

Then he dropped his towel on a lounger and strode towards the sea.

'I apologize for Luc's moodiness. It's understandable. He hasn't come to terms with losing his mother.'

Teddy said, 'I suppose he's going to follow Urban into the firm?'

'I believe that's the plan.'

Frankie stood up and carried Nina to Teddy for a kiss. The baby patted his face. 'She's beautiful,' he said.

'So is Em. And he's very clever.'

'Frankie, If anything happens to Ana and me, will you take care of Em?'

Shocked, Frankie looked up at her brother. 'Surely it's not that bad?'

'Do you promise, sis?'

'I swear I'll take care of Em if anything happens to you. When Urban gets back I'll tell him you asked us to be Em's guardians. I'm sure he'll agree. Maria! Pedro! Please put the children to bed.'

2

The Penthouse, Docklands
March 2013

Samvida

When I returned to the Penthouse after my husband's funeral, all the servants I knew had gone. Even poor old Maria and Pedro had retired to Portugal. Some bean counter at Edeldico had replaced them with agency staff. The new housekeepers and I avoided each other. They polished the antique furniture, wiped the glass walls and kept the pantry stocked with ready meals. I lay on the chaise longue where Urban and I used to make love in the afternoons, drinking wine and listening to sad songs. This stand-off continued until a new maid came to work at the Pent-house. Katya was older and more thoughtful than the others. She made time to prepare fresh food for me. I had no appetite but I was grateful for her kindness. One day she made me a perfect

Caesar salad. When she saw I hadn't touched it she folded her arms across her chest and swore in her own language.

'Madam,' she said, 'You have to eat.'

I propped myself up on my elbows. 'Please call me Vida. Everyone else does. When you say "Madam" I look around for my mother.'

'Where is your mother? Why don't you go to her? Maybe she can make you eat something.'

'Mum and Dad are on an adult gap year. They're in Costa Rica, saving sea turtles.'

'Have you no other family?'

'Only my brother Gus. He's at boarding school.'

'After my sister's husband died she wrote letters to him. She used to write about the happy memories the shared. She said it eased her pain.'

'I couldn't do that even if I wanted to. I don't have enough memories of Urban,' I said bitterly. 'We were together for such a short time. It isn't fair.'

'Life is not fair, Miss Vida. Your husband left you wealthy. Many widows are poor. My sister can only afford to eat meat once a week, but you own this superb apartment. Look around you and be thankful.'

I could see most of the master suite from my chaise longue. What I saw didn't make me feel thankful. For a start, the Penthouse didn't belong to Urban. He'd bought it through his firm, Edeldico, as an investment when Docklands was being developed. His first wife, Frankie, chose the decor. She sadly died of cancer ten years before Urban and I met. Since then not much had changed in the Penthouse. The exception was the master bedroom, which Urban had redecorated at enormous expense. It was supposed to be my wedding present, but I didn't like the ornate fabrics and dull colours his designer selected. Urban also hired a personal shopper to buy suitable clothes for me to wear in my new role as his wife. He knew I was a jeans and jumper kind of girl, and he didn't want me to show him up. When we returned from our honeymoon in the Maldives, thousands of pounds worth of outfits were waiting for me in my walk-in wardrobe. I didn't like those either. Until Katya told me to look around, it had never occurred to me to question any of Urban's decisions. For the first time I felt oppressed by the choices he'd made.

'This stuff is bringing me down,' I said. 'Please take it away.'

'Yes Miss. I will have it put in the store,' said Katya.

'No, don't do that. It'll be of no use to anyone, hidden away in the basement. I want you to have everything in the master suite.'

Katya's eyes widened. 'Why, Miss Vida?'

'Because I don't want it. And you've been kind to me.'

'I only tried to feed you. Anyone would do the same. There are high value items here. Are you sure they are yours to give?'

'They belonged to Urban, so they must be mine now. And I want to give them away.'

'Even the jewels?'

'Especially the jewels. I hate them. They're so heavy. And they're fakes. The real ones are stored in the EdeldiCo vaults. Take them, Katya. Take them and use them to help your sister.'

'Thank you, Miss Vida,' Katya said doubtfully. 'I'm very grateful, and my sister will be too. But you must sign a paper or there will be trouble. One minute, please.'

The maid hurried out of the room. She quickly returned with a housekeeping form which I signed without reading. Then she began to open drawers and inspect the contents of cupboards. Our conversation had exhausted me, so I lay down on the chaise-longue to rest. Soon I was fast asleep.

I woke up in the dark, feeling feverish. I threw off the blanket

Katya had tucked around me and went to lean my forehead on the glass wall. The sky was so thick with rain and sleet it was like looking through the bottom of a glass. Twenty floors down, the street lights of Docklands seemed to waver in the gloom. To take my mind off my loneliness I decided to try Katya's sister's idea of writing down happy memories. That's why I did something I'd never have dared to do when Urban was alive. I sat down at his desk and rummaged in it for a pen and paper. I was surprised by the mess I found. The first thing to catch my eye among outdated reports and torn receipts was a flyer for a cheap eatery. It looked as if Arlo's Café had been one of Edeldico's development prospects. Urban's world revolved around property deals. Even on that nightmare day in October 2012, I'd had to compete for his attention. It was my first time in Lisbon. I wanted to go sightseeing, but Urban had planned a full day of meetings at his regional office. For him it was one more business trip.

He had one more day to live.

———

Portugal
October 2012

'There's our guy,' said Urban, as we walked into Arrivals at Lisbon airport. He was waving to a burly man in a green uniform. The chauffeur stood to attention, took off his peaked cap and inclined his bald head. His gesture was somewhere between a bow and a salute.

'Welcome to Lisbon, Mr. and Mrs Edeldi,' he said. His English was fluent but heavily accented.

'Morning Raul,' said Urban. 'Estou feliz pore star de volta. Vida, I told him it's good to be back.'

Raul drove us to the offices of Edeldico Portugal, where a young man hurried out to greet us. He gave Urban a royal welcome, but I was left to follow three steps behind. I caught Raul looking sideways at me. It was a calculating look, as if he knew something I didn't. In the foyer, a manager nervously handed a folder to Urban. An irritated expression crossed his face, contorting the pale scar on his forehead.

'This will take hours, Vida. Would you like our driver to escort you to the mall?'

I didn't want to be left alone with Raul, who gave me the shivers.

'No thank you. I'm not in the mood for shopping. I'd rather wait here.'

Someone guided me to a cubicle and placed a latte and a selection of English magazines by my side. I looked up to see a receptionist giving me a cheesy smile. Under her arm she held a photograph album.

'I hope I'm not disturbing you, Mrs. Edeldi,' she began. The way she pronounced my name was sarcastic, as if she was hinting that it wasn't mine. The coverage of my wedding in the gossip magazines was fabulous, she said. Her team had compiled the best images to show clients. She was so convincing I felt touched. I was flicking through the pages when she made a speech that cut me to the quick.

'All of us at EdeldiCo Portugal are delighted for Mr. Edeldi. He was lonely for a long time after Mrs. Edeldi passed away. We called her A Primeira Dama, because she was our First Lady. She often visited us, with dear little Nina. A Primeira Dama spoke excellent Portuguese. May I fetch you another coffee, Miss? Sorry, Madam.'

The receptionist's tone was so spiteful I wondered if she had a crush on Urban. I tried to put the idea that he might have had a fling with her in the ten years when he was single out of my mind.

'No thanks. I'm good,' I said, handing back her album.

After Urban joined me I pushed the door shut with my foot. 'Why didn't you tell me Frankie and Nina used to come here with you?'

Being married to someone ultra-wealthy is like having a super-power. You can ruin someone's life with a single word. When Urban asked who had upset me, I didn't tell him about the receptionist's patronising speech. She'd made me angry, but I didn't want her to lose her job.

'It was just an idea that occurred to me while I was waiting for you,' I said.

'You think too much, Vida. You should have gone to the mall.'

'I can't spend my whole life shopping.'

'Why not? Lots of women do. Frankie did. Look, I'm a busy man. You can't expect me to mention every detail of my life I met you, any more than you can describe every day of your past life to me.'

'You have twenty-five years more past than I do. And the staff here know everything about it.'

Urban laughed. 'That's what they think.'

I said, 'It was the same in Milan and Vienna. I had to sit and wait for you, while everyone in the office compared me to Frankie. You have no idea how difficult it is to be a second wife.'

'I'm sorry you feel that way. I tell you what, I'll postpone this afternoon's meetings. Raul can drive us down the coast to Cascais.'

That's when I asked the fatal question.

'Why can't we take the train, like real folks?'

I'd dozed off with my head on Urban's desk. When I woke up rain was falling and the sunshine of Portugal seemed very far away. For the first time in days I wanted to be clean. Under the shower I dragged product through my hair and coaxed out the knots. I was sitting at the dressing table wrapped in a robe when my step-daughter Nina let herself in. She was wearing a black top and jeans - her uniform when she helps out at Willa's Salon - and her blonde curls were piled so high she had to duck through the door frame. Although not many young women would welcome a stepmother only three years older than themselves, Nina and I had got on well from the start.

'Hi little momma,' said Nina. 'Are you okay?'

'I'm fine,' I said. 'How was the hen party?'

'Like all the others.' Nina hugged me. 'You smell nice. And you're smiling! That's great, because I want you to look confident for your meeting with my tight-fisted cousin.'

I'd forgotten Nina persuaded me to talk to Urban's nephew about my inheritance. 'I don't want to discuss anything with Lucan.'

'You have to. He's the new CEO. You won't get the money Dad left you until Luc signs it off.'

'I don't care about the money. I loved your Dad for himself.'

Nina said, 'I know. But even neo-hippies like you can't live on air.'

She advised me to take my phone and passport, because she thought I might need them for legal purposes. I chose a navy blue suit with a plain white shirt and low heeled black courts, and threw last season's light blue trench over them. After the concierge buzzed to let us know a car had arrived to take me to Edeldico HQ, Nina kept me company in the elevator.

'I'm going home to have a nap,' she said as she waved me off. 'But I'll be back this evening to find out how your meeting with Luc went.'

3

Edeldico HQ
Archy

The new CEO sauntered into Archy's office, took possession of the guest chair and crossed one perfectly tailored leg over the other. 'How's your day been so far, Brise?'

That morning Archy had found himself alone in the elevator. Edeldico shared the building with several other firms, so this was a rare event. For once he was not surrounded by eyes he had to catch or avoid. This unexpected whiff of freedom inspired him to go on a small adventure. He had worked for Edeldico on and off for eight years, starting in his university vacations. In all that time he had never visited the roof garden. When he took a break from his screens he preferred to grab a coffee in one of the city squares, but recently he had read a report which aroused his curiosity. Consultants brought in to improve the garden were recommending a vegetable patch and a mini-orchard with apple and pear trees. Best of all, beehives would be installed. The idea of honey bees flying high above the city appealed to his imagination.

Acting on impulse, Archy hit the top button.

He left the elevator on the thirty-third floor and climbed an open metal staircase to the deserted garden. Stacks of concrete slabs had already been lifted and the vegetable beds were ready for planting. There were no beehives as yet, but in a sheltered corner tree saplings were huddled against the wall. When Archy realised the walkway went all around the top of the building, he undid the buttons on his overcoat and strolled round twice. The views over London were so stunning he hardly noticed the wintry weather.

It had been an enjoyable half hour, but not one Lucan Edeldi needed to know about. 'Everything's good, sir. Would you like an update on my current projects?'

'No. I want to discuss a more urgent matter. One with potential to affect the future of Edeldico.'

The CEO's tone of voice was ominous. Archy braced himself for trouble. He was aware that the new boss disliked him. Lucan's uncle, Urban Edeldi, had chosen Archy for an internship over the heads of dozens of eager graduates who were hammering on the firm's door. The other candidates had attended more prestigious universities and came from families who could afford to bankroll them, but Archy led the pack from the start. Once the young graduate had demonstrated his natural ability and drive, Urban began to give him preferential treatment. When opportunities came Archy's way he grabbed them with both hands. Thanks to Urban's mentoring and his own relentless hard work, his rise within the organisation had been meteoric. Inevitably, some colleagues felt challenged by his success. Lucan was one of them.

Six months previously, Urban's sudden death had upset the

balance of power at Edeldico. As his uncle's natural successor, Lucan had seized control. Potentially this had spelt disaster for Archy, but he was outstandingly good at what he did, and it was not in his nature to give up without a fight. While he was mourning his mentor he plotted ways to get on the right side of the new CEO. Colleagues higher up the food chain complained that Lucan was impossible to read. 'You knew where you were with Urban, but Lucan's a weirdo,' executives whispered in the wash-room. Archy had ignored Lucan's detractors so completely that office gossip labelled him the CEO's bitch. He didn't care. His game plan for reaching the top of the financial dunghill was to hang on tight to the tail feathers of the cock already crowing at the summit. Lucan Edeldi was that cock.

Lucan leaned over to inspect the framed photographs on Archy's desk. His obsession with family pictures was well known. Multiple professional portraits of his aristocratic wife and well groomed children were on display in the executive suite. Behind his back, Edeldico gossip said that because Lady Willa was always abroad on business and their two boys were away at boarding school, he needed decent pictures to remind himself what they looked like. Looking at his own treasured snaps through the eyes of his boss, Archy was embarrassed to realise how shabby they were.

'What's going on in this one? Basketball? I was a rugger man myself.'

'Those guys were on my team at uni. We topped the league that year.'

'Who's that? Is she your girlfriend?'

'Ex. We were both into extreme sports, but it turned out we didn't have much else in common. I kept that pic because we'd just climbed the rock face in the background. You can see five counties from the top.'

Lucan turned away from the photos and gazed in silence at the rain running down the glass wall. Archy saw this as a sign of disapproval and his heart beat faster. At last the CEO coughed, as if difficult words were sticking in his throat and threatening to choke him.

'Brise, in the past you and I haven't seen eye to eye. I hope we can put our differences behind us, because I need your help.'

The young financier breathed a sigh of relief. This was an outcome beyond his wildest dreams. 'You can rely on my support, sir.'

'It's six months since Urban passed away. As you can imagine, my family and I miss him terribly,'

Archy had overheard discreet exchanges which suggested that taking over as CEO had consoled Lucan for the loss of his uncle. Nevertheless, he nodded sympathetically.

'We're all grieving, but Urban's widow seems unable to cope with her loss. She mopes around the Penthouse and eats next to nothing. In my opinion, her behaviour is ridiculous. I mean, they were married for less than a year. You can hardly call it a marriage. I genuinely believe the girl isn't in her right mind. I intend to put pressure on her to pull herself together. Then we can pay her off and get on with business.'

Archy couldn't believe his luck. Vida, the temp who had married the CEO, was a legend at Edeldico, and this was his chance to meet her. 'No problem, sir. Send over the pre-nup and the will and I'll get on it.'

'Unfortunately it's not that simple. For a start, here was no pre-nup. Although Urban was marrying a girl half his age, apparently it never crossed his mind to get one. As for his will, because Edeldico owns multiple properties across Europe and South America we met with all kinds of delays and complications in setting it up. These difficulties were never resolved.'

Archy could hardly believe his ears. 'Let me get this straight, sir. Edeldico has assets worth many millions. Your uncle founded it as a family firm and managed it until the time of his death. Are you telling me that he died intestate, shortly after remarrying?'

'That's the bones of it. When he married Vida, Urban had no legal will.'

'With respect, sir, why was this allowed to happen?'

'I was doing my best to sort out the legal tangles when Urban told me he was engaged. I begged him to postpone the wedding, but he ignored all my warnings.'

'So, as his legal wife, Mrs. Edeldi can claim ownership of Edeldico?'

'Not all of it. I own a substantial number of shares and so does Urban's daughter Nina. Don't look so judgmental, Brise. It wasn't my fault. My uncle was fifty and apparently in perfect health. He must have thought he was immortal. Sadly, as we now know, he only had months left to live.'

First and foremost, Archy was a professional. He knew what he could achieve and what was beyond him. Immediately he realised this task was beyond his knowledge and abilities. 'I'm not the right person for this job, sir. I advise you to seek specialised legal advice.'

When Lucan rose to his feet, Archy politely did the same. The two men glared at each other with their faces only inches apart. In spite of being on the wrong side of forty, Lucan was as tall as Archy and almost as athletic in appearance. The expression on his face was so aggressive the younger man found himself backing away. When Lucan realised Archy was in retreat, he reached out and flicked the end of his nose with one finger. This apparently playful gesture reminded Archy of the immense power Lucan had over his career prospects.

'You've got it wrong, Brise. Urban's negligence created an

unorthodox situation, therefore we'll have to use unorthodox methods to resolve it. You're the best man to do this, because of your outstanding business brain. In spite of our differences, I must admit you're one of the most astute financiers I've worked with.'

'It's good of you to say so, sir.'

'What's more, your personal presentation is impeccable. I've always said you can't beat bespoke tailoring. A quality hand-made suit establishes a man's status before he opens his mouth. And although I'm not a fan of the shaved head look, I must admit it helps you to blend in with a wide range of communities.'

'Thank you sir. I promise I'll do whatever I can to help Mrs Edeldi.'

'You don't work for Vida. I'm the one who's calling the shots. You have two days to draw up a letter of agreement. Draft it yourself, and make sure it's watertight. We usually run these things past our legal nerds, but this time I want you to give them a miss. They may not appreciate the sensitivity of the situation.'

Write a letter of agreement in two days? Make it watertight, without legal checks? Alarm bells rang in Archy's head. He decided to ignore them. He'd seen enough of Edeldico's tame lawyers to know their priority was to stay on the right side of the boardroom.

'What sort of agreement? And with whom?'

'The agreement is between myself, acting for EdeldiCo, and Mrs Vida Edeldi. She doesn't know it yet, but she's going to give up her claim to her late husband's property. Leave that side of it to me.'

'You'll be asking her to sign away millions. What will she receive in return?'

'I'll give her enough to live on until she finds another sugar daddy. And there's something else I want you to do, Brise. My cousin Nina has persuaded Vida to meet with me to discuss the situation. I want you to collect her at the service entrance and bring her to the meeting pod on Floor Six. Is that clear?'

'Yes, sir.'

'And don't say a word about it to anyone.'

'No, sir.'

Lucan paused in the doorway. 'Get rid of those photos, Brise,' he said. 'They make you look like a loser. Why not frame up a shot of yourself with your parents?'

Archy was left feeling humiliated and confused. The CEO's unexpected request for help had turned his world upside down. It seemed like years since his carefree walk around the roof garden. Only one thing was clear in his mind. He had to get hold of a family portrait. After checking that no-one was within earshot, he called his contact at a photographic agency.

'Hi. I need an image from stock. A mixed race family group, taken around the Millennium, including a pre-teen boy. No, it's not for publication.'

4

Cascais, Portugal
October 2012

Samvida

I didn't tell Urban the receptionist at Edeldico Portugal had disrespected me. He'd have dismissed her on the spot. It would have been selfish and immature of me to have the woman sacked, so I vented my anger on him instead. To cheer me up he offered to ask our chauffeur to drive us to the seaside, but I refused. I didn't want to go anywhere in creepy Raul's black limo.

'Please sir, allow me to drive you there. É o meu trabalho,' said Raul.

'I know driving is your job,' said Urban. 'You're Edeldico's most trusted chauffeur. However, my wife wants to experience the joys of everyday life in Portugal. We'll be travelling to Cascais by train, so please drop us at Cais du Sodre. You can take the rest of the day off.'

Before Urban set him straight about who was the boss, Raul had been giving me scornful looks. Now he hated me. He'd stopped complaining, but I could tell from the back of his head that he was furious. I enjoyed watching his ears become redder and redder while he drove us to the station. It was a minor victory, but one I'd soon regret. By the time we reached Cais du Sodre Urban had begun to enjoy himself. He marched towards the station waving his arms and enthusing about the building's Art Deco frontage. I couldn't resist glancing back over my shoulder at Raul. He'd parked in a taxi rank and was leaning against the limo with a stunned expression on his face. I was surprised to see how devastated he looked by our decision to leave him in Lisbon.

In the crowded train Urban found us window seats. He took off his navy silk tie and stowed it in my bag before loosening the collar of his matching shirt. We'd hoped to pass as an ordinary Portuguese couple on a day out, but that was never going to happen. All the other passengers were staring at our expensive linen suits. I refused to allow them to embarrass me. In spite of the fortune we carried on our backs, I was determined to enjoy a simple trip to the seaside with my husband. At Belem the train passed a ship carved from stone, with statues of sailors gazing out over the water. Urban told me it was created to celebrate explorers from hundreds of years ago. He talked about them sailing away in little wooden ships, in a gamble to find gold. I asked him if the risk they took paid off. He thought for a minute before he replied.

'The king of Portugal backed a speculative venture and won Brazil. I call that a decent profit on his outlay.'

I said, 'The king didn't risk his own life.'

Urban changed the subject. 'Vida darling, look how the sunlight is shining on the sea. I wish we were on the water right now. We must bring the yacht down here next summer.'

The train stopped at villages with names that sounded like bad fairies from a movie. The stations of Alcantara, Caxias and Carcavello were splashed with vivid graffiti. The train took us within yards of a string of beaches. Couples soaked up late rays and children splashed through the shallows of the Atlantic. On the promenades, cyclists dodged dogs and their walkers. Clothes and bedlinen were airing on the balconies of terracotta apartments. Heat radiated through the train windows and bounced off the warm bodies surrounding us. I'd been over-excited all day, first of all about my trip to Lisbon and later over my treatment at Edeldico Portugal. I hadn't made time to eat and drink. A slight headache warned me I was dehydrating. My hair glued itself to my sweaty face while I hunted in my bag for something cooling. I found perfume but no water. I hadn't packed any because I didn't think I'd need it. In the world I shared with Urban there was always a waiter with a cold drink on a tray.

'We'll have a bite to eat before we explore,' said Urban. 'I know my way around the town. Edeldico used to keep a house on the beach. There were a few decent restaurants.'

At last the train pulled into Cascais. Urban put his arm around my shoulders to support me while we walked the short distance from the station to the promenade. The wavy pattern of the street paving made my head swim. The bright colours of the houses lining the lanes, the blue tiles and the courtyard gardens full of exotic plants whirled before my eyes like fragments in a kaleidoscope. At last he said, 'This one will do. The customers look like locals. That's always a good sign.'

The restaurant Urban chose was in a busy pedestrian street, squeezed between a private house and a souvenir shop. Pots of red flowers lined the pavement. From my seat I glimpsed the beach a few hundred yards away. Urban slipped a few euros to the waiter, who gave us a table distant from the kitchens and close to the flowers. Across from us a party of Englishmen on a stag do were knocking back beers. Urban sat facing me with his back to a group of Portuguese business people. Menus appeared with bottled water. The food smelled delicious. I began to feel better.

'There are healthy options for you, Vida. Sumos naturais, sumos detox. What would you like to drink?'

I'd been scolding Urban about his sugar intake. 'I'll have a detox juice. So will you.'

To serve us the waiter had to dodge around tables pushed together for a birthday party. On the table was a cake with 80 written on it in colourful icing. A crowd of old people were laughing and joking together. More guests kept arriving. Chairs were fetched. Urban ordered for both of us.

'Dois aipo, maca and gengibre, ovos mexidos.'

'Vida darling,' said Urban, 'What do you think of those artworks?'

'I see no artworks,' I said.

'Look again sweetheart. They're created from flotsam washed up by the sea.'

Nearby there was an outdoor exhibition of sculptures made from plastic containers, driftwood, lengths of rope and other trash. To me they looked like the contents of a recyling bin. I said, 'They're not my kind of thing.'

'Mine neither,' he said. 'But after lunch I'm going to buy some.'

I didn't like the idea. 'I hope you're not going to put them in the Penthouse.'

'Of course not. They're exactly the kind of thing I want to display at Edeldico HQ. We've been looking out for a concrete way to demonstrate our firm's commitment to environmental issues.'

'Since when was Edeldico interested in the environment?'

'We care about climate change, the rain forests and so on.'

'I worked there for six months, and this is the first I've heard of it.'

Urban smiled his slow sweet smile, the one that lit up his hazel eyes a moment too late. 'Darling, you and I have so much to learn about each other. I'm looking forward to getting to know you better.'

The drinks turned out to be apple and ginger tisanes sprinkled with celery leaves. Urban stirred his with a spoon and reached for the sugar bowl. I covered it with my hand, but he insisted on spooning the white crystals into his tall glass cup.

'I'll need a sugar rush later, when we get a room,' he said. 'As you so kindly reminded me this morning, I'm twice your age. It takes more than rabbit food to feed my passion.'

Crash! The deafening burst of sound came from close by. Urban's hand flew to his heart. Then he stood up, seized my wrist and pulled me to my feet. I was dragged behind him while he pushed and shoved his way towards the exit.

A waiter stood in our way. 'Sir, madam, your meal is ready.'

Plates of eggs with salad had appeared on our table. A waiter was picking knives and forks from between the feet of grumbling Portuguese pensioners and replacing them on a metal tray.

'A tray drop. Is nothing. Sit down, enjoy your meal,' the waiter said.

We returned to the table with downcast eyes, trying to avoid the amused glances from other diners. After that everything seemed normal, but Urban's mood had changed. Warily he peered sideways at the stag party, then over my shoulder at the booted and suited business types.

He said, 'Do you mind if we swap seats? I want to watch the entrance.'

Although it meant I lost my view to the sea, I gave up my seat to him. I tried to revive the carefree mood of a few minutes earlier by ordering a margarita, but Urban refused to join me. Instead he added sugar to my tisane and swallowed it along with his own. This annoyed me, so I stopped trying to make conversation. In silence we nibbled our spicy Mexican eggs.

At the next table, the white-haired birthday boy blew out candles and his elderly friends sang 'Happy Birthday' in Portuguese. I sang with them in English. After that I couldn't stay angry. I turned to my husband with a smile. His face was as white as a sheet and the knife and fork shook in his hands. He saw me and he didn't. His mind was in another place. He was breathing in short pants and his voice was slurred when he gasped, 'Frankie....' It was the first time he'd called me by her name.

Something was terribly wrong. With a pounding heart I cried out for help, but the birthday party were cutting the cake and the uproar drowned my voice. When I scanned the street leading to the train station I saw someone wearing a chauffeur's cap and jacket. It was Raul. He'd driven to Cascais in spite of Urban's orders. I'd never been so glad to see anyone. I beckoned urgently to him and he raced towards me.

During the few seconds it took the chauffeur to reach us, Urban's eyes had become glassy and his breath had begun to grate. He tried to stand up but a seizure overcame him. Raul flung his arms around his master's waist. I clasped my husband's hands. They were as cold as stone. Raul and I half-dragged Urban, who was stumbling on helpless feet, out of the restaurant. His arm, once so protective, was a dead weight on my shoulder. His limbs flailed, knocking over clay pots which split on the pavement, spilling bright flowers. Chairs and tables toppled over. Waiters and customers reacted to our desperate dash. Some cleared the debris to make way for us. Others froze in horror. Urban's mouth gaped and dribbled and his eyes were dull. He was struggling to breathe but he was still with me. I sensed his soundless plea for help. I don't know how we made it to the car, but it must have been through some heroic strength of Raul's or miraculous effort of my own. We flew down the motorway towards Edeldico's private clinic. Urban was convulsing in my arms. I welded my dry lips to his blue ones, straining to lock life into his body.

The odour of death filled the limousine.

5

Edeldico HQ service entrance
Archy

Lucan's orders had been crystal clear. He wanted his meeting with Urban's young widow to be top secret. That was why Archy was lurking among the rubbish bins at the service entrance. Vida was not due to arrive for another half hour, but he dared not risk being late to welcome her and escort her to Lucan. He was also keeping a lookout for stray smokers, although at two in the afternoon, most of his colleagues were at their desks. Archy was not taking any chances. If someone recognised Lucan's glamorous guest and spread the word, it would be a personal disaster for him. As requested by Lucan he'd drafted a letter of agreement between Edeldico and Vida, without consulting the legal department. He sincerely hoped the document would satisfy both parties, because the sooner it was signed, the sooner he could forget his clash with Lucan. Archy had become accustomed to the cut and thrust of the business world, but the CEO's bullying was in a different league. Lucan had begun his attack by softening him up with flattery, then a few minutes later he had called him a loser. Coming from the man who controlled his future this was devastating to Archy's confidence. But it was Lucan's scorn for his photos that hurt him most.

For Archy, university had been a revelation. At boarding school he was too different from the other boys to bond with them, but he fitted in well with fellow students on his East London campus. The three years he spent there had been the happiest of his life, but after graduation the friendship group which had been so vital to his self-respect broke up. Archy chose the safe option – a job with Edeldico and a funded MBA – while his cheerful, fun-loving basketball team and the bright, sporty girls he used to date scattered to the corners of the earth. They kept in touch on social media, but clicks on the thumbs up icon gave no clues to what was going on in their hearts and minds.

'I bet Emma hasn't got a photo of me on her desk,' Archy said to the nearest dustbin. 'And Leon and Kai have probably forgotten they ever played basketball. Maybe Lucan was right, and I am a loser.'

He forced himself to concentrate on the job in hand. Although Archy had never met Vida he was disturbed by Lucan's callous remarks about her response to bereavement. The poor woman was obviously having a breakdown, and instead of offering her help and support Lucan was making her suffer for a failure of management which was largely his own fault. Previously Archy had been unaware of the conflict between Urban's wife and the nephew who was also his business partner. Now he recalled an intriguing piece of gossip. According to the Edeldico grapevine, it all kicked off when Urban hosted a drinks party at the firm's penthouse. The event was popular with clients and more guests than expected had turned up. Lucan was detained at

HQ by a phone call from Panama, so he arrived late and in a bad mood. By then the waiters were overwhelmed and Vida was helping out by taking a tray round. When she approached Lucan to offer him a drink he refused angrily. His eyes were fixed on the string of real pearls around her neck.

'That necklace belongs to me. Hand it over,' said Lucan.

Vida tried to walk away, but Lucan took her arm and propelled her out on to the balcony. Someone overheard their conversation, which was carried on in angry whispers.

'Are you calling me a thief?'

'What am I supposed to think when I see you flaunting my late mother's necklace?'

'Urban says she left it to him.'

'He's mistaken. Mama left everything she owned to me. Hand over the necklace!'

'No way! You'll lock it up and no-one will ever see these lovely pearls again. I'm sure that isn't what your Mum would have wanted.'

'Don't you dare tell me what my own mother wanted!'

'I don't care what you say. I'm keeping the pearls.'

Once again Lucan took Vida's arm. He pushed her against the outer wall of the balcony and forced her into a corner. Then he hooked a finger under her necklace and pulled until the string broke. Precious pearls bounced off the ledge and fell all the way to the street. Passers-by twenty floors below watched them rain down from the sky and rattle off the pavement like hailstones.

That was not the end of the story. In an effort to keep the peace between his wife and his nephew, a few days later Urban presented the warring pair with valuable gifts. Lucan received a pair of antique cuff links that had belonged to his grandfather. Samvida was given a choker made of the best Brazilian emeralds. As for the pearls, they were never heard of again.

In Archy's opinion this episode helped to explain Lucan's attitude to Vida. Before Urban married her he had been a widower for a decade. By then Lucan had been Urban's heir apparent ever since he was in his teens. The sudden loss of influence over his uncle must have caused him pain. To make Lucan's situation worse, at the time everyone had expected Urban and Vida to have babies. The last thing Lucan wanted was a fertile young aunt whose children would deprive him of what he saw as his rightful inheritance. No wonder his nose had been put out of joint.

Now it occurred to Archy that there might be a darker reason for Lucan's hatred of Vida. The circumstances surrounding Urban's death were unclear. Throughout Edeldico's sphere of influence, a massive effort had been made to hush up the mystery. Archy had not yet seen a satisfactory explanation of why Urban, a fit man in early middle age who had recently passed a full medical with flying colours, had collapsed and died without warning. Within fifteen minutes of apparently suffering a heart attack, he was admitted to a clinic owned by EdeldiCo Portugal. No-one who knew Urban could understand why he had not survived and made a full recovery. But was Vida capable of murdering her husband? Archy thought not. By all accounts the couple had adored each other, in spite of the age gap of almost twenty-five years. What mattered was whether Lucan thought Vida was responsible for Urban's death.

When a mud-splashed SUV drew up at the kerb, Archy relegated all thoughts of murder to the back of his mind. The driver gave his passenger barely enough time to climb out safely before accelerating away. The young woman deposited unceremoniously on the pavement didn't react to the driver's behaviour. Like a nocturnal creature forced into daylight by real or imagined danger, Vida Edeldi blinked through her bedraggled dark curls with a stunned expression on her face. Archy tried not to stare at her, but it was difficult to resist. Vida had briefly worked at at Edeldico but their paths had never crossed, so this was the first time he'd met her in real life. He'd only seen the photographs of her wedding, which had been displayed at Edeldico HQ and shared online. In them Vida glowed with the kind of beauty which can only be conjured up by joy. Today, under a cold sky overcast with snow clouds, she looked frail and younger than her twenty-six years.

'Hello, Mrs Edeldi. I'm Archy Brise. Mr. Edeldi has asked me to welcome you. The circumstances of this meeting are rather unusual, but I assure you everyone at Edeldico wants you to feel safe and comfortable. I'm your guide for the day. Please follow me.'

Archy had said more than he intended - perhaps more than was wise - but he had no regrets. Vida did not reply, but she looked more relaxed and he thought he saw the ghost of a smile on her lips. After he hauled open the metal security gates she entered the building ahead of him. She was wearing a long blue coat and low heeled shoes. He couldn't help noticing the natural grace of her walk.

In silence the two of them passed through deserted maintenance zones, in and out of service lifts and past empty work stations. Soon after Urban's death all the equipment on Floor Six had been dismantled, in preparation for a refurbishment that had not yet been carried out. Weak daylight filtered through to the middle of the floor from distant wall to ceiling windows. Archy guided Samvida through a wilderness of upturned desks, loose carpet tiles and dangling wires. At the heart of this devastation a windowless meeting pod was being used for storage. Archy tapped lightly on its door.

'Enter,' said Lucan.

Flickering tube lights shone down from a low ceiling on to dusty stacks of furniture inside the pod. Archy was surprised to see that a state-of-the-art flat screen took up half of one wall. In a crooked swivel chair behind a cracked glass desk Lucan was waiting. A laptop was by his elbow.

'Take a seat, Vida.'

There was only one chair within reach. It was the basic stackable kind, made of plastic and metal tubes. The plastic was cracked and the bent legs were of uneven lengths. Archy expected Vida to ask for something more comfortable, but she didn't. Instead she waited for Archy to place the chair opposite Lucan and hold it ready for her. Then she sat down and tucked her bag under the seat. Archy felt angry and embarrassed on her behalf. This was no way to treat a relative who was also a shareholder. If Lucan's intention was to make his victim feel powerless and insignificant, he was going the right way about it. He was glad to see that the widow's dignity was unaffected. Vida sat on the broken office chair with the posture of a queen.

Lucan waved a hand dismissively. 'Go back to your desk, Brise. I'll call you when we're done.'

Archy was certain Vida wanted him to stay. After he promised to make her comfortable and safe she'd trustingly followed him to Floor Six without asking questions. He'd done what he could to make her feel comfortable, but he wasn't sure she was safe. Uncertain of what to do next, Archy hovered by the door with his eyes on Vida.

Vida turned to smile at him. Then she looked her late husband's nephew straight in the eye. When she spoke, her voice sounded as if it had not been used for a long time.

'Archy is my guide. I want him to sit in on this.'

'That's out of the question. He has a full day of meetings, haven't you, Brise?'

Archy, who had cleared his diary, said he could move a few things around.

'This is a private family matter, Brise. Be on your way.'

'Yes sir. I'll see you later, Mrs. Edeldi.'

It was obvious that Vida was reluctant to be alone with Lucan, but there was nothing Archy could do. It was out of the question for him to challenge the CEO, so he had no choice other than to leave the pod and close the door. Vida's gaze followed him. He felt as if he'd abandoned a helpless kitten in a thunderstorm. In spite of his own issues with Lucan, Archy decided not to return to his desk. Instead he hovered behind a filing cabinet a safe distance away, keeping his eye on the pod. Having suffered a taste of the CEO's malice himself he couldn't bear to think of Vida getting the same treatment. He hoped she would guess he was waiting nearby for her tormentor to release her.

Archy guessed that from now on, he was going to spend a lot of time watching over Vida Edeldi.

6

Edeldico HQ Floor Six
Samvida

I don't know which of us was more on edge, me or Urban's nephew. I perched on a crooked plastic chair doing my best to look confident. He fiddled with his laptop and tried not to look me in the eye. Under the cracked glass of the desk his legs twitched like a spider's in a jar. I'd expected a warm welcome at the firm my late husband founded. Instead I'd been led to a storeroom full of discarded office furniture and outdated tech. I'd have made a run for it if I wasn't afraid of bumping into more of Lucan's henchmen. Archy seemed like a nice guy, but I didn't know what nasty surprises were lurking on Floor Six. I took a deep breath and tried to stay calm.

'Thank you for agreeing to meet with me,' Lucan said. 'You must be wondering why I've taken so much trouble to ensure our discussion remains private.'

'There's no need to be secretive about my inheritance. All you have to do is give me the money.'

'If only it were that simple. Before we discuss this matter any further I want to show you something.'

Lucan inserted a flash drive into the laptop and a spacious corner office with a view over the City of London appeared on the wall screen. It was the room where eighteen months before, as a temp fresh from the countryside, I'd first met my husband.

'Why are you showing me Urban's office? Are you gloating because it's yours now?'

'Just watch, Vida.'

The screen went blank. When it sprang to life again, the camera focused on two lovers. They were almost naked, except for skimpy underwear and hoods with eye-holes. To my horror I realised I was watching my husband and myself having sex. On his desk. The recording was monochrome and silent, which for some reason made the images even more embarrassing. I couldn't look. I was shaking all over and my tongue had stuck to the roof of my mouth.

'It was a Sunday, so nobody was at work. Urban told me we were the only people in the building and he'd switched off the surveillance cameras. Who made this film?'

By the gleam in Lucan's eyes, I could tell he'd got over his initial embarrassment and was starting to enjoy tormenting me. He paused the film. 'I'm afraid I can't say.'

'Can't or won't? Who else has seen it?'

'Apart from the film maker, only me - so far. What happens next is up to you.'

I was on the point of fainting, but I didn't dare lose consciousness when I was alone with Lucan. I clasped the edge of the desk with both hands.

'Are you trying to blackmail me? Get real! Urban and I are

unrecognisable in those hoods. Anyway, nobody will care that we liked to mix it up.'

My tormentor hit a key and the hideous on-screen pantomime came to life again. Now Urban and I were kneeling. My body was curled inside his like a snail in a shell. Taking his weight on one hand he placed the other around my throat and squeezed. Then his hand slid upwards until it covered my mouth and nose. When he pulled my head back sharply I was astonished to see myself flinch. In my mind I'd been easy-going about Urban's sexual fantasies, but clearly my body had felt differently.

'You're showing your age, Lucan. Home-made porn isn't a big deal these days.'

'We'll see about that. Get ready for part two.'

Lucan allowed the action to roll on. I knew what was coming but there was nothing I could do about it. I wanted to close my eyes, but a sense of danger warned me to keep them open. An emaciated figure had joined the on-screen action. Ragged bandages were swaddled around its skeletal head and body. Sunken eyes peered through the eye-holes of a mask like those Urban and I wore. I wriggled out of my husband's embrace, slid off the desk and threw my arms around the newcomer. Urban's reaction was brutal. He grabbed the creature by its wrist and twisted one fragile arm behind its back. Around the intruder's neck hung a strip of loose cloth. Urban took hold of one end and I grabbed the other. We pulled and twisted in a bizarre tug-of war until our victim fell to the floor.

Lucan hit pause. 'That looks like criminal abuse to me.'

'It was a bit of fun,' I said, with all the dignity I had left. 'Urban enjoyed role-play - the rough kind. I saw no harm in it, and the actor was well paid. The only person who did wrong was whoever filmed us without permission.'

'You'll change your tune after you've seen part three.'

'What are you talking about? There was no part three.'

When the film started again the setting had shifted out of doors. A high fence ran alongside a stretch of rough grass and a pond coated with scum. Urban was crouching at the water's edge. He was unmasked and wore a loose black robe. At first I couldn't make out what kind of creature was trapped between his thighs. Then I realised it was a human being swaddled in rags. They put up a feeble resistance, until Urban got them by the throat. When he was done he pushed their head under the surface of the water and held it down. Several minutes passed before the struggling stopped and the victim lay still. Then a veiled young woman took centre stage. She was dressed in flowing see-through robes. Long dark hair was piled on top of her head, she wore elbow-length gloves and around her neck was a wide jewelled choker. Urban stood erect astride the prone body, while the woman knelt with her back to the camera and wound her arms around his thighs.

'Criminal abuse followed by sexual homicide,' said Lucan. 'You have been a busy girl.'

'I've never seen any part of this horrible film before,' I said. 'Where did you find it?'

'Urban gave me the flash drive a few days before you went to Portugal.'

The air left my lungs. 'You're lying,' I gasped. 'Why would he do that?'

'He made me swear not to watch the film unless something happened to him. In that case my orders were to show it to you and ask you to sign a waiver giving up your claim to his property. If you refuse to sign, the police will be informed and the film released to the media. It was Urban's way of keeping Edeldico out of your greedy little hands.'

Lucan's words opened up a new world of betrayal and uncertainty. It was hard to process. 'If Urban felt like that, why did he ask me to marry him?'

'Because you caught him in the throes of a midlife crisis. He'd become obsessed with finding a young wife who could give him more children. My cousin Nina has never shown any interest in Edeldico, and Urban has always wanted a son to follow in his footsteps. Apparently a loyal nephew wasn't good enough.'

Bitterness flickered across Lucan's face. 'You're young, healthy and naive, Vida. Perfect breeding stock. That's why my uncle married you.'

I didn't believe this, but I let it pass. I had more important questions on my mind.

'Who played the body in the water? Surely nobody died in real life.'

'We can't be certain of that. And I'm prepared to swear in a court of law that the girl in part three, the one with Urban's gonads down her throat, is you. I'd recognise that emerald choker anywhere. It's the one Urban gave you after you stole my mother's pearls.'

I shook my head. 'That is not me. As for the choker, I don't know where it is.'

Lucan removed the flash drive from the laptop and stowed it carefully in the inside pocket of his jacket. Then he said, 'Neither of us wants your homemade porn to hit the social media. Not to mention the niche pornography sites. The police take a dim view of the kind of erotica that ends with a death in real time. Fortunately there's a simple solution.'

'How can it be simple if somebody died?'

He pushed a piece of paper and a pen across the desk.

'In business anything can be done if you take it offshore. This document is a legal waiver stating that you've given up your rights to Urban's property, including his shares in Edeldico.

Immediately after you've signed it I'll destroy the flash drive in front of you. Don't worry, I'm not planning to leave you destitute. That would be bad for the firm's image. You'll receive a generous allowance.'

'And if I refuse to sign?'

'Do keep up, Vida. I've already told you I'll hand the flash drive over to the police.'

'Why? I haven't done anything wrong!'

'So what? You're a trophy wife whose wealthy older husband died unexpectedly. People will draw their own conclusions. I found that out after Urban died. I had to put a lot of time, money and effort into convincing the world he'd passed away from a heart attack.'

'But he did, didn't he? Pass away from a heart attack, I mean.'

'I suspect you know more about that than I do.'

I picked up the waiver but couldn't read it. My hands were shaking too much. I didn't believe a single word that came out of Lucan's lying mouth. All I could think of was how devoted Urban had been to Edeldico. The firm was his whole life. I couldn't bring myself to sign away my share of something the man I loved cared so much about. On the other hand, I knew Lucan was right about my image on social media. Young widow of rich older man isn't a good look.

I said, 'I can't think straight. Please, just give me whatever I'm entitled to and let me go. I promise I won't bring any harm to Edeldico. Why would I?'

Lucan must have realised I was incapable of making a decision at that moment. He picked up his phone. 'Very well. You have one day to consider your position before I go to the police.'

Archy arrived at the door of the pod very quickly after Lucan called him. I guessed he hadn't gone back to his desk. He'd hung around on Floor Six, because he was suspicious of Lucan's motives and wanted to protect me. Neither of us spoke while I followed him back to the service entrance.

The SUV was waiting to take me back to the Penthouse. While Archy was helping me into it he slipped his business card into my jacket pocket. 'Mrs Edeldi,' he said, 'I admired and respected your husband more than I can say. If ever I can assist you in any way, please don't hesitate to call me.'

The driver didn't take me to the Penthouse. Instead he stopped by the shopping centre in Canary Wharf, where he waited barely long enough to make sure my feet had hit the ground. Then he closed the doors and drove away at speed. It wasn't until I was watching him dodge through the traffic that I realised I'd left my handbag, with my passport, credit cards and phone inside it, on Floor Six.

I turned my back on the lights of the Mall and wandered through wind and rain. Lost in a waking nightmare, I lost my sense of time. When the cold became too much to bear I headed for the Penthouse.

7

The Penthouse
Samvida

Nina had said she'd come back to hear about my meeting with
Lucan. I made up my mind to tell her a version of the truth
involving intimate photos of myself and beg her to back me up. I
was frightened and confused by what had happened, but one
thing was clear in my mind. My step-daughter must never know
about her Dad's involvement in the sex film, even though it was
fake and made without permission. And I was deeply ashamed of
my own part in the role play. I'd let Urban persuade me it was
going to be fun, but after watching myself on screen I knew I'd
been fooling myself. At the moment when his powerful fingers
dug into my neck I'd feared for my life. I decided to ask Katya to
help me look for the emerald choker. It was possible she already
knew where it was kept, because she was fascinated by the
Edeldico jewellery. If I could prove my choker was different

from the one an actress wore in the third scene of the film, Lucan's attempt at blackmail would fall apart.

Little did I know what was lying in wait for me at the Penthouse.

When I stepped out of the elevator into the welcome lounge and the sensor lights came on, I couldn't believe my eyes. The place looked as if someone had been in a hurry to make a getaway. A bowl of lilies and gladioli lay smashed to smithereens on the antique carpet. Blooms were trampled on the wooden floor and one of Urban's golf clubs lay among the lilies. The front door was wide open. I tiptoed inside. There was no-one in the dining room, no-one in either of the kitchens, no-one in the home cinema. I moved on to the master suite. When I left the suite had been full to overflowing. Now it was empty. My sequined dresses, Urban's racks of identical white shirts and the fake jewellery were gone. Even the emperor size mattress had disappeared. That morning I'd asked Katya to take away the clutter. She must have called up every van driver in East London. Only the frame of the bed I shared with Urban was left standing. On it was the suitcase I brought with me when I moved in. Inside it I found jumpers, jeans, socks, underwear and two pairs of trainers. To the last, Katya had done her best to take care of me.

After the initial shock had worn off I felt nothing but relief. All I could think of was the emerald choker, which Katya must have taken along with the rest of my fake jewellery. I could no longer use it to prove my innocence, but at least Lucan couldn't use it as a weapon against me. I left my coat on the bed along with the suitcase and went to look for my step-daughter. Nina had said she'd be back that evening, but she was nowhere to be seen. Often she went straight to the Penthouse gym, so I went there to look for her. When I found the gym empty I passed through it to the garden. By then it was dark. A half moon was obscured by drifting clouds and the wind made the tropical plants under the gazebo rustle and flap. The safety lights failed, so I walked cautiously on my way to the pool. Heavy rain was rippling the surface of the water. Something shapeless was suspended underwater in the deep end. It looked like a woman's body, limbs loose, hair floating like seaweed. I blinked, unable to believe my eyes, then looked again.

The body in the pool was Nina.

For one dreadful moment I hesitated, not knowing what to do. Then I sprang into action. It was unthinkable to lose both Nina and Urban. I kicked off my shoes and dived into the pool. A pale shape loomed up beside me and long nails dug into my calves. I'd forgotten that whenever Nina's upset or angry, she takes to the water. Her hands were gripping my ankles and tugging me below the surface. I wondered what on earth she was doing. I was in no mood to play, and my lungs were aching. That's when I realised I was being relentlessly dragged down. Whatever my step-daughter was up to, she was deadly serious. Luckily the floor of the pool was only a few inches below my feet. I've never been so grateful for being tall. I allowed myself to sink to the bottom, then kicked upwards. Nina hung on to me and we wrestled in the shallow end. Her hair was plastered over her shoulders and chest, her face screwed up with fury. In fear of drowning, I kneed her in the groin and she fell backwards, splashing and howling. I scrambled out of the pool and dashed towards the gym. I made it a few steps ahead of Nina, but before I could lock the door behind me I slipped and fell. A kick from her bare karate-trained foot caught me in the eye.

Doubled up in pain I screamed, 'What was that for?'

'You've got a nerve to ask, after what you've done!' Clinging to a chest press, Nina threw up. The acid reek of wine vomit filled the air. For a heart-stopping second I thought she'd found out about the film.

'Nina, I promise you it had nothing to do with me!'

The back of her hand struck me across my mouth. Something wet and warm ran down my face.

'Liar! You gave Mum and Dad's things to the maid!'

I breathed a sigh of relief. Nina didn't know about the porn film. Her insane anger was triggered by Katya de-cluttering our suite. I tasted relief along with the blood in my mouth, but I was still in danger, cornered between a weights stack and a cross-trainer. I kept her talking in the hope she'd calm down.

'I'm sorry, Nina! I didn't think you'd mind. I'll call the agency, get Katya's contact details and ask her to bring everything back.'

'I already tried. The address she was using is fake and she's ditched her phone.'

Salty blood was trickling from my nose to my chin. I wiped my face with the back of my hand and tried to lower the tension with a question. 'Why didn't you tell me how you felt about those things?'

'You're my friend! You're supposed to know how I feel without having to be told!'

With each word she punched my chest and limbs as if I were a training bag.

'Don't hit me!' I yelled. 'I'm not psychic!'

'You don't have to be a mind-reader to understand how people feel. You just have to give a shit.'

I didn't understand. 'How was I to know you cared so much about some old clothes?'

Nina grabbed me by my sodden shirt collar and shoved me against an equipment rack.

'This isn't about the clothes! Ever since Mum died, the Penthouse has been my sanctuary. My happy place where nothing ever changes.'

She raised a hand to strike me again. This time I was ready. I pushed her, ducked under her arm and slithered closer to the exit.

'You stole my memories of Mum and Dad!' she screamed. 'It's like they died twice!'

'Look, Nina, everyone says Frankie was a lovely person, but your Dad was far from perfect. He did things he shouldn't have.'

My step-daughter's hair was sticking in damp trails to her face and her blue eyes were flashing. 'You mean his offshore accounts? Don't be stupid. Most people would park their savings offshore if they could afford the charges.'

I said, 'Lucan mentioned offshore. What does it mean?'

She stared at me open-mouthed, 'Are you serious?'

'You know I don't care about money, Nina.'

For a second she looked as if she was going to laugh. Then her face knotted up again.

'Did Dad catch you sleeping around? Was giving his stuff away some weird kind of revenge?'

'I was faithful to your father because I truly loved him. I'd have married him if he was a street sweeper.'

'You're lying! What Lucan says is true. You murdered Dad to get your hands on his money!'

Picking up up a 10kg beanbag, Nina slammed it into my belly. I grabbed her thigh and she caught me around the waist. I wrapped my arms around her and we rolled on the floor, kicking and punching. Then my opponent stopped struggling and her heavy breathing morphed into snores. Nina had passed out with one side of her face squashed into a rubber mat. There was drool at the corner of her mouth but she was breathing normally. I'd seen Nina like this before, especially since Urban's death left her a double orphan at twenty-three. I knew she'd be all right when she sobered up.

I covered Nina with warm towels, closed the door to the pool garden and checked that the heating was switched on. Then I went into the changing room, dropped my wet clothes on the floor and grabbed a cotton wrap. The fabric snagged on my engagement and wedding rings. Once upon a time I'd been proud of those sparkling rocks but now they looked grotesque. I pulled them off, went back into the gym and slipped them on to Nina's fingers.

When I was sure she was safe I carried my suitcase and coat from the bedroom to Urban's study and locked the door. I went into the en-suite to splash my face with water and was appalled by my blood-streaked reflection in the mirror. I desperately needed to talk about what had happened, but I had no-one to turn to. Kind-hearted Katya had disappeared, taking with her the emerald choker. My Mum and Dad were thousands of miles away. I couldn't disturb Gus at the boarding school where he was preparing to take A-levels. Nina, my step-daughter and best friend, had tried to drown me. As for my old friends, I'd lost touch with them after I started dating Urban.

Huddled on the chaise-longue I tried to get the events of the day straight in my mind. I was confident Lucan had been lying when he told me Urban made the film to scare me into giving up my right to inherit his property. My husband knew I married him for his brilliance and charisma, not his money. But what had he been thinking when he took his sinister fantasy so close to the limit? And where did he find actors willing to act out that grisly murder scene? Finally I understood why I hadn't been able to completely satisfy Urban's needs. His lust was for the ultimate thrill money can buy - power over life and death.

I began to wonder what would happen to me if Lucan leaked

the film to social media. That day, for the first time both Lucan and Nina had revealed that they suspected me of causing Urban's death. Who were people more likely to believe? Me, or the victim's daughter and the CEO of a respected finance firm? Then came the most frightening thought of all. What if I died suddenly, like my husband? Would my share in Edeldico pass to Lucan? If so, was this stupid, cruel man capable of committing murder to achieve his heart's desire?

There was no way I was going to hang around to find out. The flyer for Arlo's Café I'd found in Urban's desk caught my eye. I put it in the pocket of my coat along with a few coins I found in a drawer. It seemed as good a place as any to start my journey.

8

Arlo's Café, Coopers Hook
Hetty

Hetty Brill wiped a hole in the condensation on the inside of the window and peered through it. She was looking out for Chelsea, who was due to arrive to help with the lunchtime rush, when a young homeless man entered the café, bringing with him a flurry of cold damp air. Before shuffling to the counter with his head down he paused on the threshold until he caught Arlo's eye. The group of young mothers at a table near the door hauled their baby buggies out of his way, wrinkling their noses when his stink hit them. On first sight he looked like a tall twelve-year-old, but his face, which peered through tangled reddish-brown hair with a look of wary curiosity in the brown eyes, was mature. He was so thin it was a miracle the baggy sweatshirt and stained jogging pants stayed on him. His shoes, brand new and fastened with velcro, were from the local supermarket. Hetty reckoned he must have got those on the five-finger discount. Around his neck was a leather purse on a knotted cord.

'Hey, Yessy!' said Arlo. 'Where have you been? I haven't seen you since before Christmas.'

'Yes.'

'Do you want a cheese sandwich?'

There was no reply.

'Chicken? Sausage? Salad?'

Yessy stared at the food without speaking.

Arlo stirred the bowl of penne. 'Pasta?'

'Yes.'

'Meat?'

'Yes.'

'Tomato sauce?'

'Yes.'

Arlo doled out a small spoonful of minced meat and a big spoonful of sauce. He set the plate on the counter and reached over to dip a hand into Yessy's purse. When he drew his hand out again it was full of shiny stones. He let go of them as if they were red hot.

'So that's how it is,' he said. 'Pay me next time, Yessy.'

Yessy grabbed his plate with both hands and carried it outside. He sat down at a table under the awning Arlo had pulled down against the weather and began to spoon the pasta into his mouth.

Hetty went over to have a word with her ex. 'I thought you were trying to attract them posh new residents who've moved here since the Olympics?'

Arlo looked up from the tomato he was slicing

'So what?'

'Well, Yessy is going to put them off. Who's going to pay top dollar for a coffee with some little pikey stuffing his face out front? You've got to get rid of him.'

'How do you suggest I do that?'

'Next time he comes in, tell him to sling his hook. I'm gasping for a latte, babe.'

Arlo sliced a lettuce savagely. 'Is there any chance of you clearing a few tables?'

'Not likely. I have to teach a Zumba class in half an hour.'

Sulkily Hetty returned to her stool. In her opinion it was unreasonable of Arlo to ask her to help clear tables, now they were separated and she had her own dance studio. She enjoyed spending an occasional evening with her ex, when he cooked something special and they ended up sleeping together. After twenty-five years of marriage Arlo knew what she liked, but there was always a price to pay. Hetty made up her mind that the next time she stayed over, she'd be long gone before there were plates to be washed.

Arlo had given his premises a face-lift in preparation for the London Olympics in 2012. A year later the café still looked fresh. Upcycled tables and chairs, painted in Olympic colours to match the wall posters, created a homely atmosphere. A wooden booth salvaged from a pub stood in one corner. Along the plate glass frontage stools were tucked under a shelf. This was where Hetty liked to perch and watch goings-on in the street. Behind her a long table was occupied by builders in high-viz jackets. They were enjoying all-day breakfasts with safety helmets stacked under their seats. Hetty didn't rate the builders. Their healthy appetites boosted the café's takings, but on the down side they created too much work. Because of the cold weather there'd been a rush on the full English, and eggy plates were piling up.

The mothers huddled protectively around their toddlers were recuperating from the school run. They could be relied on to put away a couple of expensive coffees each - that was why Arlo turned a blind eye to the supermarket croissants they were passing around under the table. On the counter sandwich fillings were ready under a perspex screen alongside a big bowl of pasta. Arlo didn't do complex menu choices, but in case things got busy he always had home-made soup on hand. Sometimes it actually was home-made.

Sleet was lashing down outside and snow was forecast. According to the free newspapers tucked into the rack, this was the coldest spring in fifty years. When a woman with white hair paused to shake raindrops from her umbrella before stepping indoors, Hetty averted her eyes. These days she rarely spoke to her elderly cousin. She'd grown tired of Irene rabbiting on about her career as a local councillor and how the manager of the accounts department of the pickle factory had begged her not to retire. If everyone in Coopers Hook knew as much about Irene's past as Hetty did, her reputation would take a dive and no mistake.

'Isn't it cold for the time of year? I nearly got blown away crossing the street. Sorry to trouble you, Arlo, but can you spare me a pint of milk? I don't want to walk all the way to the mini-mart in this weather.'

'No problem, Irene. Has the lift in your block been mended yet?'

'Don't make me laugh,' said Irene. 'Morning, Reed. Will there be anything to eat at the Champions' meeting?'

'Er, yes,' said Reed Rankhorn, who as usual was treating the corner booth as his personal office. 'Sandwiches.'

'Lovely. Viv and I will see you then.' On her way out Irene smiled and waved at the community policeman who was sitting in a corner nursing a coffee.

'Morning Jammy,' she called out. 'See you later!'

'Don't encourage him,' Hetty muttered under her breath. She caught Arlo's eye and he shook his head in Irene's direction. One of the few things they agreed on was the wisdom of keeping well clear of coppers - even the ones who couldn't arrest anybody.

'Reed mate,' said Arlo, 'Are you ready for another cup of tea?'

Reed was sorting crumpled receipts he took from his cargo pockets into two piles. One was tucked under a treacle tin filled with sugar lumps and the other beneath a ketchup bottle. The environmentalist was project manager for a local regeneration scheme. Attracted by his charm and rugged good looks, Hetty had attended a winter festival he'd organised. She didn't intend to repeat the experience. Salads made of weeds, home-grown pumpkin soup and pizza baked out of doors in a clay oven were well out of her comfort zone.

'Yes please mate. By the way, I'm holding a Champions meeting at eleven. We'll want tea, coffee, half a dozen rounds of sandwiches and a packet of biscuits.'

'Sure thing,' said Arlo. 'I'll make cheese sandwiches. Everyone eats cheese.'

'Except vegans. But we only have two of those and they can't make it today.'

Suddenly he looked more cheerful, and Hetty knew why. Reed controlled a substantial budget for community engagement. His outlay on tea and sandwiches for residents' meetings, or coffee and ciabatta rolls for corporate volunteers, formed a significant part of Arlo's takings.

Hetty hitched up the hem of her skirt. 'Reed, can I be one of your Champions?'

Reed kept his eyes on his invoices. 'Of course - if you're genuinely interested in regeneration. And if you're prepared to work with Yessy.'

'Yessy? Are you winding me up?'

'Not at all. Now he's back from wherever he's spent the winter he'll be taking over the heavy work at Plain Ease. Feeding and cleaning the hens, turning compost and so on. I'm too busy with paperwork. I hate the end of the financial year.'

'Tell me about it,' said Arlo, handing Reed his tea.

Hetty sniggered at the very idea of losing sleep over tax returns. Arlo grinned and brought her the latte she'd asked for. He'd sprinkled a chocolate heart on top.

'I've had three calls from the finance department about the hospitality gazebo,' said Reed. 'The invoice has gone missing. I hope some over-enthusiastic community gardener hasn't composted it.'

Perched on a stool, Hetty crossed her legs. 'Reed,' she said, 'There's a box labelled "Invoices" propping open the door of the shed at Plain Ease.'

'So there is! I started a new system then forgot all about it. The invoice may be in there.'

Hetty said teasingly, 'Shall I come down to the garden and help you look for it?'

'There's no need for you to get your hands dirty,' said Reed.

'I don't mind a bit of dirt,' said Hetty.

At the bus shelter on the other side of the street, Puja's grand-daughter and her friend were talking to a stylish young woman. Hetty's eye was caught by the expensive blue trench coat the stranger was wearing. 'Them posh kids ain't got enough sense to dress down when they go slumming,' she said to herself. 'She's asking to get mugged, wandering around Coopers Hook in a coat worth more than some people's cars. I wonder what she's got in that tatty old suitcase?'

After Bushra and her mate caught a bus the girl in the smart coat was left alone in the shelter. Buses came and went but she stood motionless, staring through sleet towards the café. Everything around her was on the move, but she seemed to be frozen in time. For some reason the girl made Hetty think of Urban Edeldi. Since her patron's sudden death six months before too many things reminded her of the old days. She sighed, thinking of the fun times she and Urban had enjoyed together when she was a hostess at Salthouse Salsa in Shoreditch and he was making a name for himself in the City. Images of the time when she was young and her lover was a king among men were seared into her memory.

With an effort Hetty dragged her thoughts back to the present and the young woman under the bus shelter. 'I know I've seen her before somewhere. She's probably been to one of my salsa nights. Maybe she'll pay for a course of lessons if I offer her a ten per cent discount.'

She waved to the stranger through the window of the café. As if the random greeting had released her from a spell, the young woman sprang into action with a smile. Hetty caught her breath. Under the bed at her studio was a pile of gossip magazines splashed with that smile - above a six-figure wedding dress. Vida Edeldi, Urban's widowed bride, was crossing the street towards the café.

Hetty thought Vida was even prettier in real life than in her pictures, but she couldn't have said why. Her hair was glossy and her brown eyes were striking, but her style wasn't glamorous. Her long legs were too muscular to be elegant. As for her boobs, Urban had liked a good handful, but Vida was thin. Too thin.

Vida shut the café door behind her and stared at Hetty, rubbing her naked fingers together to warm them. Her face was marked with bruises and she had a black eye. Hetty wondered who had beaten her up and where the rings were which had set

Urban back half a million. Most urgently of all, she wanted to know what Vida was doing in Coopers Hook.

'Hello,' said Vida. 'I'm Sam.'

9

Hetty and Urban
1985 - 2012

Hetty never asked Urban what brought him to Salthouse Salsa in the first place. To her, it wasn't important. She only cared that he kept coming back. The first night he showed they danced belly to belly until closing time. After that he bowled into Salty's most evenings and made a beeline for her. After the other private dancers noticed his fat wallet they were all over him like a rash. They were wasting their time, because he only had eyes for Hetty.

At twenty-two, Hetty was working morning shifts at the pickle factory and taking dance lessons most afternoons. She knew she was running out of time to make it as a professional dancer. Occasionally she was hired for a local show, but gigs at some church hall where you had to get changed in the toilets was a long way from the glittering West End career she craved. To pay for her lessons she worked evenings at Salty's, partnering lonely single men who were desperate for female company. Now and again she snogged one of them to earn a much needed tip, and sometimes old man Salty asked her to be nice to one of his wealthy associates. Hetty was pleased when Urban told her she was special, because he was also special to her. He was the first boyfriend she'd had who paid for everything without her having to twist his arm.

Urban was engaged to Frankie and Hetty was dating Arlo, but that didn't bother them. They were having too much fun. From the beginning they both knew they were going to sleep together, but Hetty put it off as long as she could. She did this because Urban enjoyed spoiling her with expensive gifts, and in her experience after you'd done the deed with a man the presents became few and far between. When at last she ran out of excuses they made plans for their first night together. She was thrilled when Urban offered to take her for a long weekend in Jersey, because Bergerac was her favourite television programme. She'd only watched it on her Mum's tiny black and white screen so she was excited to see the locations in real life.

The car ferry to St. Helier ran from Weymouth. When Urban drove the two of them there in his red Porsche, Hetty was surprised to find out what a long way it was from East London to Dorset. She had no idea England was so big. The journey took even longer because whenever they saw a secluded spot Urban insisted on parking up and seducing her on a blanket he kept in the car. Hetty was worried about missing the ferry, so she was relieved when at last Urban put his foot down to get them there on time. She spent the boat trip walking round and round the deck. Due to Urban's enthusiastic lovemaking she was too sore to sit down.

Their hotel was within sight of Elizabeth castle, but Hetty wasn't given time to admire the view. Urban was in too much of a hurry to get to their room. After a turbulent half hour she limped to the bathroom down the corridor to clean herself up. When she returned he was emptying thick brown envelopes out of a leather briefcase and shoving them into a plastic bag.

'I have to meet a client,' he said. 'Wait for me in the bar. We'll eat when I get back.'

Hetty sat alone in the hotel bar drinking gin and waiting for her lover. Since they left London she'd had nothing to eat but a sausage roll on the ferry, so by the time Urban showed up she was tipsy. He paid her tab and promised to make it up to her. At the best restaurant on the island he ordered two steaks and a bottle of champagne. Hetty drank more than her share of the fizz and the rest of the evening was a daze. She woke up the next morning hurting all over. When she noticed a bruise on her neck Urban said it was a love bite. She soon forgot her aches and pains when he took her to a jeweller's and bought her a heavy gold chain. It was the best tip in the history of Salty's. When the other hostesses saw it they were green with envy.

For the next six months, every few weeks Urban would drive the two of them to Weymouth to catch the Channel Islands ferry. His Porsche attracted attention on the car deck, but he refused to drive anything else. Hetty kept hinting she'd like him to take her to Paris in it, but he never did. Occasionally she persuaded him to take her for a drive around the island, but mostly she waited in the hotel while he followed up on his business deals. She developed a taste for champagne and built up an impressive collection of gold jewellery.

After what turned out to be their final trip together, they got back to London in the early hours of the morning. As usual, Urban hailed a black cab to take Hetty from London Bridge to Coopers Hook. He was helping her into the taxi when two heavies lurched out of the shadows. One of them swung a knife at Urban and the other crashed a steel-toed boot into Hetty's left knee. Urban threw a fistful of notes at the cabbie, who didn't need telling to drive like the clappers.

The next morning Urban called Hetty to apologise. It had been a misunderstanding, he said. He'd defaulted on a loan and his client had overreacted. She accepted his apology even though it was pointless. Her knee was shattered and with it her dream of becoming a professional dancer. She didn't know it then, but it would be a long time before she saw Urban Edeldi again.

One day fifteen years later Hetty happened to be in Shoreditch. A nail bar had opened where Salthouse Salsa used to stand. For old times' sake she went inside. When the manicurist jumped as if she'd been stung, Hetty looked up to see Urban standing over her. One hand flew to her neck where the gold chain used to lie, before she sold it along with the rest of her jewellery to help Arlo buy his café.

'Hetty Brill! It's great to see you again,' said Urban, bending over to kiss her cheek. 'If you're wondering what I'm doing here, I bought the building when old man Salty retired. Your manicure's on the house.'

Urban looked exactly as he had when they last met, except for the white scar on his forehead. When he saw Hetty staring he touched it and said, 'This scar is my souvenir of our trips to Jersey. How's your knee?'

For once in her life she had no words.

While the manicurist was giving her the most careful French polish of all time, Hetty told Urban about Arlo and Chelsea and the café. He'd been widowed and was bringing up his daughter Nina alone. Although he was still mourning Frankie, it wasn't long before he got down to business.

'Are you available for work, Hetty? I've set up my own finance firm and I'm looking for a runner I can trust.'

'Not really. I already have two jobs. I work in the café and I teach salsa.'

'We can call it salsa if you like.'

Urban had lost none of the charm Hetty remembered, so it wasn't long before he talked her into doing errands for Edeldico. While Chelsea was at school she'd pick up a package at one address and drop it off at another. Sometimes she made bank deposits with the reference "salsa". Once she'd got used to the extra money she couldn't stop. Arlo missed his wife's help at the café, but he knew better than to question her.

Driven by nostalgia rather than desire, they went to bed together a few times. Hetty didn't enjoy these trysts. Afterwards she had to go home and run around after Arlo and Chelsea, which spoiled the mood. And Urban's tastes were more extreme than in the eighties. When he pretended to strangle her with her tights she called a halt to their fling. Back in the day, the only thing he'd wanted to put around her neck was a gold chain.

When Urban suddenly passed away Hetty was left in a difficult situation. She didn't know what to do with the large sum of cash she'd recently collected from her usual sources. When Urban was alive she'd always passed the takings directly to him, secure in the knowledge he would protect her. His nephew, who had taken control of the firm, didn't answer her calls.

Hetty waited to see what would happen next.

10

Arlo's Café
Samvida

On a back street in Coopers Hook tacky pink signage spelled out 'Arlo's Café'. I hesitated under a bus shelter, trying to decide what to do next. I couldn't afford to go inside. After paying my fare from Canary Wharf I only had two pounds left in the pocket of my trench coat.

Two women a bit younger than me came out of the café, crossed the street and joined me under the shelter. They were teasing each other with open cans of fizzy drink in their hands. The short one was a Londoner of Asian heritage. When her friend, who was Black and as tall as me, tumbled and spilled her drink on my coat I lost it. Anger had been roiling inside me for twenty-four hours and I couldn't help yelling. When I calmed down they were watching me open-mouthed.

'Folu, you're such a muppet! Look what you did,' said the Asian girl.

'Shut up Bushra! It was your fault. You pushed me,' Folu said, in an accent I didn't know. She took a tissue from the pocket of her overalls and dabbed at my coat.

Bushra hadn't taken her eyes off my face. 'Who beat you up?'

'What's it to you?' I snarled.

Folu backed away. 'My bad! I'm sorry I messed up your lovely coat.'

'Maybe the coat isn't hers. It looks like she had to fight for it.'

For me, this comment was a reality check. I'd been living among the ultra-wealthy so long I'd forgotten you can't walk around a rough part of London with a black eye, wearing a designer coat over an old jumper and jeans, without attracting attention. No wonder Bushra thought I looked suspicious. It was time to come up with a cover story.

'The coat's mine. I got it from a charity shop,' I said.

'Yeah, right,' said Bushra, climbing aboard a waiting bus.

As she followed her friend on to the bus Folu thrust a five pound note into my hand. 'Get your coat cleaned. Maybe it is not enough but it is all I have.'

When the bus drove away there were tears of gratitude in my eyes. Thanks to Folu's generosity I could afford something to eat. The thought of a cup of tea and a slice of toast made my mouth water. I was on the point of crossing the road to Arlo's when I noticed the young man sitting at a pavement table outside the café. He was unwashed and so thin his scruffy clothes hung off his back. He looked homeless, but someone was taking care of him, because on his table was a plate of pasta. When he saw me he stopped eating and put down his spoon. The poor guy looked as if he was overwhelmed by a mixture of strong emotions. Astonishment, bewilderment and delight were chasing each other across his dirty face, but the strongest emotion was joy. This complete stranger was staring at me as if I was a dear old friend he'd never expected to see again. When he picked up his plate and held it out as if to invite me to share the food, I was so freaked out I became rooted to the spot.

A strange woman staring out of the window of Arlo's Café broke whatever spell I was under. When she smiled and waved I felt as if was being thrown a lifeline. Because of the trauma I'd experienced I was craving human contact, but my encounter with Bushra and Folu had taught me a valuable lesson. I needed a cover story to explain why I was in Coopers Hook, and I needed it fast. Fortunately I had form at name-changing. My freethinking parents named me Samvida because it's unusual. When I was at school in the country everyone called me Sam, but when I moved to London I switched to the more sophisticated Vida. I decided to become Sam again and stop suppressing my Midlands accent. That way people were unlikely to connect me with the Vida Edeldi on social media. I made sure the fiver Folu had given me was in my pocket, crossed the street with my suitcase rattling behind me and pushed open the door of the café.

'Hi,' I said to the woman who'd greeted me from the window. 'I'm Sam.'

When her mouth shut like a steel trap I realised she'd mistaken me for somebody else. There was a confused expression in her green eyes, as if she was trying to think of something to say. From the grey roots showing through her up-swept blonde hair I guessed she was in her late forties, but the way she carried herself made her look younger.

'I'm Hetty?' she said. It sounded like a question.

I said, 'Do I know you?'

Hetty looked startled, as if she'd expected me to say something else. She opened her mouth to reply then closed it again.

We stared at each other in silence, trying to figure out what we had in common. At last she said, 'I think I've seen you at my salsa nights. I own the Wicker dance studio.'

'Sorry,' I said. 'I don't know the place. I'm new around here.'

'Come to one of my classes. I'll give you a card.'

When Hetty reached for her bag her hand shook, and it wasn't from cold. Inside the little restaurant it was steamy as a sauna

'I can't afford dance lessons,' I said. 'I'm unemployed. And homeless.'

Hetty slid off her stool. When she walked a few steps in her high heels she limped slightly on one leg.

'I love your coat, Sam.'

'Thank you. I bought it from a charity shop.'

Hetty laughed out loud. 'You got yourself a bargain. Mind if I try it on?'

'It won't fit you,' I said.

'I'll make it fit,' said Hetty. She barely came up to my shoulder, but when she put her arm around my waist her grip was as tight as a vice.

I was relieved when a man with long brown hair emerged from the corner booth and rescued me from Hetty's clutches. In his hand-knitted jumper, muddy cargo pants and scuffed safety boots he looked too country for Coopers Hook. Although he was only about thirty his mustache was like something from a Victorian photo - long, waxed and pointy at the ends.

'Hi. I'm Reed Rankhorn. Are you interested in becoming a Champion?'

'Not really,' I said. 'I only came in for something to eat.'

'The poor kid's starving,' said Hetty, releasing me. 'Arlo, give Sam a cup of tea and a slice of toast.'

The café's owner was a strongly built man of about sixty who looked as if he had once been athletic. His cheeks were rosy and his grey hair was thick and curly. When he brought over my tea and toast I noticed he also had a limp. Bustling around the busy café, serving food and clearing tables, he looked as if he could do with some help.

'Sit down, Sam,' said Reed, leading me to a big round green table. His kind blue eyes were full of concern. 'Those bruises look painful. Are you in some kind of trouble?'

'Big trouble. I lost my job.'

'Do you live in Coopers Hook?'

'No, but I might settle. It depends on whether I can find work and somewhere to live,' I said.

'Well, keep in touch. I project manage the community garden at Plain Ease, as well as several other regeneration projects across East London. Property around here is selling like hot cakes. I'm hoping to recruit some of the new residents. You're welcome to sit in on our Champions' meeting.'

'What's a Champion?'

'Champions are residents who support local regeneration projects. Most of their time is spent on practical tasks, but they also gather feedback, take part in focus groups and attend planning sessions. Today we're going to talk about our market gardening enterprise.'

This sounded like a job opportunity.

'How much are Champions paid?'

Reed frowned. 'We don't grow food for profit, Sam. We do it to feed our community. When the social contract breaks down because of climate change due to global warming, the food chain will collapse. If we have a safe space where we can grow our own food and set up a co-operative sharing business, we'll have a chance of survival. The Champions are working to achieve this. They're volunteers but they claim expenses. And when we harvest our crops they'll get all the organic vegetables they can eat.'

I wasn't sure about being paid in broccoli, but in my situation I had few options.

'Can I be a Champion, Reed?'

'Not without an address, Sam. But you fit into another category my charity supports. Being homeless, you're eligible for free accommodation at a social enterprise hostel. You'd have to spend a few hours every day doing manual work on regeneration projects. You wouldn't get paid, but you'd have a roof over your head and a few pounds a day for food. How does that sound?'

'It sounds perfect. How do I apply?'

Reed pulled a crumpled application form from his trouser pocket and smoothed it on the table.

'Name?'

'Sam Gumby,' I said.

That one was easy. Gumby is the name of Mum's cat.

'And how old are you, Sam?'

I knocked five years off my age, hoping it would improve my chances. 'Twenty-one.'

'What was your last job? Do you have references?'

'That's going to be difficult, Reed. I used to work in my uncle's shop. Yesterday I caught my older cousin stealing from the till. When I challenged him, he beat me up and threatened to kill me if I told anyone. That's why I ran away.'

I was proud of myself for coming up with such a fine story. There was even a seed of truth in it. But it didn't satisfy Reed.

'I understand you had to take yourself out of harm's way, Sam. But I need at least one reference.'

'Please, Reed, give me time to sort my life out.'

Just then a man of about my age walked in. He was a

younger version of Arlo except for his face, which was a masculine version of Hetty's.

'What kept you, Chelsea? I have a business to run too, you know.'

Hetty threw on her puffer coat and grabbed her fake designer bag.

'See you later babe,' said Arlo, holding the door open for her.

His shoulders slumped as she ran past him without a word.

'Don't tell me Mum's been making herself useful for once,' said Chelsea. He was stacking a tray with cups so fast they made a noise like chattering teeth.

Arlo sighed. 'That'll be the day.'

Reed called out, 'Chel, you're the very man I want to see. This is Sam Gumby. Sam, Chel manages TimePad, the social enterprise hostel I've been telling you about. Chel, Sam is unemployed and homeless and she's applied to be a Champion. Have you by any chance got a spare bed for her?'

'Some kid left this morning. I was going to look at the waiting list but as it's you who's asking, she's in.'

I couldn't help asking Reed if it was okay for me to jump the queue.

He shrugged. 'Business owners like to do me favours, because I control the regeneration budget.'

11

The Mansions, Coopers Hook
March 2013
Irene

Irene slammed shut the street door of her block too late to stop an icy gust of wind following her indoors. The blast sent dust monsters rolling across fractured floor tiles to gather under the wheelchair parked in a corner. Junk mail and free papers clogged the space where the doormat used to lie. Among them was an envelope addressed to her. She picked it up and popped it into her bag with the pint of milk she'd fetched from Arlo's. Only a few months ago her neighbour Puja used to do her food shopping, bring it up to her flat with the post and stop for a cup of tea and a chat. But along with all the other tenants who used to live in The Mansions, Puja and her family had given up the struggle against eviction and moved out. She often popped round to see Irene, but it wasn't the same as having her downstairs.

It wasn't any warmer in the hall than it had been in the street, but Irene was relieved to be out of the rain, The only light came through the cracked transom above the door. Because the windows had been broken so many times they'd been boarded up to deter squatters. In Irene's opinion it would be a good thing if a few well-behaved squatters moved into The Mansions. With house prices sky-high, even well-educated people were desperate to find somewhere to live. They'd be company for her and Viv, and one of them might figure out how to fix the lift, which was of the old-fashioned cage type. Even when The Mansions were built in the fifties the mechanism had been slightly out of date. Modern engineers took one look, shook their heads and went away. There'd been an 'out of order' notice on it since before the Olympics, and Irene doubted whether it would ever be operational again. Rubbing her hands together to warm them before climbing the stairs, Irene thanked her lucky stars that she was still good on her feet. However, a firm grip on the handrail was essential. To make matters worse most of the landing lights had blown. When the last few bulbs gave out she and Viv were going to have to stay indoors in the evenings. Since Viv had her stroke they were always home before dark, but it was nice to know they could go out if they felt like it.

Irene's second-floor flat opened off a wide landing with the lift shaft in one corner and the staircase in the other. She had to walk across the landing to reach her front door. As she passed the large window she looked out over the roofs of Coopers Hook. She knew the names of many of the inhabitants of those homes. It was a long time since she'd been Councillor Mrs. O'Callaghan with a full in-tray on her desk at the town hall. She'd had to give up her civic responsibilities when she began caring for Viv, but she did what she could for the community. She was looking forward to the Champions meeting later that morning. It was always a pleasure to see her old friends again and make plans for the food growing project at

Plain Ease. When she was safe inside the flat Irene turned her key in the lock. Her kitchen was the first door on the left and the bathroom was at the other end of the corridor. There was space in the cupboard between the two rooms to store their vacuum cleaner, bedlinen and towels. On the right was the sitting room and two good-sized bedrooms. Although the whole place needed fresh wallpaper and a lick of paint, it was spacious, well lit and cheap to run. She and her family had lived there comfortably for almost fifty years.

Irene went into the kitchen, where she was starting tomato plants on the window sill. When the weather improved she intended to plant them out in the community garden at Plain Ease. The kitchen filled up with a peppery scent as she reached for the scissors tucked between trays of seedlings. By the time Viv had shuffled to the kitchen from her bedroom Irene had cut the letter from the landlords into shreds.

Viv leaned her walking stick against the table and lowered herself into a chair. 'You can stop worrying about identity theft, Mum. Nobody wants to be us.'

'It was you who told me never to throw away anything with our address on it.'

'Forget it. We're on the point of being evicted.'

'Over my dead body.'

'I think we ought to read the letters to find out what they have in mind.'

'We already know they're trying to force us out so they can turn The Mansions into investment properties. Are you hungry?'

'A bit. Will there be food at the Champions' meeting?'

'Sandwiches, Reed said. But you know what he's like. He'll probably forget to order them. We'd better eat something before we leave.'

Irene tipped cornflakes into china dishes painted with flowers and added a drop of milk. Then she made two teas, one in a mug for herself and another in a lidded beaker for Viv. The women ate together at the table by the window, because Irene liked to keep an eye on the street. Her flat overlooked Arlo's Café, the gate of Plain Ease and a row of railway arches. Directly under the window was a bus stop. While she ate, Irene watched every bus that paused by the shelter and observed the people who got on and off.

'The new community policeman was in Arlo's when I went to get the milk. He calls himself Jammy. He says his mates gave him the nickname because his surname's Preserve. I said hello to him.'

'Mum, I hope you're not going to start telling tales on the neighbours.'

'Of course not. You know I've never been a grass. Not even when I was a councillor. But I might make Jammy aware of one or two things. He may not notice them otherwise. He seems like an easy-going kind of chap, which isn't a bad thing. The last one was the type who lived on his nerves.'

'Is Plain Ease open yet?'

'Reed's van is parked across the gates. I expect he's gone to look after the hens. And guess who's sitting outside Arlo's stuffing himself with pasta?'

Viv sprinkled sugar on her cornflakes. 'Is Yessy back at last? I wonder where he's been all winter. The poor kid must be frozen, sitting outside in the rain. Arlo should let him eat indoors.'

'Yessy stinks, poor lad. It's best to keep him in the open air. I suppose he'll go back to sleeping rough at Plain Ease. I don't know why Reed allows it.'

'He allows it because Yessy does all the heavy work in the

community garden. And he's the only one who can work the compost toilet. '

'What's the point of the compost toilet? Whose idea was it to have a loo for demonstration purposes only?'

'It was a donation from a sponsor.'

'Viv, do you think it's Reed who gives Yessy his dinner money? '

'Not likely. Reed's as tight as a crab's arse. Have you ever seen him pay for a cup of tea? '

'Come to think of it, there was money in Yessy's purse long before Reed set up Plain Ease.'

While Viv was eating her cornflakes, taking care not to spill them, Irene stood up to get a better view of what was happening in the street. Yessy was gobbling up pasta as if he hadn't eaten a square meal in weeks. Reed was rummaging around in his van as if he'd lost something - probably paperwork. Meanwhile, in the front window of Arlo's, a familiar face was staring out through a hole wiped in condensation.

'Hetty was in the caff again this morning. I wish she'd leave Arlo alone.'

'It's none of our business, Mum.'

'I'm ashamed to be related to that woman. She makes out they're separated, but she runs back to Arlo whenever it suits her. He's a lovely man who deserves better. If I was him, I'd tell Hetty where to go. I hope she isn't going to show up at our meeting.'

Viv put down her spoon. 'That won't happen. Can you imagine Hetty gardening? She'd ruin her manicure.'

'But she fancies Reed!'

'She's kidding herself. Reed must be twenty years younger than Hetty.'

While Viv laboured through the slow process of getting ready to go out Irene did the washing-up with one eye on the window. In particular she was monitoring a secluded corner under the railway arches. In the past she'd seen Hetty hanging around there with booted and suited City types. Brown envelopes had changed hands. What was her younger cousin up to? Irene thought she knew.

At the bus stop three young women were chatting together. Irene knew two of them. Puja's grandaughter Bushra was probably on her way to university. Her friend Folu lived at the new hostel Arlo and Hetty's boy managed. Irene knew for a fact Folu was running three cleaning jobs, but for months she'd seen her walking up and down by the arches every evening at ten. Once she'd asked Folu who she was waiting for. The girl had kissed her teeth and said nothing. Irene thought this was very rude.

The third girl was a tall, thin stranger with long dark hair. Over jeans and a jumper she was wearing a smart blue trench coat. Irene said aloud, 'I hope that girl knows how to stand up for herself. If she walks into Arlo's in that coat Hetty's likely to walk out in it.'

'Mum, are you talking to yourself again?' Viv called from the bathroom.

'I said, be careful with the flush. It's been catching, and if it breaks we'll have to pay to get it fixed. We won't get any help from the landlords.'

Looking down at Bushra, Folu and the stranger, Irene tried to imagine what it felt like to be them. She found it impossible to put herself in their shoes. At twenty she'd been married and pregnant with Viv. Two years later Rob came along. He was a wild kid, but the army made a man of him. How different her life might have been - if only. If only her Jim hadn't dropped dead of a heart attack at fifty-four. If only Rob hadn't been on duty when the bomb went off. If only Viv hadn't had a stroke the day after her no-good boyfriend went back to his wife.

In her bedroom Irene brushed her white hair and applied bright red lipstick. In the bottom drawer of the dressing table which Jim's mother had given her as a wedding present lay an ancient manilla folder. Carefully Irene extracted a dog-eared sheet of paper. Her protected tenancy agreement lay in her hands, written down in black and white, exactly as she remembered it.

'Don't let them grind you down,' she said to herself. 'So long as you pay your rent, they can't evict you.'

'What's that, Mum?' Viv was at the door. Irene slipped the folder under a pile of cardigans.

Viv took firm hold of her mother's arm in preparation for their trek downstairs. 'Maybe we should accept the inevitable and find ourselves somewhere new to live, like Puja did. If I'm honest, Mum, I fancy a ground floor flat in one of those smart new blocks.'

'Don't talk like that, Viv. You're playing into the hands of the landlords. They're trying to break our spirit. They want us to give up and move out. That's why they won't repair the lift. Be careful on the stairs, love, and take your time. There's no hurry.'

12

Arlo's Café
Samvida

While I was enjoying my second free cup of tea, two elderly women who were well wrapped up against the cold entered the café. The older one was pushing the younger one in a wheelchair. I pointed them out to Reed, who looked up from completing my application form.

'Yes, those ladies are Champions,' he said.

I'd been watching a group of women who were laughing and joking together at a table close to the door. Babies and toddlers were climbing all over their mothers, some of whom were pregnant. The snippets of conversation I overheard - about kids' birthday parties, local schools and the cost of child care - reminded me how much Urban and I had wanted to start a family. There was no need to wait. Because we were wealthy, child care was no problem. I was longing to have babies and Urban wanted to have more children before he got too old to play with them. He said he didn't care if we had boys or girls but I knew he secretly wanted a boy. Even Nina was on board with our plans. She was looking forward to having a younger brother or sister. I was so sure I'd conceive while we were on our honeymoon in the Maldives that I became depressed and tearful when I got my period. In spite of Urban's disappointment, he'd been matter-of-fact about the situation. It had only been a few weeks, he pointed out, and if necessary we could afford fertility treatment. Anyway, I was young and we were both in good health, so I was likely to fall pregnant very soon.

We went on trying for a baby until the day Urban died. If I had fallen pregnant, I'd probably have belonged to a cheerful gang of mums like the one in Arlo's. It made me feel sad to think that now I was single again it was possible I'd never have children. In the dusty meeting pod on Floor Six Lucan had called me naive and told me the husband I adored only wanted me as a breeder. This proved he was a liar who knew nothing about me. The truth is, I was fine with being a baby machine. I'd happily have popped out a dozen little Urbans and Samvidas.

The woman using the wheelchair stood up and began to walk with a stick. Although she was unsteady on her feet she made good progress - until the baby buggies got in her way. The other woman was trying to collapse the wheelchair and park it in a corner, but it was difficult in the confined space. Before long the wheelchair got tangled up with the buggies and the woman with the stick was clutching the counter for support. Distracted by their socialising, the mothers barely noticed the difficulties the older women were suffering. Some of them carried on talking while they reached behind them to move their buggies with one hand. The result was a tangle of wheels, trailing blankets and screaming toddlers.

Reed, whose head was bent over his paperwork, didn't notice

what was happening. I was about to go and help the two elderly Champions when a policeman took charge of the situation. He must have been sitting behind us all along, but I hadn't noticed him. He was only a community officer, the sort who can't arrest anyone, but the sight of his blue uniform sent a shiver down my spine. Ever since Lucan made me watch me the sex movie I starred in without my knowledge I'd felt an overwhelming sense of guilt. Even though I knew I'd done nothing wrong the thought of being anywhere near a police officer was terrifying.

Smiling with relief, the woman with the stick sat down next to me. When she spoke her voice was slightly slurred. 'Thank you Jammy,' she said. 'I don't know why babies need prams the size of caravans.'

As she took a chair next to her daughter the older woman said, 'We appreciate you keeping it local, Reed. At least we didn't have to fight our way through the buggies to get on a bus.'

Reed said, 'Ladies, this is Sam. Sam, meet Irene and her daughter Viv. Irene is an expert forager. You can learn a lot from her.'

Irene and Viv were unwrapping their layers of woollens. They both wore their long hair up. The mother's was white, the daughter's brown streaked with grey. Both of them had pretty old faces with pointed chins and piercing dark blue eyes. They'd made an effort to look smart for the meeting, with red lipstick and gold earrings. When Arlo brought over a tray of tea, sandwiches and biscuits, they greeted him like an old friend.

The next Champion to arrive was a middle-aged Asian woman. While she made her way through the crowded café she kept her eyes on the floor. She wore a loose brown waterproof, a purple hijab and wellington boots decorated with a floral print.

'Morning Puja. Good to see you,' said Reed. 'This is Sam.'

Puja welcomed me with a kind smile. She'd just settled down

with a cup of tea and a biscuit when someone sat down beside her. I hadn't seen the young woman come in. If I had I'd probably have left immediately, because it was Bushra from the bus stop. She was wearing a hijab printed with green and yellow designs that matched her brown jacket and trousers. Her nails were painted dark green and her tote bag was so full it had to have a chair to itself.

Reed said, 'I'm glad you were able to join us, Bushra.'

Bushra hugged Puja. 'Nan, it's okay for me to miss my lecture. My friend's taking notes.'

Puja patted her granddaughter's arm and helped herself to another biscuit.

Reed said, 'Massive thanks to everyone for turning out in such awful weather. Before we begin our planning session, I want you to welcome Sam to the group.'

Everyone said, 'Welcome, Sam.' Nobody asked me where I'd come from or how I'd got my black eye. And that was all it took to make me a new woman. I was no longer Urban's pampered wifey. I was homeless, unemployed, abused Sam Gumby, local Champion.

Reed asked us to draw the things we'd most like to see in our market garden. I know nothing about growing vegetables, so I drew a shed like Dad's. Irene sketched squares with crop names neatly printed: rocket, chard, garlic. Viv made a grid of wide paths with ACCESS written in capital letters. Puja doodled cartoon sunflowers.

Bushra's drawing of tall plants I recognised from Mum's garden looked professional. I was embarrassed because I'd made such a fuss over my coat, so I tried to say something nice.

'Your picture is amazing, Bushra. What are those flowers called?'

Without looking at me she muttered, 'Hollyhocks.' I don't

think she's ever going to like me. I wish I hadn't been so rude to her and Folu.

I was so interested in everyone's drawings that I didn't notice how fast the sandwiches were disappearing. Suddenly Irene asked if everyone had finished eating. Without waiting for an answer, she produced an empty tin box and began to pack it with what was left of the food. Puja brought out a Tupperware bowl and set up in competition. Soon there was nothing left on the plate but curly slices of bread peeling away from grated Cheddar. I'd missed out on the biscuits. I took the tired-looking scraps and wrapped them in a paper napkin, because for the first time in my life I didn't know where my next meal was coming from.

I was stowing the bread and cheese in a side pocket of my suitcase when Chel tapped my shoulder. 'Chop chop Sam,' he said. 'The rush is over. Grab your stuff. I can show you the room if you get a move on.'

TimePad turned out to be inside a large house that must once have belonged to a wealthy merchant. It was a few minutes walk from Arlo's Café, on a street that must once have been the height of fashion. Around the windows were sprays of plaster flowers. Where the plaster was chipped you could see layers of bright colour. The facade was painted white, but the organic shapes and dots of colour made it look as if it might burst into bloom at any moment. Inside were stunning wooden staircases, thin room partitions and the smell of paint. The hostel had only been open for a few months. I was one of the first homeless people to stay there. Chel showed me to a narrow room with a high ceiling. At the far end was a high sash window. Along one wall was a set of bunk beds and by the other was a small chest of drawers. In one corner was narrow wardrobe with a hanging rail at the top and two shelves near the floor. Everything was white except the cheap carpet, which was dark grey. Pinned to the wall was a sheet of paper printed with the rules of TimePad. No smoking. No sub-letting. No noise because of shift workers.

'Here you go,' said Chel. 'Lock-up's at eleven. You don't need a key. I live on the ground floor, so if you want anything you know where to find me. I'll come back later to check you're okay.'

I was already going off my new landlord, who was standing far too close to me. Chelsea is usually a woman's name, so he wasn't what I'd expected. 'Don't bother, I'll be fine. Your name's unusual for a man. Was it Hetty's choice?'

'No, Dad's. One of his football heroes had it for a middle name. Catch you later, Sam.'

The top bunk was made up with an old chair cushion and a couple of moth-eaten blankets. There were no pillows or sheets on the bottom bunk but the mattress looked clean. By then I was exhausted, so I dropped my coat on the floor and passed out on the bed fully dressed. I surfaced long enough to nibble some bread and cheese and stagger to the bathroom, but I didn't fully wake up until early the next morning. When I regained consciousness I was alone in the room. I could hear voices and footsteps on the landing and the blind on the high sash window was letting in watery daylight. My coat was hanging from the rail and someone else's clothes were folded on the shelf. When I remembered Reed was expecting me at my new place of work I got up and raised the blind. The view outside was bleak. One floor down was an enclosed back yard. Beyond it was a landscape of cranes dangling over building sites flanked by crumbling Victorian warehouses.

In the bathroom, a Black girl was washing at the row of basins. When she turned around I realised it was Folu. I hoped she'd be more ready than Bushra had been to make it up.

'Hi, Folu,' I said. 'We spoke yesterday, remember? My

name's Sam. Thank you for the money. I'm sorry I was rude to you.'

'Don't worry about it. You and I are room-mates now, so we must be kind to each other.'

I'd splashed my face and hands with water before I remembered I had no towel. When Folu offered me a ragged cloth I took it and dried myself while we talked. She was just back from one of her cleaning jobs and getting ready to go to another.

'This place is okay, Sam. It's better than living on the street. But you will have to be careful.'

'Careful of what?'

'You'll find out. Tell me, who hurt your face?'

I was telling Folu my cover story about a thieving, violent cousin when a guy in a hi-viz jacket came in and broke the mood by pissing without closing the cubicle door.

'Catch you later, Folu,' I said.

'Wait for me,' she said.

13

Lady Willa's Salon
Archy

Archy was in a state of high tension when he arrived for his appointment at Lady Willa's. The glitzy atmosphere in the foyer did nothing to relax him. On the wall was a display of the salon's creative triumphs, including a huge shot of Willa accepting her umpteenth industry award. Every nerve in Archy's body was begging him to run away while he still had his dignity.

Lucan had briefed him about dramatic events at the Penthouse.

'One of the maids has done a runner, taking with her several thousand pounds worth of household and personal items belonging to my late uncle. The agency claims that Vida signed for the removal of the goods. I can't be bothered to pursue the woman across Eastern Europe, so I've written off the loss. What concerns me is that my cousin Nina reported the theft. Vida has vanished off the face of the earth.'

Since helping Vida Edeldi into a cab after her secret meeting with Lucan, Archy had researched her background more thoroughly than any due diligence case.

'She may have gone abroad to visit her parents.'

'Impossible. Her passport and phone are in my safe and I've cancelled her credit cards and allowance.'

'How did you get hold of Mrs. Edeldi's things? Sir, are you sure it's legal? She can't be leading a normal life.'

'Of course it's legal, Brise. The firm paid for everything she owns. That's why she left her handbag with me for safekeeping. Anyway, Vida's life hasn't been normal since Urban passed away. She's been skulking in the Penthouse ever since, as if she had something to hide.'

This was confirmation that Lucan suspected Vida had murdered her husband.

'Surely your cousin has Vida's contact details?'

'Nina isn't picking up. I want you to track her down and find out what she knows about Vida's disappearance.'

'Shall I try Miss Edeldi's flat in Fulham?'

'Make it look like a chance meeting. Nina helps out at my wife's salon. Get yourself a haircut.'

This was Lucan's idea of a joke. He didn't know how close to the bone it was. Archy had never been to a barber. He didn't know what his hair looked like, and he had no intention of finding out. He'd worn a buzz-cut since he was ten - self-inflicted when money was scarce. By growing a full head of hair he risked destroying the neutral appearance he'd spent years cultivating. On the other hand, a visit to Lady Willa's was his best hope of making contact with Vida. After giving Lucan's suggestion careful thought, Archy had resolved to make an appointment with one of Willa's top stylists. If not having any hair turned out to be a problem, he was ready to blag his way through.

An impeccably groomed receptionist greeted him. 'What are we doing for you today, sir?'

Archy ran a finger around the inside of his shirt collar, which suddenly felt too tight. 'I have an appointment with Franco.'

'Franco will be free momentarily. May I take your coat?'

Within seconds, his overcoat had been spirited away and he was following someone slender as an avatar through a maze of mirrors. In the salon's inner sanctum, heads were being wrapped in foil, painted with gels and trimmed with flying scissors. On the work station where he was left to await his fate, tools with teeth lay ready. The mass of bodies and reflections flowing past him on all sides appeared chaotic at first, but he soon became aware of an underlying calm. After the competitive rage of the financial world, he found the buzz of the salon reassuring. It was like watching a ballet where everyone knew their role and performed it joyfully.

A bearded face appeared over his shoulder. It was Willa's prize-winning senior stylist. 'Hi. I'm Franco. What brings you here today, Archy?'

It was a good question. Archy wasn't sure of the answer. Ambition, cowardice, fear?

'My boss sent me. He's married to your boss.'

'Understood,' said Franco. 'Let's talk follicles.'

The stylist began to palpate Archy's scalp with powerful fingers, while he lectured him in a broad Scottish accent about growth programmes. Archy wasn't listening. He was intent on scanning the mirrors in an effort to locate Nina. It was proving to be more difficult than he had expected. There were hundreds of images of her on social media, wearing designer dresses and shoes. In each of them her hair was a different colour. Here in the salon droves of twenty-something assistants in monotone outfits were running up and down. Any one of them could be Urban Edeldi's only child.

The puzzle was too hard to solve. Weariness took over Archy's body and weighted his eyelids. Swaddled in satin and lapped in luxury, with Franco's theories about bone structure rumbling on as a background to his thoughts, he felt more relaxed than he had for years. It dawned on him that he'd been allowing rampant ambition to crowd out everything that made life pleasurable. It was years since he'd had a proper girlfriend, months since he'd spoken to any of his old friends and weeks since he'd been on a date. As far back as he could remember, his whole life had been work followed by more work. Scholarship, university, summer jobs - they'd all led up to his internship at Edeldico. A promotion which seemed to promise the world had followed. And the result of his efforts was being ordered to spy on two recently bereaved young women.

Archy decided that after he'd had his pretend haircut he'd take the rest of the day off. He made up his mind to go home and review his contacts - maybe text one of those women he'd promised to call. It was time he found a friend to have a drink with, before the world forgot him and he was left alone with the dream. At his rented studio flat, if emergency sirens didn't keep him awake it was his neighbours, fighting or making love. Often, by the sound of it, they did both at once. When at last he fell asleep, a dream followed. It was always the same dream. He'd woken from it, with tears rolling down his face, at every stage of his life and in many different places. The dream had followed him to the dorm at boarding school, his university hall and tents halfway up mountainsides.

Archy's eyelids began to droop. He was on the verge of nodding off when he caught sight of the back view of a young woman with curly blonde hair. There was something about her that was familiar and endearing, as if they'd known each other in a former life. It was a shock when her front view rounded the corner of the mirror he was facing and spoke to him.

'Hi! I'm Nina? I'm sure we've met, but I can't remember where?'

She looked so much like her late father Urban that Archy was struck dumb.

The interruption to his creative flow annoyed Franco. 'Archy is a new client. Please get him a drink.'

'My pleasure. Breakfast tea, flat white, glass of Sauvignon?'

A few minutes later, Nina reappeared with peppermint tea in a stylish white cup. A minuscule biscuit nestled in the saucer. By then Archy had recovered from his lapse in resolve and was discussing his growth management plan with Franco. It sounded more challenging than the Cresta Run.

'You tend to over-complicate things, Frank,' said Nina. 'Archy has two choices. Grow it or not.'

The stylist gave her a stern look. 'Aren't you needed in reception?'

Nina's face lit up and she clapped her hands. 'Now I remember! You used to work for my Dad.'

Franco rolled his eyes. 'Why don't you two have a lovely catch-up while I'm prepping my next client?'

'Perfect,' said Nina with a grin. 'I'll give him a head massage while he tells me how much he enjoys working for my mean cousin.'

'Sounds good,' Archy said. He wasn't sure where this was going, but he hoped it would lead him to Vida.

Nina's fingers assaulted his bare scalp without mercy. The pleasurable pain reached down his neck into his shoulders, squeezing out embedded coils of tension he didn't know existed.

His limbs were longing to relax into the treatment, but he forced himself to stay alert. He dared not lose focus again. It was essential to control this conversation in order to get the information he needed about Vida, without making her step-daughter suspicious.

'Unfortunately I can't satisfy your curiosity about your cousin,' he said tactfully. 'Humble drones like me don't see much of the CEO.'

'Do you think the firm will go under now my Dad's dead?'

The bluntness of the question took Archy by surprise. He thought for a moment before replying. 'I'm sure we'll survive. Market confidence is up right now.' Her fingers caressed his neck. 'Some of the financial journalists say EdeldiCo is over-extended. Isn't there a risk there'll be a gap in funding after my stepmother claims her inheritance?'

Nina seemed to be a fan of the direct approach - the type who liked to put her cards on the table. Archy liked her style. He threw back an even blunter question.

'Mrs Edeldi recently had a meeting with the MD. Why don't you ask her?'

For a second, Nina's fingers stopped pounding Archy's scalp. 'My stepmother isn't interested in business. She says money doesn't matter to her. I think it must be true, because she's ridiculously generous. She gave away all of my Dad's things, along with everything he ever bought her.'

'Good news for some charity.'

'No such luck. She gave it all to one of the maids.'

Nina's fingertips dug in hard. 'Ouch,' said Archy.

'After I found out what Nina had done with Dad's stuff, I got high and we had a fight.'

'I'm sorry to hear that. I hope you and your stepmother have been able to make it up?'

In the mirror their eyes locked.

'You didn't come here to get your hair cut. My cousin sent you to find Vida,' said Nina, removing the towel from his shoulders.

Franco arrived to reclaim his chair before Archy had time to reply. He gave the stylist a generous tip and followed Nina back to reception. Their faces flickered across the mirrors and were multiplied to infinity. It was astonishing how his senses had been revived by her perfume and the touch of her fingers on his skin. He recalled his decision to forget about work for a few hours. He was going to speak to a mate, look up a lover, take a friendly girl out for a drink.

'Nina, what time do you finish work? Can we get that glass of Sauvignon?'

She shook out his overcoat and helped him into it. 'There will have to be ground rules. I don't want to talk about Vida. Or Lucan.'

'You have no idea how happy that will make me,' said Archy.

14

Plain Ease
Samvida

'Plain Ease is a Meanwhile Space.' When Reed talked about his projects, you could hear the capital letters in his voice. 'Once upon a time it was a pickle factory. In a couple of years a block of flats will be built on it. MEANWHILE it's a community garden.'

It was my first morning in Coopers Hook. I'd thrown on a hoodie against the rain and run all the way from TimePad to Plain Ease. When I arrived at the gates a white van painted with the logo of an environmental charity was parked at the entrance. Reed was in the driver's seat.

'Hi Sam. Did you sleep well?'

'Like a log. Thanks for finding me a bed.'

'It's what I do. Hop in!'

We drove a hundred metres along an unmade road between building sites. Cranes reared up like dinosaurs behind hoardings decorated with stencilled graffiti. Where the track opened out Reed parked up. Rain was pounding in sheets on the windscreen and roof, so we waited in the van for it to stop. 'Welcome to Plain Ease, Sam,' said Reed, when the rainstorm had passed and we could hear ourselves speak. 'You'll be working here five days a week, from ten until four. Technically you're a volunteer, but you can claim up to £5 a day for food. I'll need receipts. How does that sound?'

'Perfect.'

'Promise me you'll provide a reference.'

I crossed my fingers and promised.

We climbed out of the van on to a stretch of tarmac where weeds were bursting through. Reed called it the Yard. Big wooden boxes were lined up at intervals across it, creating a kind of maze. Each box was a metre square and built on a pallet. Numbers were stencilled on their sides. Reed made it clear these boxes were a big deal.

'These are our mobile gardens, Sam. They're designed to be transported by fork-lift truck. When the building work starts we'll move them to the next Meanwhile Space. Come into the poly-tunnel and I'll tell you about our market gardening project.'

Inside the poly-tunnel, which looked like a giant plastic tube, trowels and empty plastic seed trays were laid out on trestle tables. On the floor were sacks of potting compost. Reed told me vegetable seeds were going to be started off in the trays and transferred to the mobile gardens when they were strong enough. Later they'd be harvested and delivered to local restaurants. Plain Ease was going to become a small business, but it wouldn't make a profit. Any money left over after the costs were covered would be used for development.

Next, Reed took me to a shipping container with windows and a door cut into it. 'This is the Hub of our enterprise,' he said.

The space inside the Hub was split into two sections. On the right, waterproof coats waited on hooks with muddy rubber boots lined up below them. Watering cans were clustered around plastic crates overflowing with grubby gardening gloves. Spades and forks were propped up in a corner. A smaller room on the left had a notice taped to the door. 'Staff Only', it read. Against the wall was a long workbench with a box of teabags and an open carton of milk at one end. The rest of the bench was laden with plants in need of TLC and mugs advertising local charities. On the floor under it were crates full of packets of vegetable seeds, canvas tote bags printed with logos, laminated information sheets and packs of bottled water. A cheap metal desk piled high with receipts, handwritten notes and letters with fancy headings stood under the window. The rest of the Hub was tidy and well organised. I could tell somebody worked hard to keep it that way. As soon as I saw Reed's desk I realised he was not that person.

Since the day before I'd eaten nothing but left-over bread and cheese and drunk only tap-water from the washroom at TimePad. My head felt as if it was about to float off my shoulders and my stomach was rumbling. Reed took a vacuum flask and a packet of cereal bars from his backpack.

'We're off grid here, but I bring hot water. Yesterday's milk should be okay.'

The milk had gone off, but I was so hungry the tea tasted delicious. I swallowed a cereal bar pretty much whole and secreted another in my back pocket for later. When a fresh wave of rain pattered on the roof an excited clucking floated in on the breeze.

'The weather is putting the rescue hens on edge,' said Reed.

I almost asked him who the hens had rescued, but I wasn't sure he'd get the joke. Instead I asked if they lived in the wooden hut behind the bushes on the far side of the yard.

'That's the compost toilet. That's for display purposes only. Arlo lets us use the café's facilities.'

I'd never heard of a compost toilet. I was trying to get my head around the concept when Bushra walked in. She was wearing Doc Martens boots with jeans and a tie-dyed tunic and headscarf.

'My Nan's on her way,' she said. 'We waited for the rain to stop.'

'I've just remembered I promised to pick Irene and Viv up in the van,' said Reed. 'Bushra, can you take Sam to the poly-tunnel and get her started on the seed trays?'

Bushra gave me a hard stare, so I asked Reed to show me the hens. He agreed immediately, as I'd guessed he would. I already knew the twelve battery hens he'd rescued were his pride and joy, because he'd been telling me all about them while we drank our tea. The hen-house was at the top of the community garden. It had been built by volunteers from recycled wooden uprights and wire netting, at a total cost of 49p for nails. At one end of the run was a shelter with perches, food trays and water drips. The eggs were collected from boxes full of straw. Reed and I had to stoop to get through the padlocked gate, but once inside we had space to walk around.

When the hens came to greet us Reed picked one up and gave her to me to hold. Under her feathers my hand touched his. The hen was settling down in my arms when something very scary happened. Lying under the shelter was what looked like a pile of rubbish. Suddenly it rolled over and a tail appeared at one end. Thinking it was a fox I clutched the hen tightly. Then a young man crawled out from under empty pellet sacks and stood up, rubbing his eyes. It was Yessy, the homeless guy who'd offered to share his food with me. I'd mistaken his matted hair for a fox tail.

When Reed told Yessy off he sounded more resigned than annoyed. 'You know you're not allowed to sleep in the hen-house.'

'Yes.'

'Don't let me find you here again.'

'Yes.'

'This is Sam, our new Champion.'

'Yes.'

Yessy's eyes were searching my face eagerly, looking for a sign of recognition. When I gave him a thumbs up he grinned and returned the gesture. Like Hetty, he must have mistaken me for someone else. I was starting to think I had a doppleganger in Coopers Hook.

While we were walking back to the Hub, Reed complained it was impossible to keep Yessy out of the hen-house. 'I keep changing the code on the padlock, but he cracks it every time. I think he watches me from the bushes when I put the numbers in. And he comes and goes from the community garden as he pleases. He must have found a hole in the fence.'

Irene and Viv were waiting for us in the yard. They were wearing identical rain hats, waterproofs and Wellington boots. Viv was using her wheelchair with a waterproof cover over it.

'You were late so we started walking,' Irene said to Reed.

'Sorry,' said Reed. 'I had to give Sam her induction. I hope you didn't get wet.'

'We don't mind the rain,' said Viv. 'It's nice to be out.'

Irene looked up into the trees. 'Spring's very late this year, but just look at those rooks! They're getting on with building their nests. Nothing stops nature.'

The old mother and daughter chose to clear debris from the mobile gardens. Viv pulled out dead roots while Irene trotted up and down to the compost heap with a wheelbarrow. Puja was in the Hub sorting the gloves into pairs. She was the one who tried to keep everything tidy. As Reed returned to his desk he reminded me I was supposed to be working in the poly-tunnel. It was time to face my fears.

Bushra was trowelling potting compost into plastic trays. She didn't look up when I walked in. I screwed up my courage and said, 'I'm sorry I was so rude to you at the bus stop. I was having a really bad day.'

To my relief she turned to face me with a smile. 'Forget it. Everyone has bad days. Would you like to see my uni project?'

'Yes, I'd love to,' I said, looking around for an art folder.

She stood her trowel upright in the compost sack. Two minutes later we were standing in the middle of a muddy flower bed looking for signs of new growth.

'I'm doing an MA in textiles,' said Bushra. 'I make organic dyes to use in my designs. Reed lets me grow the dye plants at Plain Ease. Look, I have samples. '

'Most of them are yellow,' I said, rummaging in her tote bag. 'Is that your favourite colour?'

'Yellow is what you get. There are more shades of yellow plant dye than any other colour, but they fade. When you look at a tapestry embroidered hundreds of years ago, all the trees are blue. The embroidery wool would have been dyed green at first, but over the centuries the yellows faded.'

I picked out a pink scrap from among the coils of fabric. 'This colour is lovely.'

'It's called madder. There's a madder plant over there. You can keep that piece. Here, have this this little sewing kit as well. I get them free from my fabric supplier.'

After Bushra left I asked Puja about the compost toilet. Before she gave me the key she made me swear I only wanted to look at it. There was nothing much to see. The inside of the hut was pristine and smelled of pine. A metal lavatory pan reflected light from a window in the roof and a scoop lay on top of a bucket full of wood chippings. I was about to leave when I heard two people talking outside. When I stepped back in surprise, my foot nudged the bucket and chippings spilled out on to the floor.

A woman spoke first. 'Hetty's grandmother was my mother's sister, so I've known her since she was a baby. She's always been a chancer. Now I think she's mixed up with very bad people. I've seen her swapping packages with toffs in suits.'

'You mustn't judge people by their clothes,' a man's voice said. 'Yessy looks like a down and out, but he can afford to eat at Arlo's.'

'There's more to Yessy than meets the eye. There's always the price of a dish of pasta in the purse around his neck, but nobody knows where the money comes from.'

The voices faded into the distance. When I opened the door a crack I saw Irene and the community policeman walking away across the yard. The wheels of his bike were juddering over the holes in the tarmac. I scooped to gather up the spilled wood chippings. When I went to replace them in the bucket I noticed what looked like the edge of a brown paper package sticking out. By digging carefully among the chippings I managed to undo it at the top.

The parcel was full of used banknotes.

For a moment I hesitated - but there was never any real doubt in my mind about what I was going to do next. I couldn't report my find to Reed, because he was sure to call the police. I was on the run, in fear of my life, after being accused of sexual homicide and murdering my husband, so an interview with the local coppers was the last thing I wanted. And I needed money to live on. A fiver a day was barely enough to pay for food. I didn't know how I was going to afford toothpaste, soap and tampons.

Working fast, I hid big handfuls of ten and twenty pound notes inside my clothes and trainers.

I closed the brown paper on the rest of the cash, covered it with wood chippings and locked the door of the compost toilet. In the Hub, Puja took back the key without asking questions. When I went out into the Yard Irene and Viv were waiting by the van for a lift. Reed was on his phone, winding up a conversation.

'I have to go to another site, Sam. Puja will lock up. As it's your first day you can finish early.'

Folu was at work when I got back to the room we shared. While I was using the kit Bushra had given me to sew banknotes into the hem of my blue trench coat, I reviewed my situation. I had a job, a roof over my head and the five hundred pounds I'd liberated from the compost toilet. Best of all, a community garden in Coopers Hook was the last place Lucan would think of looking for me. For the time being I was safe.

15

Arlo's Café
Hetty

It was the first sunny day in Coopers Hook for weeks. Most of Arlo's regulars had seized the opportunity to get out and about. Only Arlo, Hetty and Chel were in the café when a diesel engine grumbled into life in the street outside. The two men rushed to peer out of the window. Looking over their shoulders Hetty saw a flash of sunlight ricochet off a grey van's side mirror.

'Why are you two so jumpy?' she said. 'Dozens of vans go past here every day. What's so special about that one?'

'It's not the van that makes me jumpy. It's the guy inside it,' said Arlo. 'You'd better take a head count of your tenants tonight, Chel.'

'Not me. It's their own lookout if they ain't indoors before lockup. Anyway, I reckon I could take that foreign geezer. Dad, have you got any spare toilet rolls in the store? We've run out at TimePad and I ain't got time to go down the cash and carry.'

Wearily Arlo said, 'Go and have a look.'

'Which foreign geezer does he mean?' said Hetty, when Chel had left through the kitchen door..

Arlo was pouring himself an espresso. 'You know who he's talking about. It was you who got us into this mess in the first place. You borrowed from your so-called business contacts and made me sign for it. Then you spent the lot on your precious dance studio and left me high and dry.'

'You owed me. I gave you thirty years of my life. It was time I had something for myself.'

'I wish I could have something for myself. Maybe a season ticket for the football. But I can't even afford to take a day off. All I ever do is stand behind this counter, try to earn enough money to pay the debt you saddled me with and hope the geezer in the grey van doesn't break both my legs.'

'Stop moaning and drink your coffee,' said Hetty.

Yessy slunk in, looking over his shoulder. Hetty scowled at him. Since he'd settled back into life under the protection of Reed and the Champions he looked clean and well fed. However, with his tangled hair and slept-in clothes he was a long way from being the ideal customer.

Arlo took a few coins from the wallet around Yessy's neck and threw them into the till. 'Pasta?'

Yessy licked his lips. 'Yes.'

'There you go, mate.'

Yessy waited.

'Meat sauce?'

'Yes.'

'Salsa?'

'Yes.'

As usual, Yessy took his food outside. Reed, who'd just

parked on a double yellow line, paused to give him a high five before bounding into the café.

'You're perky today, Reed,' said Hetty.

'I always feel better when the sun shines. I hope it stays like this for our big event at Plain Ease on Saturday. Can we rely on your support, Arlo?'

'Sure, no problem.'

An event at Plain Ease meant trails of mud across the café floor and devastation in the washroom. In Arlo's place, Hetty would have told Reed to send one of his volunteers to clean up after his punters. But Arlo wouldn't complain about being put upon, for fear of offending his best customer. His only compensation was the extra income he earned from selling food and drink to the locals who attended Reed's fairs and festivals.

'Will you be wanting any refreshments for your guests?' Arlo asked hopefully.

'Not this time. Irene is going to lead a foraging tour. Puja will encourage punters to eat the plants they've gathered, by showing them how to make green smoothies. The theme will be food for free.'

Hetty and Arlo exchanged glances. They'd both been listening in when the last Champions' meeting took place around the green table. Their ears had pricked up when when Reed enthusiastically put forward a plan to generate more income for his market gardening project.

'Several local restaurateurs have signed up to buy our produce, but until we start the harvest, every penny counts. Irene, I'd like you to lead a foraging walk. If you show people which wild plants are edible, they can harvest them. And Puja can demonstrate how to make green smoothies with the plants they've foraged. You'll do that, won't you, Puja? Thanks. We can price the event high and our only outlay will be on avocados.'

Irene said, 'Who's going to pay good money to listen to me going on about weeds?'

'Lots of people will jump at the chance, Irene. All the top chefs are using foraged ingredients these days. Believe it or not, you're bang on trend.'

Remembering this conversation, Arlo said, 'I could make smoothies in the café. I can bung an avocado in a blender just as well as Puja. If you want to do the green thing I'll throw in a few nettles.'

'Ha! I love your sense of humour, Arlo. I'm due to meet a sponsor. See you later.'

Reed stepped aside to allow Folu, Sam's room-mate, to pass him in the doorway. The factory cleaner rarely put in an appearance at Arlo's. She never had any money, even though, according to Irene, she was holding down two jobs. Sometimes Bushra treated her to a can of fizzy drink and Sam occasionally bought her a meal. Hetty was sure Folu's immigration status was illegal. Whoever had got her into the UK was probably creaming off her wages.

'Some people don't deserve their good luck,' said Arlo. He was watching Reed's van clear the pavement, just as a traffic warden rounded the corner. 'Morning, Folu. Day off? What can I get you?'

'This is not a day off for me, sir. Unfortunately I am out of work. I am looking for a new job.'

'My deep fat fryer needs scrubbing,' said Arlo. 'Will you do it for a fiver?'

'Yes please.'

She slipped around to the business side of the counter, just as Chel came out of the kitchen. He glared at her. 'What are you doing here at this time of day?'

Folu bowed her head. 'I asked your good father for work. He

has asked me to scrub his fryer.'

'What happened to the cleaning jobs I got you?'

By the sound of it, Chel was taking a cut of Folu's wages. Hetty picked up a free paper and pretended to be enthralled by an article about bollards.

'I cannot scrub floors on my knees any more. It is too hard. And the chemicals make me sick.'

'Think you're too good for hard graft, do you? Well, my Dad ain't going to bail you out.'

Arlo said, 'Steady on, Chel. The poor girl wants a better job. We've all been there.'

Folu raised her head and looked Chel in the eye. 'I am skilled at kitchen work. And I am an excellent cook. I can make jollof rice and fish soup and piri piri chicken.'

'What good is that foreign muck to us? Does this look like one of them flash new restaurants? We're running a good old English caff. Go on, sling your hook.'

Folu turned her back on the two men and stalked towards the door, holding her head high. Hetty felt sorry for her - a refugee's life was hard enough without this kind of rough treatment - but Chel had a point. The café made barely enough money to cover its sky-high business rates. And then there was the debt to Edeldico. Arlo couldn't afford to take on staff.

'You were too harsh with her, Chel. I'd have given the girl a day's trial. The kitchen needs a deep clean. There's a load of grease congealing down the back of the grill.'

'Dad, even if we could afford her wages, you don't want Folu working here. She's a flake. I got her three perfectly good cleaning jobs and she's packed them all in.'

Hetty looked suspiciously at her son. 'I hope that's not down to you, Chelsea.'

Chel threw his arms up in exasperation. 'How's it my fault?

Folu's lucky to get any kind of job. Who knows where she blew in from? And have you seen the way she hangs around by the arches every night? I wouldn't be surprised if she's on the game.'

When a gang of builders walked in, filling the air with banter, Arlo sprang into action. Hetty finished her latte and refreshed her lipstick. When she got up to leave Chel stood in her way.

'Mum, you know you said Folu's problems was down to me? What did you mean?'

'Ain't it obvious? The girl can't go on scrubbing factory floors with bleach. She's pregnant.'

'Never. Folu's skinny as a rake.'

'She's six months gone, take my word for it. And if it's yours, don't come running to me for help. You should know better than to sleep with them skanks from TimePad. That job is your one chance to be a manager. Lose it, and you'll never make anything of yourself. And as for you, Arlo, don't you dare employ her. This is a business, not a charity. Folu will have to look out for herself.'

Arlo stopped taking the builders' order to gape at their son. 'Chel, what have you done?'

'I ain't done nothing, Dad! Folu probably don't know who the daddy is, but I swear it ain't me!'

Jammy chose this moment to walk in and approach Hetty. Immediately Arlo and Chel remembered something urgent they had to do in the kitchen..

'Good morning Mrs. Greer.'

'The name's Brill. Arlo and me are separated.'

'Do you have a few minutes to spare, Miss Brill?'

'No I don't. I have a business to run.'

'I just wanted to warn you that concern has been expressed for your safety.'

'Is that so? Which smart-arse has been sticking their nose into my business?'

'I'm not at liberty to share that information.'

'What am I supposed to have done?'

'It's not about anything you've done. It's about what other people might try to do to you. I understand strangers have approached you in the vicinity of the railway arches.'

'Who told you that?'

'A concerned neighbour saw you talking to a stranger in a smart business suit. The kind of person sometimes referred to as a toff. You gave him a large brown envelope. This neighbour was afraid you might have been acting under duress.'

Hetty looked at Jammy thoughtfully for a moment. Then she smiled.

'I know what you're talking about, Officer. I wasn't acting under nothing. As you probably know, I run a dance studio at the old Wicker pub. The toff, as you call him, was interested in taking dance lessons. There was a brochure about my classes in the big brown envelope.'

'I see,' said Jammy, 'I'm relieved to hear it. Thank you for clearing the matter up, Miss Brill.'

Hetty watched the policeman make a hurried exit and walk quickly away from the café.

'Actually, that ain't a bad idea,' she said to Arlo.

'What's that, babe?'

'Brochures for my classes at the Wicker. Maybe I should have some printed up.'

16

The Roof Bar, Coopers Hook
Archy

Archy always enjoyed Edeldico's social payback days. It was a relief to get out of his tiny glass office, where he felt like a specimen in a test tube, and get his hands dirty on a practical project. Today he also had the fun of watching the reactions of his cosseted colleagues to everyday life in Coopers Hook. From their daily commutes these City boys and girls had learned, in theory, that civilisation extended east of Liverpool Street. When they were faced with the reality they behaved like Martians on their first trip to Earth. From the station, a diverse wave of warm bodies carried the group, via the street market, to a multi-storey car park, where they fought their way into a coffin-shaped lift smelling of urine and chips. By the time they reached the top floor, all the sharp-elbowed shoppers laden with bags had baled out and the volunteers were left to find their own way. They huddled together on a bare landing with a trapped draught howling around them. When Archy hammered with his fist on the thick metal door that led to the roof they flinched and tried to hide behind each other.

Only Nina stood firm at Archy's side. Her presence was the reason why he was enjoying this corporate day even more than usual. It seemed miraculous to him that a month after their first meeting he was spending so much time with his late mentor's daughter. They weren't exactly dating. Archy hadn't even tried to kiss Nina yet. Her friendship was more than he'd dreamed of, and he didn't want to push his luck. But there was definitely a strong connection between them. The feeling he'd first had at Willa's salon that he and Nina knew each other in a former life had never left Archy. From a few words Nina had let slip, he guessed she felt the same way.

On the day they met, he'd been waiting when she emerged from Lady Willa's salon. Over a glass of sauvignon at a nearby wine bar, the two of them clicked. Since then, they'd been skating, taken long walks along the Embankment and tried out several new restaurants. Nina had even popped into Edeldico HQ one afternoon to see Archy. She'd avoided Lucan but showed a interest in the firm's annual report. Afterwards, the MD had made a point of mentioning her visit.

'I hear you've made contact with my cousin. Have you any news of Vida?'

Archy couldn't very well say that Nina had refused to talk about either Lucan or her missing stepmother. 'Not yet. I'm working on it.'

'Why don't you take Nina with you on the next payback day? In a new environment, maybe she'll relax her defences and tell you where Vida's hiding.'

Archy wasn't sure how Nina would react to being asked to take part in building a garden on the roof of a multi-storey car park, but he extended a tentative invitation. When she accepted without hesitation, he felt delight and terror in equal parts.

The heavy door to the car park roof creaked open. Behind it stood a young man with a hipster mustache. His sweatshirt bore the logo of the environmental charity contracted to run the project. Like the team from Edeldico he was dressed for manual labour. Archy held out his hand.

'Archy Brise. We spoke on the phone.'

'Reed Rankhorn, project manager.'

'Pleased to meet you, Reed,' said Nina. 'Great mustache.'

Reed grinned, exposing large white teeth.

When the EdeldiCo team emerged on to the roof they were blasted by an icy wind bearing the stench of diesel. Archy made a quick tour of the proposed Roof Bar, assessing the task his team had volunteered to complete. Planks of wood were deposited in neat piles every few metres. One complete structure had already been built as an example. Each was of a different design, but all of them included seats and a planting box. Ready in a windblown corner were the fixings for a big screen, with a mixed bunch of recycled garden chairs stacked nearby. In a sheltered corner near the doors, hundreds of labelled pot-grown plants were lined up. In the centre of the roof stood the battered frame of a red car.

'Cool, isn't it?' said Reed. 'My charity's been shortlisted for a design prize for this project. And it's all totally do-able. Here you are, I've had the instruction sheets laminated. Look, this is the plan. Seating, raised beds, shrubs, herbs. And we're going to plant a tree in that old Porsche. We're delighted to have Edeldico working with us. You guys are going to make a difference today.'

With ten minutes all the tasks were allocated and targets had been set. Ignoring bursts of freezing rain, the Edeldico team were applying their inborn competitiveness, usually employed in the pursuit of financial gain, to building street furniture out of wood. It soon became obvious that some of them had never used a saw before.

Nina said, 'City boys and girls always have to win, don't they? Everybody wants to finish first. I hope we don't lose any fingers.'

'The guys have an extra incentive today,' said Archy. 'Lucan has donated a magnum of champagne as a prize for the fastest worker.'

'Is that so? He's not usually so generous. I expect he's trying to keep them sweet. Since Dad passed away an awful lot of staff have given in their notice. Headhunters are sniffing around.'

'How on earth do you know that?'

'I keep my eyes open. And my ears. Sometimes I overhear very interesting conversations. You'd be surprised what people tell their hairdressers and beauticians.'

Archy and Nina were using the list Reed gave them to count out shrubs and herbs, which had to be ready to fill the finished planters, while they kept tabs on their team's progress. When they moved the containers gusts of wind snatched up scents of rosemary, lavender and sage. Nina paused to sniff the air. 'Isn't it a lovely smell? My Mum would have loved this project. She was always pottering about in our roof garden at the Penthouse. Did your parents like gardening, Archy?'

Archy was distracted by trying to make sense of the Latin names on the plant labels. Without thinking he said, 'I don't know.'

Puzzled, Nina put down the lavender plant she was holding.

'There's a picture of your family in your office. It was taken in a garden. Whose garden was it?'

'Ours of course,' said Archy.

He realised he was digging himself into a dangerous hole, and tried to talk his way out of it.

'Dad did the garden. Mum wasn't keen on working out of doors. Her pale skin burned easily.'

'Are you kidding me? In the photo it's your Dad who's White, not your Mum!'

'Hiya mate!'

A stocky young man was steering a trolley laden with cardboard boxes out of the lift. In one hand he held a fat brown envelope. With the other he was pushing curly brown hair off his forehead.

'Are you with EdeldiCo, mate?'

Archy didn't answer. He was too busy thinking of a way to get himself out of the mess he'd got himself into. He'd forgotten what his pretend parents looked like in the pretend family picture he'd bought from the image bank to please Lucan. He couldn't believe he'd been so stupid. Nina would probably never speak to him again.

'Yes, I'm from Edeldico. Hi.'

'Chel. From Arlo's Café? Arlo's my Dad. I've brought the wraps and ciabattas you ordered. Vegetarian is in the white bags. You didn't order no vegan, did you?'

Reed, who was setting up an urn next to the gutted Porsche, waved a styrofoam cup in the air.

'Talk to the guy with the mustache,' said Archy.

'You want me to deliver the goods to Reed? Will do - in a minute. First off I have to deliver this package to a Mr. Lucan Edeldi.'

'He's our CEO. Do you want me to sign for it?'

'I wouldn't if I were you, mate. Personally, I never sign my name to nothing.'

'Okay, I'll give it to him.'

Archy reached for the envelope, but Chel wasn't in a hurry to hand it over. He was standing too close to Archy for comfort and staring into his face, looking fascinated.

'What're you lot doing up here, if you don't mind me asking? Are you making a film? We've been tripping over film crews in Coopers Hook since the Olympics.'

Archy allowed his arm to fall to his side. 'We're making a garden. There's going to be a bar and a big screen.'

'A bit windy for a boozer, ain't it?'

'It'll be all right in the summer. And there's an amazing view.'

'How did they get permission to start a business on a car park roof?'

'I have no idea. The bar is a social enterprise. It's nothing to do with me.'

'Then why are you here?'

'Edeldico is sponsoring the project, so we're doing a spot of corporate volunteering. We call it a payback day, because we're giving something back to the community.'

Chel thrust his face closer to Archy's. 'What's your name? I've seen you somewhere before.'

'May I have the letter addressed to Mr. Edeldi? I'm kind of busy right now.'

When Chel was safely back in the lift Nina said, 'That guy thinks he knows you.'

'Well, I don't know him. Maybe I've been in his café. More likely he's trying to drum up trade.'

Nina leaned her back against the concrete wall. 'You're messing with my head. I need a fag.'

As far as Archy knew, it was the first time since they'd met that Nina had felt the need to smoke. She told him she'd given it up, along with drugs and alcohol, because getting high had damaged her relationships with the people she loved. If the cravings had come back, it was a bad sign. Archy didn't want to be the person who sent his revered mentor's daughter into a spiral of self-destruction.

'Have I done something to upset you, Nina?'

'I hate it when people lie to me. I thought you were different.'

'What did I do wrong?'

'You said you'd never met sandwich guy, but he obviously knew your face.'

'I swear I never saw - what's his name? Chel? I've never seen him before in my life.'

'And you knew the way here, didn't you?'

'So what? It's not a crime.'

'But you told everyone you'd never been here before. You're such a liar, Archy Brise. Who among this lot smokes?'

Archy watched her trying to blag a cigarette from his colleagues. She was unsuccessful, because nobody on the roof was smoking. The most competitive were recklessly wielding saws and hammers. They all wanted to be the one to take home Lucan's magnum of champagne. Others were using their phones to catch up with the financial markets. Stragglers were taking a break and enjoying the sandwiches Chel had brought. Reed was serving up hot drinks and chatting to a group of women who were showing a keen interest in environmental management.

For Archy, crunch time in his fledgling relationship with Nina had come far too early. Leaning on the safety wall and gazing out over Coopers Hook, he wondered if he'd ever be able to tell her his real story, now that she'd labelled him a liar. He'd known from the outset of their friendship that one day he'd want to tell her the truth about his childhood, but he thought he'd have time to find the right words. Under his breath he practised opening sentences.

'The thing is, Nina….What happened was…As far as I know….'

When he turned around Nina had gone.

17

Plain Ease
Irene

'Remember the first rule of foraging. Never eat anything unless you know what it is,' said Irene.

Fifteen wannabe foragers, who had paid what seemed to Irene a huge amount to be shown which weeds were edible, were milling around in the Yard. They were tapping every word she said into their iPads or scribbling them in notebooks. Each forager was clutching an empty brown paper bag. The weather was perfect for their expedition. Although temperatures were low for April, the rain had held off and the sun was shining. When Irene arrived at Plain Ease Reed had been nowhere to be seen. She went to speak to Bushra, Folu and Sam, who were chatting by the gate.

'Bushra love, will you come with me on the foraging tour? I want someone to keep an eye on the time while I'm talking. I have to bring the group back by eleven. Your Nan is going to show them how to make green smoothies.'

'Sorry Auntie. I promised Grandad I'd help him in the shop.'

Folu said, 'Not me. I have to look for work.'

'You've got three jobs already,' said Irene crossly. 'Why do you want another one?'

'I don't want more jobs, Auntie. I want one better job.'

'Sam, what about you?'

'I'll be there. Reed's had to go away for the weekend. He asked me to support you.'

Already the guests were nibbling and sharing leaves they'd plucked from the undergrowth. Sam was busily checking their tickets and making them aware of housekeeping details. Irene was delighted when she asked them to spend some money in Arlo's in exchange for using the café's facilities. Since Sam signed up as a local Champion Irene had been impressed by her willingness to get her hands dirty. The young woman was a force of nature and a born leader. She looked like a catwalk model, but her grace was powered by muscle.

'What's this plant?' the guests were muttering to each other. 'Can you eat it?'

'We'd better start the tour before they make themselves sick,' said Irene, nudging Sam.

The group set off down the path that led to the heart of Plain Ease. Irene paused where long blades of sheep sorrel were pushing through clumps of hogweed. When she was a councillor she'd addressed much bigger audiences, but a lot of water had gone under the bridge since then. She tried not to let her nervousness show.

'Sorrel has health benefits, but it tastes sour. Hogweed is better value. I cook the young shoots the same way as asparagus.

Before the flowers open, you can use them like broccoli. And the seeds are good for flavouring bread.'

By the time the group reached the woodland edge, where a dainty white flower was thriving, Irene was into her stride. 'That's lady-smock. Yes, you can eat it. The flowers look pretty in a salad and the mature leaves are hot and peppery. At the bottom of the stem you'll find young leaves that taste like cress.'

While they were slowly making their way to the very bottom of the community garden, the group flung a torrent of questions at Irene. Her throat grew sore and her head began to ache. She was wondering why she'd let Reed talk her into this, and how she was going to get through another hour, when a piercing whistle rang out. Instantly the foragers stopped haranguing her. Sam took her fingers out of her mouth and yelled, 'Follow me to the graveyard!'

The young Champion guided the foragers through a gap in the hedge. Where an overgrown path led from Plain Ease to an abandoned graveyard, Irene took the lead, the others following her in single file between high banks where carrot flowers swayed above their heads. Sam brought up the rear. After a short walk they reached a broken gate opening on to a Gothic land-scape of uneven marble slabs and leaning stone angels spotted with lichen. The roots of self-seeded trees had bullied their way to the surface, pushing aside even the heaviest marble grave sculptures. Escaped garden varieties combined with wild plants to make a knee-high jungle. For a week Reed and Yessy had been fighting to free the ruined gravel paths from invading brambles. They'd lost the battle. Taking Sam's hand to balance herself, Irene climbed on to the plinth of a monument and called her group together.

'No-one's been buried in this graveyard for fifty years. The Champions would love to turn it into a nature reserve, but most likely the land will be sold for development. Over there you'll find a patch of salad burnet. It tastes like cucumber, so you can add it to your smoothies along with the cleavers you already have in your bags. And maybe a few dandelion leaves.'

'What's that flower?'

Sam pointed to a starry cluster of blossoms a few metres away. To everyone's delight it turned out to be wild garlic. The foragers wandered off to rummage in the undergrowth for the elusive delicacy. Some distance away, beyond the furthest grave, Irene noticed a woman wearing a thin white frock. She hadn't noticed anyone dressed like that among her group, who were straying all over the place. It was difficult to take a head count.

'One of them's gone off on her own, Sam. Will you round up the others and start walking back? We have to give Puja time to make the smoothies.'

'Okay. Will be all right on your own?'

'I'll be fine. I know this place like the back of my hand.'

While Sam was gathering the guests together Irene set off to find the woman in white. When she found herself tumbling over sunken gravestones and rotting tree trunks she began to feel uneasy. This was no place for a woman her age to have a fall. If she broke her hip and had to stay in hospital for weeks, Viv would be left alone. Then the landlords would throw them out of their flat before you could say Jack Robinson. It didn't bear thinking about.

While she watched her step and tried to forget her problems, she kept her eyes on the ground. When she looked up again the unidentified woman was nowhere to be seen. Irene kept on going. It would never do to leave one of her foraging group behind, after they paid so much money for the tour. Tiredness and anxiety tumbled Irene's thoughts and her vision became blurred. Then the sun came out from behind a cloud and she saw the woman standing knee-high in the grass. She was bending over with her back to Irene. Like a fifties housewife she'd tied her fair hair up in a scarf. A hazy recollection surfaced from among Irene's oldest memories. For a moment she was little Reen again. She was late going home and she'd be sent to bed without her supper.

'Aunty!' she called out. 'I'm over here!'

The white-clad figure straightened up and turned around. It was her cousin Hetty.

'What are you doing here, you nosy old freak?' said Hetty. 'Did you call me Aunty? Have you finally lost your marbles?'

Irene's mind snapped back to the present. 'I was pulling your leg. In that dress, and with your hair up, you're the living image of your old Nan. She'd turn in her grave if she heard you being disrespectful.'

A woman's jacket was slung over a nearby gravestone. At Irene's feet a cracked marble slab revealed a deep crevice in the earth. Next to it lay a bulging supermarket bag-for-life. A few banknotes had fallen from the bag and become entangled in the long grass. Hetty had been retrieving the cash when she was interrupted.

'My Nan wouldn't give a monkeys what I said, you old fool. Anyway, she ain't buried here. But someone very close to you is. Ain't that so, Irene? Wasn't they buried at the expense of the parish, in an unmarked grave?'

Irene went pale. 'I've got to go. I didn't mean to pry. I thought you were one of my foragers.'

Hetty looked around. 'Where are they?'

'Sam took them back to Plain Ease.'

'There's no end to her talents, is there?'

'What do you mean? Sam's a good girl.'

'There's more to Sam than meets the eye. And you're no better than me, Irene. I've got a bone to pick with you!'

'I'm the one who should be picking bones!'

'Why did you shop me to that copper? You're no better than a grass.'

'You've got a cheek calling me a grass. Your Nan grassed up her own sister!'

Hetty straightened up and folded her arms. 'Are you saying you grassed me up because of something that happened years before I was born?

'I am not a grass!'

'If you ain't, how come Jammy is all over me?'

'Maybe it's because you've done something you shouldn't.'

'Somebody told him they saw me talking to a business contact by the arches. Was it you?'

Irene turned away from Hetty and began to stumble up the path.

'Come back and listen! Have you been spying on me?'

'There was no need to spy. Anyone could have seen you from our block.'

'But you and Viv are the only two people living in The Mansions. It must have been you who grassed to the police. What did you tell Jammy about me?'

Clutching the heavy supermarket bag to her chest, Hetty followed Irene up the path to Plain Ease.

'If you must know, I told him about about the packages.'

'What packages?'

'The ones you give to toffs. Or they give them to you. Be grateful I didn't tell him about all the other stuff I've seen you passing around over the years. What's more, your Chelsea has been trotting around with big brown envelopes ever since he was old enough to get the bus by himself. I know all about you, Hetty

Brill. You do other people's dirty work, and you've brought up that kid to be as big a crook as yourself.'

'You're lying. You can't have seen all that from the second floor. Not at your age! '

'My eyesight's as good as it ever was. The likes of you never look up, so you don't know who's looking down. What do you think Viv and I do all day while we're sitting at our window? We watch the street. Not much goes on in Coopers Hook that we don't know about.'

'But why did you shop me to the police? What's in it for you?'

Irene leaned her back against a tree trunk and faced her accuser. 'You're out of order for bringing toffs here, Hetty Brill. It's toffs who want me and Viv to give up our home, so they can do it up and charge the new tenants a fortune in rent. Who's got that kind of money? Only other toffs. You mark my words, in five years time rents around here will be so high, no-one but toffs will be able to afford to live in the area. Then where will the likes of you and me go?'

Hetty's hands were on her hips and her face was inches away from Irene's. 'If you ever snitch on me again, I'll tell Jammy what you done!'

'Don't try that trick on me. It was you who set up the deal. If I go down for it I'm taking you with me.'

When Sam ran towards them Irene turned her back on Hetty. 'Sam, where are my foragers?'

'In the Hub with Puja. Are you all right?'

Hetty swung the muddy bag-for-life behind her back. 'Irene's safe with me, Sam.'

'Nobody's safe right now. Take my arm, Irene. Come on, Hetty. We've got to get out of here.'

18

Plain Ease
Samvida

I was helping Puja to wind up her green smoothie session when I heard screaming. The foraging party looked up for a moment, then went back to sorting and sharing the edible plants they'd collected under Irene's supervision. 'Don't worry,' I shouted over their chatter. 'It must be kids. I'll go and tell them to play somewhere else.'

Another scream rang out as I was leaving the hub. It came from the direction of the hen-house. I began to run. The hens were huddled together, clucking in terror. Among their upturned feeding dishes Yessy lay motionless on his side with his eyes closed. His jogging pants and shirt were splashed with blood. More blood was congealing around his nose and mouth and his hair trailed in the dirt. His skinny arms were stretched out as if begging for help. One hand clutched the padlock from the gate, his bony fingers winding through it like a knuckleduster. At the moment when he lost consciousness he must have been trying to protect himself.

Without help and equipment I could do little to help him, so I raced back to the Hub. When I got there I was relieved to see Jammy cycling into the yard. I was no longer as frightened of the community police officer as I had been when I arrived in Coopers Hook. I kept my distance from him, but I was used to seeing him in Arlo's. It helped that he was relaxed about his duties. I'd never seen him challenge anyone.

'I was on my way to the station when I heard someone shouting,' he said, leaning his bike against the wall. 'So I changed direction. When I was approaching the entrance to Plain Ease a grey transit van shot out of it and nearly sent me flying. The van was speeding on the wrong side of the road. I wasn't able to get its number because I was having trouble staying upright.'

Suddenly we were surrounded by fifteen people wearing anoraks and walking shoes. Each of them was clutching a brown paper bag, as if they were preparing a communal attack of nausea. At the edge of the crowd Puja hovered with a tray of bright green drinks. Someone must have suggested taking the smoothies out of doors. It looked like the garden party from Hell.

'Someone call an ambulance. There's been an accident,' I said

'I'm on it, Sam,' said Jammy.

Puja handed the tray of drinks to a man in a flat cap and hurried into the Hub.

'That's a pity.' The woman who spoke was clutching a handful of weeds like a bouquet. 'We've had a really lovely time learning how to forage. It's such a shame the day's been spoiled.'

As the police officer on the scene it was up to Jammy to take charge of the situation. To my surprise that was exactly what he did. I hadn't seen this masterful Jammy before. He said, 'Take it easy folks. Who's been hurt? Does anyone here have medical training?'

While the foragers were shaking their heads and edging towards the exit, Puja reappeared. She was holding the first aid kit I'd replenished the previous day and a bowl of clean water.

'Good job Puja,' said Jammy.

Leaving Puja to close the foraging tour and sign the participants up to the mailing list, Jammy and I headed back to the henhouse. We were relieved to find the gate was unlocked. Jammy crawled through it and I handed him the kit and the water. Then I watched from the path while he checked Yessy's airways, breathing and pulse. When Jammy dabbed the homeless man's face with damp cotton wool water ran down his cheeks, making streaks in the dirt and blood. Suddenly his eyes flickered open. Like a tranquilised animal waking to find itself tied up, Yessy went into a panic. He lashed out with his arms and legs, spilling the water and making the hens squawk and flutter.

Jammy said, 'You're safe now. Keep still. Where does it hurt?'

Yessy rolled over on to all fours and clambered to his feet. He tried to run but somehow Jammy managed to catch him. Gently the policeman held the homeless man in his arms until the adrenalin drained away, pain kicked in and choked sobs rattled in his throat. By the time the forager in the flat cap came to let us know an ambulance had arrived, Yessy was sitting beside Jammy on a log, catching his breath. When I smiled at Yessy he grinned up at me and wiped his eyes with his fist. As always when he looked at me his mauled face shone with happiness. The change for the better which came over him in my presence was like watching a balloon being inflated. Whoever Yessy thought I was, she'd been kind to him.

While I was packing away the first aid equipment I wondered what I should say to Jammy. Until that day I'd never spoken to him, so I'd been surprised and touched when he spoke to me by my name. And I knew it would look odd if I didn't give him credit for helping Yessy. However, he was a policeman and I was on the run. I didn't know whether Lucan had carried out his threat to contact the police about the doctored sex tape, because it had been weeks since I spoke to anyone from my old life. For all I knew Jammy had a picture of Vida Edeldi, sex offender, on his phone - or wherever they keep wanted posters these days.

'I'm sure he'll be very grateful to you, officer,' I said formally.

'Maybe,' said Jammy. 'But I won't hold my breath. Have you any idea who did this?'

I shook my head.

'Did you see the van that nearly knocked me off my bike?

'No, sorry. I was busy with the foraging tour.'

While we were talking we'd taken our eyes off Yessy. I heard a shout and looked around to see him tearing away up the stony track, narrowly avoiding a collision with two paramedics carrying a stretcher.

'Another refuser,' said one. 'What a waste of time.'

'On the plus side,' said the other, 'It doesn't look as if any of his bones are broken.'

Wearily they began to trudge back up the path to the yard.

'The van was very close to Plain Ease,' said Jammy. 'And the driver was in a hurry to get away. My guess is they tried to drag Yessy into the van and met with more resistance than they expected. I'll try to track it down.'

'Sounds like a plan,' I said. 'Sorry, but I have to go and help Irene.'

Without another word I turned my back on Jammy and headed for the old graveyard. I didn't tell Jammy his informant was wandering around on her own, because he'd have insisted on going with me to fetch her. I was no longer afraid of the community policeman but I didn't want to be his friend.

19

Looker Inc
March 2013
Yessy

On the day Quila disappeared Yessy found gold floating on the water. While the other slaves were shivering in the latrines he crept to where run-off formed a shallow pond. In the morning sunlight a yellow crust on the pool's surface sparkled and shone. He waded in, scooped up handfuls of the crust and tried to cram it into the leather purse which hung from a thong around his neck.

When a ganger's whip cracked down on Yessy's shoulders Quila appeared from nowhere. Her body was skin and bone swaddled in strips of fabric. Strands of dark hair escaped from her head cloth. A length of rough towelling was wrapped around her mouth and nose, almost completely concealing her face. The brown eyes shining from her protective rags were the only clue to her humanity. On one foot she wore the remains of a trainer. but the other was bound with strips of filthy cloth.

Pointing to where Dudu, the head ganger, was marshalling a work party of barefoot slaves, Quila said, 'No beat him. Big man call us.'

The ganger lowered her whip. Like Dudu she wore thick denim work clothes with a leather apron and heavy boots. 'Go. But I better not catch him off limits again.'

Yessy's ragged sweatshirt and jogging pants dripped foul water while he and Quila ran to join Dudu's team. 'No go there,' Quila scolded him. 'Next time I no save you.'

Slaves herded together by gangers were shuffling into the huge hangar known as the Pit. When the last barefoot slave had been driven inside heavy doors slammed shut, padlocks clicked into place and the stench of decay permeating Looker Hill became intense. A circular conveyor belt juddered into motion. The slaves picked up trash from the floor and flung it on to the belt, creating a glacier of waste. Meanwhile the gangers took handfuls of glittering pebbles from the deep pockets of their aprons and scattered them over the refuse. Light from broken windows high overhead made the rolling belt sparkle like a table spread with cloth of gold.

'Plenty gold today,' Quila said to Yessy.

Along the length of the belt starving human beings were dipping into the stream of trash flowing past them. The strongest of them struggled for the best positions like guests at some night-mare banquet. The slaves flung plastic, glass and metal into the bins behind them while they stuffed crumbs of mouldering food into their mouths. They scrabbled with their bare hands among rancid vegetables, bloody towels, broken glass, dog turds and rusty blades. Scarred fingers explored the ragged rims of tin cans for fragments of food and tore apart joints of rotten meat. While they worked they plucked shimmering stones out of the decaying mass and stashed them inside their ragged clothes. Meanwhile gangers with whips patrolled the line pocketing anything of value.

'Move it, you idle junkies! Work faster!' Dudu yelled. The head ganger dominated the vast space inside the hangar. He seemed to be everywhere, skimming his whip across the slaves' backs and claiming valuables the other gangers had been slow to hide.

Rising dust tormented Yessy's tongue. He tried to cover his face, but too late. Choking and spitting he fell on all fours in the dirt. Quila tore a strip of cloth from her own rags and wrapped it around his nose and mouth. 'Up! Work or they kill you!'

'Quila!'

The ganger who called to them was a sturdy old woman, dressed like the others with the addition of a surfer cap to keep her hair in place. On her broad back she carried a sack full of round tin basins pierced with holes. Quila took two and handed one of them to Yessy. Working together, the friends scooped muck up from the floor and sifted it. They heaped shapeless objects caked with dirt into the sieves and shook them, sharing the sparkling nuggets they found among shreds of metal, plastic and glass. Yessy stowed his golden treasure in his purse. Quila tucked hers inside her rags.

Every few minutes a dumper truck backed up to a wide elevated gap at one end of the Pit. Dudu ran up a flight of concrete steps to collect a handful of banknotes from each driver. After the money changed hands the tailgate was raised and all kinds of waste tumbled through the air.

'More gold!' Dudu yelled, stowing the cash in his apron. Gangers threw handfuls of shiny stones on to the stinking piles and slaves raced to grab them.

One slave stopped work to watch the others squabbling. When he pulled his makeshift mask aside a strong Black face was revealed. 'They are lying,' he said. 'Their gold is fake. When you believe their false promises, you make them your masters.'

'Zan, we are your masters. Take him!' roared Dudu.

Two of the gangers seized Zan, tied his wrists behind his back and dragged him away.

Yessy and Quila, who had stopped to watch Zan's act of rebellion, didn't notice when Dudu approached them from behind. The big ganger kicked Yessy's thigh, making him fall to the ground in pain. Then he looped his supple whip around Quila's narrow waist.

'Hey, pretty thing,' said Dudu.

Quila scrabbled at the whip with broken nails. 'What you want?'

'You know what I want.'

'If you like me, set me free.'

Dudu released his whip, took hold of Quila's chin and made her look into his eyes. 'On the other side of the fence you're just another junkie. I can make you special.'

'Get lost!'

The ganger let go of Quila. 'If you want something from me, you've got to pay.'

'I don't want nothing.'

'Remember how good it was to have shoes on both feet?'

Dudu dangled a trainer in front of Quila's face. The laces were missing, its fabric was stained and there was a hole in the toe. She gazed at it longingly.

'Is for left foot! I got right foot already.'

The ganger displayed the ruined shoe on the palm of one hand. When Quila reached out to touch it, he snatched it away. 'What will you give me for this pretty thing?'

'I will give you my dinner,' she said.

Dudu snorted in disgust, dropped the trainer and walked away.

'My feet hurt so bad!' Quila retrieved the shoe, tore off the rags tied around her left foot and crouched to pull it on. Then she bound up Yessy's feet in her discarded toe-rags.

'You and me both got new shoes,' she said.

'Yes,' said Yessy.

Night had fallen when the gangers led their teams out of the Pit into freezing rain. The slaves stumbled over rough ground to a tent formed from tarpaulins. Outside it bowls of cold water waited on a bench for them to wash the dirt from their hands. Tia was waiting by the entrance. As the slaves filed in they opened their mouths and she placed a pill on their tongues. Quila held out her hand and Yessy spat his pill into it. She swallowed both drugs and sighed with relief.

Inside the tent woodsmoke drifted in the air. Over a fire burning in a hole in the ground a deep cauldron was suspended. Tia ladled oily soup from the cauldron into metal trays. Another ganger placed a slice of bread on each tray. Yessy and Quila found a log where they could sit together. They were eating with the spoons chained to their trays when Dudu walked in. He strode up to Quila and flung her tray on the ground.

'You owe me for one trainer,' said Dudu.

'I can pay. Look, I have gold.'

Quila pulled out the shiny nuggets hidden among her rags. He dashed them out of her hand.

'You know what I want,' Dudu snarled.

She pulled off both of her trainers. 'Take them back.'

'We had a deal,' he growled.

Dudu ripped off Quila's scarf and grabbed a handful of her long dark hair. He wrestled her on to the earth floor and knelt over her with a thigh on each side of her narrow body. She beat her fists on his leather apron in an effort to escape from his weight. Yessy tried to pull her free but Dudu knocked him to the ground with a single blow. The slaves gathered round to watch the fight.

Tia shouted, 'Let her go! We're supposed to be off grid. We do not want a riot!'

The old woman had distracted her fellow ganger. He lost his

balance and Quila pushed him over. She ran out of the tent followed by Dudu and a scream rang out. Tia looked at Yessy. 'Your friend Quila is taken,' she said. 'If you are wise you will forget her.'

Slaves dropped to the floor and scrabbled for the golden stones Quila had dropped. The gangers drew their whips. In the confusion Yessy took his chance and hid behind the largest log. After the gangers marched the slaves away to the lock-ups Yessy crept out of the tent and went to look for Quila. He crawled on his knees over scrub, ignoring the scuttering rats he disturbed. When he reached the high fence which enclosed the business premises of Looker Recycling Inc he followed it until he reached the tall gates. For once they were open. In the light of a full moon Yessy glimpsed a country road winding through woodland beyond the gates.

On the concrete yard Dudu and Tia were standing by a transit van. The ganger who had driven the van through the gates was standing by and waiting for orders. Lying flat on his belly in the undergrowth, Yessy watched and waited. Dudu opened the rear doors of the van and shone a torch inside. A young man climbed unsteadily out. Tia and the ganger supported him while Dudu bound his wrists. The next person to leave the van was a woman whose legs barely supported her. Another man had to be dragged out of the van. He fell to the ground with his head lolling to one side. Tia helped him up while Dudu tied him to the other two captives. All three of the new slaves looked as if they had been shut up for hours in the cramped quarters inside the van.

Dudu pulled out the cash he had collected from the lorry drivers who dumped their cargoes of waste. He gave a handful of it to Tia, who counted her share and passed a few notes to the third ganger. Then everyone except Dudu left in the direction of the sheds where the slaves were locked up at night. Tia led the way with a firm grip on the weakest captive. The other ganger followed, kicking them when they dragged their feet.

When the group had vanished into the night Dudu climbed into the driving seat of the van and lit a cigarette. Under cover of darkness Yessy scampered across the yard, climbed into the back of the van and curled up under a pile of dust sheets. Soon afterwards the doors slammed shut and the engine started. The windows in the back had been painted over, leaving a tiny gap through which Yessy watched the gates closing.

Dudu didn't turn on the headlights until they reached the motorway heading south. From the back of the van Yessy memorised every road sign, noted each landmark and registered changes of direction. Finally the van pulled into a petrol station. Without warning the doors were flung open and Dudu's face appeared. Acting on instinct Yessy jumped and ran. Taken by surprise, Dudu had no hope of catching up with an escaped slave fuelled by panic and adrenalin.

'You can run but you can't hide!' Dudu roared, shaking his fist. 'I'm coming to get you!'

Yessy didn't stop running until he reached Plain Ease.

20

The Gentlemen's Club
Hetty

Hetty retreated into the shadows of the square. She'd dressed as conservatively as she knew how, in a woollen coat and calf-length tweed skirt. A beanie hat was pulled down over her fore-head. At the last moment she'd ditched her trainers in favour of red courts with four inch heels. In sensible shoes she knew she'd never have enough courage to challenge Lucan Edeldi in his lair. When a youth wearing a coat smothered in gold braid swaggered towards her she swore under her breath. As usual some pain-in-the-neck was hanging around to spoil her plans. She leaned against the wrought iron railings which protected London's most exclusive gentlemen's club from the outside world and took up a pose calculated to stop any red-blooded male in his tracks.

'You can't stand here,' said the doorman. 'Move along please.'

'I hope you don't think I'm a working girl?'

'If you are, you're too long in the tooth for our gents.'

'I heard they like them young. Go and bother somebody else, sonny. I'm waiting for a friend.'

'Yeah, yeah. I've heard that line before.'

'If you must know, I'm meeting a business contact.'

'In them shoes? You're having a laugh. On your way, darling.'

Who did this creep think he was? Hetty would have walked away if there hadn't been so much at stake.

The sudden death of her old friend and lover, Urban Edeldi, had hit her hard. Six months on the loss of income caused by from his passing was starting to bite, and Hetty was beginning to fear she'd to have to stand on her own two feet in future. No more suspect pick-ups, no more dodgy deliveries, no more money-laundering in return for a generous cash payout. Hetty's only hope of continuing her profitable under-the-radar arrange-ment with Edeldico was to convince the new CEO he needed her as much as she needed him. But so far, Lucan had proved impos-sible to pin down. That was why she'd chosen the high-risk strategy of ambushing him at his club. Now the only thing standing between Hetty and success was this pimped-up nobody.

'Are you gonna piss off or do I have to fetch the manager?'

The doorman was standing so close to Hetty that she could smell alcohol on his breath. When she wrinkled up her nose and waved a hand in front of her face, he took a step backwards.

'You stink of beer. Get out of my way or I'll tell my friend you've been drinking on the job.'

Booming voices echoed along the pathway. A party of middle-aged men in bespoke suits was approaching the club. At the heart of the group was Lucan, who was telling a story which made his companions roar with laughter. The doorman reacted to the men's presence like a bull to an electric prod. Within seconds he was in position between limestone columns at the top of a flight of steps. The braid on his uniform glistened in the light of brass lanterns. While he was hauling open the club's carved wooden doors, Hetty, thanks to decades of experience of dancing in high heels, mounted the steps two at a time. Inserting herself between the suits she tucked her hand into the crook of Lucan's elbow. For the first time in many years she was blagging her way into a bastion of male privilege on the arm of a multi-millionaire. Glowing with renewed confidence, she was on the verge of achieving everything she had ever longed for.

'I told you I was meeting a friend,' Hetty said to the doorman.

Her opponent showed no sign of backing down. 'Mr. Edeldi, are you acquainted with this lady?'

Hoping she had enough dirt on the Edeldi family to force Lucan to acknowledge her, Hetty looked up at him and smiled. He avoided her gaze and tried to answer the doorman. He was opening and closing his mouth but no sound was coming out. Clearly he hadn't inherited his uncle's ability to think on his feet.

'Mr. Edeldi knows me all right. I'm his salsa instructor.'

Lucan raised his eyebrows so high they almost merged with his hairline. 'Ah, yes. Salsa.'

Hetty glanced triumphantly at the doorman. It would be fun to tell Lucan the man had been drinking on the job. She didn't care if he got the sack. It would serve him right for questioning her. But she had no chance to speak, because Lucan had her by the arm. Instead of offering to buy her a cocktail in the ladies' bar, as she'd hoped he would, he nodded to his friends to go on ahead and led her to a remote corner of the hallway. To add insult to injury, when she tried to sit down in an armchair Lucan ordered her to stand up.

'How dare you disturb me at my club, Hetty?'

'I had to come here because you ain't been answering my calls.'

'That's right. I had no reason to speak with you.'

'Have you gone straight at last?'

'I don't know what you mean.'

'Oh yes you do. You know me, and you knew about my arrangement with Urban. And I know all about you and your dodgy deals, because I've been with Edeldico from the start. I've moved an enormous amount of money for you guys.'

'Yes, and you've been well rewarded. But it's time to put an end to all that. Will you accept a lump sum in settlement?'

Hetty sank into the forbidden armchair. The conversation was going better than she'd hoped. The new CEO had fallen for her bluff. He'd admitted she'd been paid for money-laundering, without even asking her to prove she held information damaging to Edeldico's reputation.

'A bribe, you mean.'

There had been inexplicable disappearances from Coopers Hook, and Hetty thought she knew what was going on. Now she was sure she was on to something big - maybe big enough to destroy Lucan's career. She decided not to accept his first offer.

'A lump sum is no good to me. Arlo and Chelsea would find out and I'd end up clearing their debts as well as my own. What I need is a regular income to fund my studio and pay the bills. Fifty here, a hundred there, straight into my pocket in used banknotes. That's how I was paid when I was working for your uncle. There's nothing like hard cash in small amounts. It's almost untraceable. If you let me collect money owed to Edeldico I can clean it through Arlo's café or TimePad and take my cut.'

A look of relief had flashed across Lucan's face when she

turned down a one-off payment. Guessing that Edeldico had cash-flow problems, Hetty dared to push her target harder.

'Everyone likes cash in hand, don't they Lucan? Maybe even you could do with some.'

'You're living in the past, woman. Everything's digital these days.'

'Not me. I'm strictly old school.'

'If I refuse what are you going to do about it?'

'For one thing, I can get you into trouble with the law. I didn't work with Urban all them years for nothing. I know how international financiers like you launder your money and duck out of paying tax. What's more, I'm in touch with one of the private dancers from Salty's. She runs her own agency now. She told me what goes on at gentlemen's clubs. I don't think you want your posh missus to find out what you and your mates get up to.'

'In the circumstances,' said Lucan, 'I'm prepared to give you a few small jobs for old times' sake. You can pick up and transfer cash from the same enterprises you used to handle for Urban. Take five percent, and stash the rest wherever you think is appropriate. But when it comes to passing the profits on to me, I want it done digitally, by bank transfer into my golf account. And shuffle it around a bit before it gets to me. I'll make sure you get my details. Is that clear?'

'As crystal,' said Hetty.

When she passed the doorman on her way out he touched his cap and said, 'Good evening, Madam.' A cutting remark was on the tip of her tongue but she bit it back. It would be useful to have an inside contact in a flash joint like this. After all, Lucan wasn't the only stupid rich man in London. As she sashayed past her new friend Hetty slipped him a generous tip.

At Bank she paused in a doorway close to the underground

station. There she took off the high heeled shoes and pulled on her trainers for the journey home. 'Lucan ain't a patch on his uncle,' she said to herself. 'Urban would never have fallen for a trick like that. With him in charge EdeldiCo will go to rack and ruin. Never mind, I'm sorted for now.'

When she was offered a seat on the Tube Hetty knew she was showing her age, but a sudden weariness made her take it. Light and shadow clashed, air whooshed along tunnels and wheels screeched as the train burrowed under the City. Tired commuters sheltered behind newspapers or technology. Across the aisle a woman dressed entirely in fun fur rested her head on her sleeping boyfriend's shoulder. Hetty felt as if she was the only wide awake person in London.

When the train reached Mile End the aisle emptied. Hetty looked around to check out her dozing fellow travellers. Next to her a young woman was fast asleep. She was heavily made up and wore a top bearing the logo of a West End store. A carrier bag with the same logo lay between Hetty's trainers and the shop assistant's ballerina pumps. A colourful tangle of belts, bangles and scarves was threatening to spill out on to the floor. From the corner of her eye Hetty sized up her neighbour. 'Nice skin, but you can hardly see it under the slap. She's shattered, probably been on the beauty counter all day, but she found the time to blow her staff discount on accessories. She should be more careful with them things. Anyone could help themselves while she's asleep.'

At Stratford East she headed for the Overground. It was April but the air was cold as January. She walked fast to keep warm, averting her eyes from the pink signage left over from last year. In Hetty's opinion the London Olympics had been a waste of money. Arlo disagreed. He thought its legacy was good for business. The only legacy Hetty cared about was the affordable housing Londoners had been promised would be built after the event. The day Chelsea moved into his own brand new flat would be the day Hetty admitted the Olympics had been a success.

By the time she left the train at Hackney Central she didn't feel a day over forty, because she'd added a new belt and a designer scarf to her outfit. At the gates a guard winked at her. Pleased to find she could still pull, she winked back. While she was waiting for the bus to Coopers Hook she said to herself, 'I wish I'd seen that shop girl's face when she realised her bag had left the train without her. I bet she'll never doze off on the Tube again.'

21

Coopers Hook Laundrette
Samvida

Two days after the foraging tour I offered to treat Folu to break-fast at Arlo's. I was supposed to meet Bushra, but my room-mate was having a bad time and I wanted to cheer her up. She was trying to find a new job in a restaurant, because fumes from the chemicals she had to use in her job as a factory cleaner were making her ill. It wasn't going well.

'What you need is a mug of tea and one of Arlo's fried egg sandwiches,' I told her.

Folu went pale. 'That is not what I need, Sam.'

'But you love food,' I said.

'I do. But I don't want anything to eat right now. When I have my own café I will cook you the best meal you have ever eaten. My speciality is a spicy fusion of African and European flavours. It is so delicious it will make you cry.'

Although I was afraid Folu would never earn enough money

to start her own business, I told her I couldn't wait to taste her speciality.

I wasn't hungry either, but I wanted to talk to Arlo about Yessy. I hung around until he had a moment free to speak to me.

'Arlo, have you seen Yessy since he was beaten up?'

'Yes, he's been in. He doesn't look well.'

'Have you any idea who hurt him? Jammy thinks it was someone driving a grey transit van.'

Arlo leaned across the counter and spoke in a whisper.

'Don't ask questions, Sam. Yessy must have got on the wrong side of some dangerous people.'

Bushra was waiting for me outside the launderette. She was lugging a bag overflowing with raw Indian cotton. She said, 'You took your time Sam. Look, my Nan found this amazing fabric at the Hub. It's left over from the Olympics. I'm going to dye it green. Will you help me?'

The launderette looked tiny from outside, but it went deep into an old terraced house. It hadn't had a refit for at least twenty years. The machines were battered and plastered with hand-written signs. Chipped formica shelves sagged in corners. The walls were clad with peeling wood-look plastic. By the time we got there it was mid-morning. Shift workers, students and pensioners were loading and unloading machines, or waiting on the benches for cycles to finish. The air smelled of cheap soap, bleach and sweat. A woman wearing a white track suit and silver sling-back shoes was folding towels on a table near the door. She asked us if we wanted a service wash. Bushra shook her head.

'Soap powder?'

'I have everything I need, thank you.'

In the depths of the launderette, industrial size washing machines rattled and churned. Bushra chose the one with the most warning notices stuck to it.

'This one will do. The attendant can't see it from her desk.'

Just then, someone arrived to collect their laundry. The attendant fetched two full baskets. The customer wasn't happy. Every item had to be taken out and examined. Things got shouty.

'Nobody's watching us. Let's do it.'

Bushra pulled open the washing machine's heavy door. The hinge swung low, as if it was worn out from processing the dirt of Coopers Hook.

'Are you sure, Bushra? This machine looks very old.'

'They're all old. The owner doesn't replace them until they fall apart.'

'Why don't people save up and buy their own washing machines? They'd soon get their money back if they didn't have to pay to use this place.'

'You sound like my Nan. Neither of you understands that launderettes are for people who can't save up, because they barely have enough to live on from day to day. Give me a hand, Sam.'

We squashed the fabric into the machine, cramming in layer upon layer. It took both of us to push the door shut. Then Bushra pressed a button.

'Aren't you going to put the dye in with it?'

'The fabric has to be wet to take the colour, so I've put it on a short wash.'

'What, no soap?'

'Of course not. It would leave a deposit on the fibres. Look, Irene and Viv are here.'

Irene was trying to manipulate Viv's wheelchair, which was full of dirty washing, through the door. Viv followed with her stick, unsteady on her feet. The attendant was still squabbling with the service customer, but some students came to Irene and

Viv's rescue and parked them near the door. Bushra waved and Irene came over to speak to us.

'I've not seen you two in here before,' she said.

Bushra laughed. 'We don't do much washing, Auntie.'

'Viv and I are in here most days. I used to do my washing by hand, but it's too much for me now.'

'Look, Viv's trying to put a load on by herself,' said Bushra. 'She'll fall over if she's not careful.'

'I'll go back and give her a hand. Then we'll pop over to Arlo's until the cycle's over.'

By the time Irene and Viv waved goodbye, the short cycle on our machine had come to an end. Bushra asked me to block the attendant's view. Then she took some sachets from her tote, tore them open and emptied them into the machine with the fabric. Both of us sat on the bench, watching the coarse fabric rotate inside the big machine, until it was as green as madder leaves. I asked Bushra what she was going to do with all that green material.

'Maybe I'll put up a big tent at Plain Ease to display my designs.'

'There's an awful lot of it, Bushra.'

'It's more eco-friendly to fill the machine up. And I found plenty of dye sachets in Grandad's stockroom.'

'What make is it?'

'I don't know. The writing is in Bengali. We speak it at home, but I can't read or write it.'

The cotton convulsed in the drum. Through the thick glass it looked like a map of the world, green with patches of the original oatmeal. A dribble of green water rolled from the base of the machine. The broken hinge burst open. A trickle became a splash, then a flood.

'Run for it!' Bushra was off, scampering along benches,

making for the door. I was about to follow her when I remembered that the dyed cloth was marked with the logo of Reed's charity. I couldn't risk bringing trouble to Plain Ease and blowing my cover. Fortunately, the scene in the launderette was chaotic. People were falling over each other while they tried to rescue their own washing from the swelling green flood. As for the attendant, she was struggling with the straps of her silver shoes. No-one was looking at me.

I yanked at the soaked cloth and it uncoiled into the bag. The writhing mass vomited out green fluid, like a space monster. Strips of paper appeared to be caught in its wrinkles, but I had no time to worry about them. I hauled the soaking green mass from the machine into the laundry bag, picked it up and ran. I made it into the street just as the attendant managed to unbuckle her sling-backs and ran after me barefoot, splashing through green puddles. Fortunately, I could run faster than she could, even when I was carrying a bag of wet washing. A crowd had gathered outside to see what was going on. I pushed my way through. There was no sign of Bushra, but Irene and Viv were there. Viv was standing up, leaning on her stick. The wheelchair was empty. Irene called me over.

'Throw the bag on the seat and run. After I've helped Viv to walk home I'll meet you at the garden.'

I dumped the bag on the wheelchair, grabbed its handles and ran all the way to Plain Ease. Luckily, Reed wasn't there. I found Bushra hiding in the Hub. Tears were rolling down her face.

'It's a disaster, Sam. I put ten pounds into that machine.'

Bushra was inconsolable. She sobbed and sniffed on my shoulder. We huddled together, wondering if the launderette assistant had sent out search parties for us. When Irene came to retrieve the wheelchair, we were so glad to see her we didn't argue when she told us off.

'You two have made a shocking mess of our launderette. Don't worry, I told the attendant I'd never seen either of you before. I'm going back to help her mop up. Whatever were you thinking of, Bushra? And wherever did you get that horrible green dye? It's splashed halfway up the walls. The owners will have to redecorate.'

'Isn't that a good thing?' said Bushra, wiping her eyes.

'Not for Viv and me it isn't. The prices will go up.'

When Irene had left with two pairs of borrowed rubber boots on the seat of the wheelchair, I put my arm around Bushra's shoulders.

'Cheer up,' I said. 'At least you have your green tent. Help me spread it on the hedges to dry.'

Together we dragged the tangled fabric out of the laundry bag and spread it over a hawthorn hedge. A soggy brown envelope slid from among the wet folds and hooked itself on long thorns. Wet lumps of coloured paper fell to the ground. Bushra picked up one of them and smoothed it out in her hand.

'Look, Sam! It's a twenty pound note!'

I picked up another lump. A tenner. Money had was falling at our feet.

'This money wasn't in the cloth. It must have been hidden in the washing machine.'

'Bushra, what are we going to do with it?'

She ran to the Hub and came back with two of Reed's logoed hessian totes.

'Help me pack the money into these. I'll dry it out at home.'

'But it's not ours!'

As the words left my lips I remembered the cash I'd taken from the compost toilet. I'd spent some of it. The rest was hidden in the lining of my blue trench coat, which was hanging up in my room at TimePad. That money wasn't mine, but I took it anyway.

Now it felt like mine. I had no right to blame Bushra for helping herself to this windfall.

Bushra said, 'There's hundreds of pounds here.'

'We should give it back.'

'Who can we give it to? It's probably stolen.'

'We could tell Reed. Or donate it to charity.'

'No! This is my chance, and I'm not going to throw it away. There's enough here to pay for my degree project and hire a market stall. And I'll share it with you.'

So we filled the bags with lumps of machine-washed money, and Bushra carried them back to the house where she lives with Puja and her Grandad.

It's hard to tell right from wrong when you're broke.

22

Timepad
Samvida

For months after I escaped from the Penthouse to Coopers Hook, I hardly ever thought about sex. Being forced to sit in a room alone with Lucan and watch a film of myself making love was enough to destroy anybody's libido. And because I didn't know who made the film and added the fake third scene, I always felt I was being watched. To make things worse, I was exhausted from my job in the community garden. I was used to physical work, because my father is a cabinet-maker and I often helped him when I lived at home. But I wasn't used to doing it for several hours at a time. Some days I didn't know which hurt more, my back or my feet.

I've always found it hard to trust men, and with good reason. When I was ten a boy called Joe was made to sit next to me at school. We'd been in the same class since Year 1, but I don't remember us ever speaking to each other before that day. It was the last lesson before home-time and I was sitting alone at a desk right at the back of the classroom. Joe had misbehaved so our teacher told him to sit with me. It was a common punishment for boys, because they thought it was shameful to sit with a girl. At the end of the lesson Joe was ordered to stay behind. He wouldn't stand up to let me go by, so I pushed past him.

Joe put his hand up my skirt.

I was so shocked I didn't scream or cry or slap him. Walking home from school with my best friend I couldn't speak while she chatted non-stop. At last she asked me why I was so quiet.

I said, 'Joe put his hand up my skirt.'

'You're lying. Joe's a good boy. His Mum is my Mum's friend. He plays at my house.'

I ran all the way home and said to my mother, 'Joe put his hand up my skirt.'

'Sue's little Joe? Are you sure?'

'I'm sure.'

'Are you quite, quite sure?'

'Yes, I'm quite, quite sure.'

Mum rang the school and the next morning we went to see the head teacher. She was a motherly woman with tired eyes. I told her that Joe put his hand up my skirt.

'Are you sure?'

'I'm sure.'

The head teacher looked at my mother, 'Joe's mother is a Parent Governor.'

'I know. Sue and I work together.'

'I've spoken to Joe. He says he didn't do it.'

I said, 'Joe put his hand up my skirt and touched me on my pants.'

Mum put her arm around my shoulders. 'But can you prove it? Did anyone else see what he did?'

I shook my head.

'I'll try to persuade Joe to apologise,' said the head teacher.

Joe wouldn't apologise.

My former best friend began to walk home with someone else.

Mum told me to forget the whole thing and be more careful with boys in future. When I told her our teacher had made Joe sit beside me she only shook her head. I felt betrayed and confused. I knew I had allowed something to be taken away from me but I didn't understand what it was. I was angry with Joe but angrier with myself. After what happened with Chel I felt the same help-less anger.

When Folu and I showered we usually took it in turn to keep watch. This was because some of the guys who lived at TimePad couldn't be trusted in a unisex bathroom. One day when Folu was on night shift Reed asked me to help Yessy turn the compost. I got so dirty I had to shower on my own. None of the other tenants was around, so I thought it was safe to be in the bathroom alone. I was wrong. When I swung the cubicle door open, wearing nothing but an old towel Puja gave me, Chel was there. He was so close to me that I caught a whiff of his cheap aftershave. It was obvious he had something on his mind - and he came right out with it.

'When you told Reed you'd been abused, Sam Gumby, I think you was lying.'

I pulled the towel more tightly around me and reached for my coat, which I'd left hanging on a nearby hook. 'My cousin beat me up and threatened to kill me! You saw the bruises!'

By then I'd told my cover story so many times I'd begun to believe it myself. To be fair, it was almost true. I'd invented a thieving, murdering cousin, but he was modelled on Lucan. As for my bruises, on that awful night by the pool Nina was so high she could have drowned me if I hadn't fought back.

Chel took the coat out of my reach and rubbed its silvery fabric between finger and thumb, admiring the quality. I was afraid he'd notice the thickness of the hem, where I'd stowed the cash I found in the compost toilet, but he had other things on his mind. He stroked a sleeve and said, 'Kids who live at TimePad don't wear gear like this.'

'I found it in a charity shop.'

The story sounded unconvincing, even to me. As for Chel, he laughed in my face. 'Don't try to kid a kidder, love. The losers who wind up here are all on the run from something, same as you are. Their clothes are nothing but rags, and they can't look me in the eye. You're different, Sam Gumby. You look at me like you own my skin. I think you've broken out of something big.'

'Reed believes me. That's why he took me on at Plain Ease.'

'A posh bird like you, working down the old pickle factory? I've seen what people chuck over the fence there. Listen, Sam Gumby, you can either pick up takeaway boxes and bags of dog shit or you can accept the offer I'm going to make you. If you want me to scratch your back you have to scratch mine. It's your choice, babe.'

'My back doesn't need scratching. And I'm entitled to keep my room as long as I do my job.'

'Do you think I couldn't get rid of you if I didn't like your face?'

At first I'd thought Chel was just being mean. Now I was afraid he was planning to hurt me. A cold shiver ran down my spine.

'Luckily for you, Sam Gumby, I do like your face. And your legs. And the rest.'

I was terrified, because I didn't know what Chel was going to do next. The only thing I had to hide behind was a thin bath sheet. When I began to shake from fear and cold he grinned as if he thought tormenting me was fun.

'Don't panic, Sam. I ain't going to rape you. I'm offering you a deal.'

'What kind of deal?'

'The kind where both of us get what we want. And you can go on living at TimePad without having to mess with that community garden nonsense.'

'I like volunteering at Plain Ease. It's hard work but I enjoy it. And Reed looks after me.'

I mentioned Reed because I thought his name would bring Chel back to his senses. I was wrong.

'You're not listening, are you? Most of the girls get my point right away, but you're obviously a bit thick. Here's the Noddy version. Because I'm the manager of TimePad I can sign you off community service. It makes no difference to me what you do during the day. You can scrub rich people's floors, flip burgers or give strangers blow jobs in taxis, it's all the same to me. So long as you share my bed whenever I invite you to, you can stay here.'

The idea of sleeping with a bully like Chel made me feel sick. 'I'm not interested in your deal. I'd rather carry on as I am.'

He clicked his fingers. 'Then I'll evict you like that, for breaking the rules. There are lots of rules at TimePad. Sometimes I make up new ones for fun. You must have broken at least one of them.'

If I'd had anywhere to go I'd have walked out of TimePad then and there. The trouble was, I had nowhere to go. I had to think of a way to appease Chel so I could keep a roof over my head.

'Don't look at me as if I'd been brought in on somebody's shoe, Sam Gumby. It's a fact of life that if a girl wants to get ahead she has to put out. This is a hard old world and we've all got to make the most of the assets we was born with. Believe me, a girl as beautiful as you can get anything she wants from men.'

Mum told me you should never say no to a man. You only have to avoid saying yes. I hoped her method would work on Chel.

'Look,' I said, 'I've had a hard day at work and I'm shattered right now. Can I have time to consider your offer?'

'Okay, Sam Gumby. You can think about it. Just remember there's a massive waiting list for rooms at TimePad.'

Chel gave me what he thought was a sexy wink. At that moment I felt as if I was totally in his power, which of course was exactly what he wanted. He was proving that he could do what he liked with me. Although I was determined not to give in to his threats, I was aware of my own weakness.

The door opened and another tenant put his head round the door. It happened to be the man who pissed in front of Folu and me, when we were bonding on my first day in the hostel. I've never been so glad to see anyone.

'What do you want?'Chel growled.

'The ballcock in the end toilet is broke. Want me to fix it?'

'Me and Sam was having a nice chat, until you showed up. On your way!'

Ballcock guy didn't seem surprised to find the hostel manager in the bathroom, talking to a woman wearing only a towel.

'The bird will wait. The cistern won't. A plumber is going to cost you big bucks. I'll do the job for twenty if you get the parts.'

Chel said, 'Fifteen.' Then he went off to order a new ball-cock. Repairing a toilet or sleeping with me, it was all the same to him. Both were to be bargained for and got for the best price.

When Folu came home, I hugged her tight. 'Now I know what you mean about being careful.'

She hugged me. 'Did Chel hurt you?'

'No. At least, not physically.'

I'd been wondering why there were no locks on the room doors at TimePad. Now I knew. The next morning I went to the pound shop and bought a packet of wedges. From then on I put one of them under the door of our room every night when Folu and I went to bed, to jam it shut.

I never felt safe around Chel again. He'd taken my pride away from me, just like Joe did.

23

The Rising Star, City of London
Archy

According to the Edeldico grapevine, some colleagues spent more time in the Rising Star than they did in their own homes. Archy was not one of them, but this afternoon he'd left his desk early to secure the intimate table in the bay window. He'd been sitting there like a lemon for half an hour, with a bottle of expensive Chardonnay for company. An over-tipped cocktail waiter had twice refreshed the ice bucket and colleagues were giving him funny looks on their way to the bar.

However, Archy remained confident that Nina was going to show. Although it was only a few weeks since they met he felt as if he'd known her forever. She was the impulsive kind, someone who'd throw a glass of wine in your face when angry, rather than devise a public humiliation. Desperate to be forgiven, Archy had grovelled for this meeting. He understood why his mentor's daughter was disappointed in him, because she'd caught him out in a lie. He'd told her that his mother was White and his father Black, forgetting that, in the family photograph he'd bought from stock, it was the other way around. He couldn't believe he'd done something so stupid, after all the years he'd spent creating an identity for himself.

To make matters worse, Lucan was beginning to suspect Archy was not fully committed to the search for Urban's widow. That morning, he had asked if there were any clues to Vida's whereabouts.

'Not yet, sir, but I'll let you know the minute I have news.'

'Put some effort into it, Brise. Urban's estate can't be finalised until Vida signs the waiver. By the way, what's going on between you and Nina? She's way out of your league.'

'You advised me to get to know your cousin, sir, and I'm following your instructions.'

By the time he caught sight of Nina through the paned bow window Archy had begun to give up hope. His first glimpse of her lifted his heart. She was slicing through the crowds as if she were on a catwalk, wearing her favourite thigh-length brown boots. Her burgundy coat was wide at the bottom but narrow in the middle, flattering her small waist. Her blonde curls framed her face like a cloud of glory. He realised Nina had made an effort to look smart for their meeting, and his heart fell. In his experience women always dressed up when they intended to give a guy a hard time.

When Nina walked into the Rising Star a sea of suits parted before her, and the waiter hurried over to pour the wine. In spite of his nerves Archy relished the moment. Being seen with a woman who bore the firm's name would turbo-charge his status at work. He knocked back the last few drops of a confidence building bourbon and stood up to greet his guest. She sat down in the chair Archy pulled out for her but kept her coat on. On her lap, she smoothed long leather gloves that matched her boots. Her cheeks were pink and her blue eyes glowed with anger.

'I can't stay. I only came to tell you how much I hate it when friends lie to me.'

Relieved that Nina thought of him as a friend, Archy said, 'I had no intention of lying to you.'

'The couple in the photo aren't your Mum and Dad. And the little boy is not you.'

Throughout his adult life Archy had feared that one day the elaborate persona he'd built for himself would crash and burn. At this moment, when it looked as if the calamity was finally going to happen, he was astonished to experience a sense of inner calm. There was something cathartic about abandoning the impossible struggle to be someone else, and he was doing it for the best of reasons. In order to earn a place in Nina's life he was going to have to tell her what he knew of the truth.

'Lucan asked me to have a family photo on my desk, so I bought that shot from a picture library. I have no idea who the models were.'

'Why didn't you use a picture of your real Mum and Dad?'

'Because they're dead.'

'I know that. One of the first things you ever told me was that your parents are both dead, like mine. It's one of the main things we have in common.'

'Not quite. My parents didn't leave me a trust fund. Thoughtless of them, wasn't it?'

'But I have more photos of me with my parents than I know what to do with. Why haven't you?'

'I'm not sure. It's possible my parents didn't even own a camera.'

'Don't be ridiculous! Everyone has a camera. I won't listen to any more of this bullshit.'

When Nina stood up Archy took her hand and squeezed it so tight her rings bit into their fingers.

'I promise I'm telling you the truth, Nina!'

'Stop that! It hurts!'

Immediately Archy let go of her fingers. 'I'm sorry, but I can't bear you thinking I'm a liar. Stay and I'll tell you everything I know about my childhood.'

Nina sat down again. 'Well, start at the beginning. You've never told me where you were born.'

Archy emptied his glass and allowed the waiter to refill it.

'I'm pretty sure I was born in Brazil. I don't know exactly where. When I was four someone smuggled me into England. I don't know who it was. All I can remember about that time is being dragged on and off boats and planes. I ended up in Coopers Hook, where I stayed with a woman I knew as Aunty. I think she must have been a child-minder, because there were always lots of kids at her house.'

'You didn't learn that accent in Coopers Hook.'

'No. When I was eight I was sent to boarding school. I was told I'd won a scholarship.'

'Who did you stay with in the holidays? Was it Aunty?'

'No. I never saw her again. I spent every holiday at school.'

'If I'd had to stay at my boarding school all year round I'd have gone out of my mind. At least I had Dad to go home to.'

Nina's shocked response opened up a new train of thought for Archy. It had never occurred to him that there was anything wrong with living at school all year round. When other boys packed their cases and left at the end of term he had never expected to go home. Back then it was possible he'd been able to fully recall what happened to his parents. Perhaps a younger Archy understood that for him there was no more home.

'It wasn't too bad. There were several other boys who stayed

155

at the school all year round. We spent the holidays taking endless courses. Karate, swimming, self-defence, survival skills. I was being prepared for a military career. But when I was fourteen something happened that changed my life.'

'If it was gross, you can spare me the details.'

'It wasn't gross, just weird. One day a cricket match was rained off and the teacher put on an old movie. The first scene was shot in a cemetery. A little boy was looking at his Mum and Dad's gravestone. I don't know what happened after that. The rest of the team booed it off because it was in black and white.'

'You're talking about "Great Expectations". We read it at school. Are you seriously telling me Charles Dickens changed your life? Don't wind me up!'

'I haven't read the book but the film blew me away. The boy's parents had died when he was a baby, like mine, and like me he couldn't remember their faces. I got emotional because someone had cared enough to make a movie about a boy like me. That's when I made up my mind to be a success. Even though I was alone in the world, I wanted to make it to the top. Success in business has been my aim ever since.'

Nina's lips quivered. For a heart-wrenching moment Archy thought she was going to laugh at him, and his world teetered on the edge of an abyss. Then a tear rolled down her cheek.

'I get it, I really do. Not the bit about "Great Expectations". That is weird. But I understand how you feel about losing your parents. Some mornings I wake up thinking Mum and Dad are asleep in the next room. When it hits me that I'm never going to see them again it's like falling off a cliff.'

When Archy touched her hand she didn't pull away. He held up his glass.

'Here's to us orphans!'

Nina linked her wrist around his and they drank with their

arms entwined. The rings on her right hand sparkled in rays of sunshine shining through the window panes.

'Don't you remember anything about your Mum and Dad?' Nina asked.

Archy longed to open up about his recurring nightmare. Screams in the night. A door caving in. Running through the darkness, panting for breath, his small arm aching in a man's harsh grip. Then he remembered that if you want to nurture a friendship with a sympathetic woman, it's best not to throw your childhood traumas in her face too soon.

'Nothing at all, I'm sorry to say.'

Nina drained her glass.

'Book a fortnight's holiday, Archy. You and I are going to fly to Brazil and try to trace your family. I'll be interested to go because Mum's brother used to live there. I think he must have been the black sheep of the family, because nobody would ever talk to me about him. Don't argue. I'll call you.'

It took them several minutes to make their way out of the packed bar. Edeldico colleagues flocked to offer them drinks, but Archy pressed on with a protective arm around Nina's waist. Outside he stopped a black cab and helped Nina into it. When he was waving her off he stepped backwards on to the feet of someone close behind him. The feet belonged to Chel.

'Careful mate! I was delivering something to your boss when I seen you and your lady through the pub window. You're punching well above your weight these days, ain't you? After we bumped into each other at the Roof Bar I kept trying to remember where I knew you from. It me took ages to figure it out, but I got there in the end.'

'You're mistaken. We don't know each other.' Archy tried to push past Chel, but the hostel manager stood firm.

'It's your eyes I remember. They've got the same look as

when you was a kid, like you'd seen something so bad you had to blank it out. You're Archy, ain't you? At junior school I took the mickey out of you at first, because you didn't speak hardly no English, but we made friends after a while. We used to kick a ball around in the park sometimes. Come on mate, you must remember me. I'm Chelsea, the boy with a girl's name.'

Chel was a pest and an unwanted link with his own messed-up infancy. But it didn't matter now that Nina had accepted him for himself. Archy gave in to the inevitable. 'Maybe you're right. I must admit your name rings a bell. Sorry, I really have to get back to the office.'

24

Coopers Hook Dock
Hetty

Sunset was drawing shadow monsters across a derelict gasworks on the banks of the river. From the passenger seat of a parked van, Hetty stared out at the massive piles of brick rubble and heaped metal girders that surrounded her. Less than five miles from her dance studio, she felt as if she'd been transported to an alien planet.

'I've lived around here my whole life, but I've never been here before. I don't like the look of it.'

'Get out!'

'I can't walk on them rocks in these shoes. Why can't I wait in the van?'

'Go on, get out!'

Like many East London hard men, the driver was of medium height, with broad shoulders and a shaven head. His facial features were delicate, almost feminine. Hetty wanted to ask him who shaped his eyebrows, but she wasn't about to push her luck here, in the middle of nowhere. She opened the door and half-jumped, half-slid down on to uneven ground. The driver started the engine and within seconds, the van was racing away. Hetty was alone in an urban desert, powerless to do anything but scream and swear.

'Come back, you miserable sod! How am I supposed to get home?'

She yelled abuse until the van rolled out of sight, more in order to relieve her feelings than from a belief that the driver could hear her, or that it would make any difference if he did. Trying to keep her balance on uneven chunks of concrete, she was filled with an unfamiliar emotion. Hetty could not remember the last time she had been afraid. It dawned on her that, even though Urban was dead, in her recent dealings with EdeldiCo she had been behaving as if she still basked in the protective glow of his power. What a mistake to make. Alone and exposed in this unearthly place, she was at the mercy of people with no respect for the old ways. Gentlemen's agreements, my word is my bond, trust me, I'm a banker, had all disappeared into the mists of time, like flip charts and fax machines. Why had she been abandoned in this wasteland? For once in her life, Hetty was shaken to her core.

'I'll find a few little jobs for you,' Lucan had said, when Hetty waylaid him at his club. He'd kept his word. He knew she had enough inside knowledge to disrupt his privileged lifestyle, because, during many years of being Urban's money mule and occasional lover, Hetty had learned lots of EdeldiCo's dirty little secrets. After that, fat brown envelopes had once again begun to come her way, delivered by cute but clueless young city suits who showed no interest in their contents. However, as an insurance policy, Hetty had bribed the club's doorman at Lucan's club to keep her up to date with the CEO's activities. If the supply of brown envelopes ever dried up, she was going to have plenty to tell his wife, Lady Willa.

Hetty knew that blackmail wasn't the most positive start to a business relationship, but it had always worked for her. She'd insisted that cash was the only way to go. By now it must be obvious to Lucan that she'd been absolutely right. He'd be a fool not to make more use of her, because it was a no-brainer that EdeldiCo could benefit from her many talents. She was so sure of success that, when she received the message that a driver was waiting to take her to a business meeting, she'd hurried down to the arches without telling Arlo and Chel where she was going.

Now, alone and unprotected in this wilderness, Hetty was torn between sprinting for safety and the opportunity to negotiate a profitable deal. In the end, it was her feet, not her business sense, that helped make her mind up. She wouldn't get far on this surface, not even in flat shoes, never mind four-inch heels. Her best chance of a positive outcome was to impress her handlers, and she felt supremely confident of doing so. Hadn't she worked her arse off for them? Didn't she meet all her targets? Hetty went through a mental check list. 'Be a go-between EdeliCo and their partners in whatever financial scam is flavour of the month. Tick! Deliver portable assets to forgers without asking questions, like I used to do for Urban. Tick! Find creative ways of concealing large quantities of used notes. Tick!'

However, she had to admit that learning how to manage money online had been challenging. Hetty was not a fan of internet banking, and there had been times when she was forced to ask Chel for help. But she'd got there in the end. Tick!

When an elegant figure emerged from behind a pyramid of distorted girders, Hetty was astonished to find herself facing Lucan Edeldi. Arms folded across his chest, prematurely white hair ruffled by a chill wind, he resembled his uncle so closely that Hetty's heart melted. She could almost imagine it was Urban standing there, ready to whisk her away on one of their trips to Jersey, young lovers the two of them. But when the CEO of EdeldiCo spoke, this romantic illusion was broken.

'What game are you playing this time, Hetty Brill?'

Immediately she was on guard. 'What do you mean, game? I live a quiet life these days. How are Lady Willa and the family?'

'Don't try to distract me. I know you're up to something.'

'You've got it wrong, Lucan. I admit, me and Urban got up to a bit of funny business, back in the day. Things is different now.'

'They certainly are. I only agreed to keep you on for old times' sake. But I expect you to keep your side of the bargain. You promised to deposit ten thousand pounds in my golf account last week, but I received less than half that amount. Where's the rest of my money?'

It was the question Hetty had been dreading. The cash retrieved from the old cemetery had been delivered as promised, but some of what had been tucked away in the compost toilet, along with all that had been stashed in the launderette, ready for her to collect and spread over numerous bank accounts, had gone missing. She had high hopes of retrieving it, but meanwhile, what was she to say to Lucan?

'Give me time. I've worked harder for you than I ever did for Urban. He used to ask me to pick up cash from drops, or hawk knock-off goods to fences. Once in a while I'd have to negotiate with a forger, but mostly I was feeding dummy accounts in high street banks. Since I've been working for you I've done all that and more, and I've had to learn to do it online. Keeping up with technology ain't easy at my age. And it's not as if you're on the breadline Lucan. You can afford to wait.'

'I've been using what you bring in to cover my personal

expenses. The boys' school fees, golf, the subscriptions to my club and so on. At this point in time, Edeldico needs every penny it can raise. Our clients have been nervous since Urban died, and we can't finalise his estate because my uncle's widow has gone missing. Have you any idea where she's hiding?'

'How would I know?'

'You knew everything about Urban. Tell me if you get news of Vida. I'll make it worth your while.'

When Vida, alias Sam, had appeared without warning in Hetty's manor, it had seemed like a business opportunity beyond her wildest dreams. She had soon realised that her hot property was useless to her without a buyer. Now Lucan was presenting himself as a potential purchaser. Hetty did a quick mental calculation. She could tell the CEO where to find Sam, take his money and keep her head down for a while. Or she could keep the information to herself, in the hope that in the long term, keeping on the right side of Urban's wealthy widow might lead to even greater rewards.

Seeing Hetty hesitate, Lucan said, 'I'm concerned about Vida. She has no means of support, and I'd never forgive myself if she came to harm.'

Hetty made up her mind. 'Okay. Give me a few days to get the money together, and I'll try to trace Vida. Is that all?'

'There is one more thing. Do you know a block of flats called The Mansions? The building is in EdeldiCo's property portfolio. We've marked it for development, but some old woman living there has a protected tenancy. I want you to find a way of making her move out.'

'You mean Irene?' said Hetty. 'She's my cousin, but that doesn't mean she'll listen to me.'

'If The Mansions isn't empty by the end of the month, I'll be forced to call in my debts. Edeldico pays your son's wages through that hostel we sponsor. And we made a substantial loan, with his cafe as security, to your husband.'

Out of habit, Hetty said, 'Arlo and me are separated.'

'Good. That means you won't mind if EdeldiCo closes down his business. Which is what we're going to have to do unless your cousin moves out. I don't care how you do it. Just get it done.'

Lucan signalled to a sleek black limousine that was creeping toward them. He took a pay-as-you-go phone from his pocket and handed it to Hetty. 'Let me know when she's gone.'

Hetty grabbed his sleeve. 'Please Lucan, don't sack Chel. The job at TimePad is the only chance he's ever had to make something of himself. And I beg you not to foreclose on Arlo. If you do, he and Chel will make me give up my studio. I'll get Irene out of her flat, I promise.'

He shook her off. 'If you don't, I'll make sure you and your family suffer.'

'I'll do whatever you say, Lucan. Can I have a lift to the Overground?'

Lucan got into his limousine and the chauffeur drove off. While she was limping back to civilisation, Hetty decided not to expose Sam to Lucan - yet. She'd keep that trick up her sleeve. But how was she going to make Irene and Viv leave The Mansions, when their bitter family history ruled out any possibility of getting the old woman on side?

'Blackmail's no use,' Hetty said to herself. 'She's got as much dirt on me as I have on her.'

In order to persuade her elderly cousin to leave the flat that had been her home for over fifty years, a more subtle approach was needed. By the time Hetty saw the lights of the overground station, she had a plan.

25

The Wickers Dance Studio
Hetty

By the time Hetty got back to the studio, tired and angry from her face-off with Lucan, night had fallen. Chelsea was waiting for her, kicking his heels under a dim street light. 'Mum, is something dodgy going on at EdeldiCo?'

Taken by surprise, Hetty dropped her keys. While she was scrabbling for them, Chelsea went on, 'After I made the drop for you at EdeldiCo HQ this morning, I bumped into this guy who went to my junior school. I seen him once before, last month, at one of Reed's projects. He works for EdeldiCo now, and not in the post room, neither. He's running the show. When we was kids, he didn't speak no English, but now he's earning big bucks. How does that work?'

Urban had set his firm up in the eighties, in order to buy out small businesses that were in financial difficulties. How those businesses got into trouble was a matter with which Hetty had never concerned herself. Twenty years on, it would have been easier for her to tell her son which of Edeldico's enterprises were not dodgy.

Straightening up, Hetty said, 'It's none of our business.'

'He was drinking in the EdeldiCo local, with all them city whizz kids. His suit was top dollar, and his bird had massive rocks on her fingers! See?'

The pictures had been taken through the window of the Rising Star. The faces of the couple were blurred, but the jewels on the woman's right hand stood out. Having trawled the internet for months for images of them, she instantly recognised Vida Edeldi's wedding and engagement rings.

'Do you know their names?'

'Archy is his name. I don't know hers.'

Since the day Urban's widow had walked into Arlo's and introduced herself as homeless Sam, the whereabouts of her jewellery had rarely been far from Hetty's thoughts. The intriguing sight of Samvida's rings, on the hand of Urban's only child, set off a chain of wild speculation. Was Samvida on the run from Nina? Or were Nina and Samvida working together, in order to carry out some kind of scam against Edeldico? If that was the case, Nina must be in touch with her stepmother, but how? As far as Hetty knew, Sam possessed no devices. Alternatively, it was possible that the two young women were in competition for Urban's fortune. And how did Lucan fit into the puzzle?

Searching for clues, Hetty examined the image closely. What she saw made her heart miss a beat.

'Chelsea, you say you remember this guy from junior school?'

'Yeah. He was one of them refugee kids.'

Hetty swallowed hard. 'You're right. Something dodgy is going on.'

'So why don't I get a piece of the action? If Archy can make it to the top, so can I! I'm management material too.'

'Don't kid yourself, Chel. TimePad is a dumping ground for kids who don't belong anywhere else. Edeldico sponsors it as a tax dodge. You only got the manager's job because you're my son.'

'How can you say that? Ain't I helped Dad with the café, ever since I was big enough to see over the counter? Nobody knows Coopers Hook like I do, not even you! That's why Edeldico took me on!'

Bitterness flooded Hetty's heart. She'd begged Urban to give her boy a chance to better himself. In the end she'd had to settle for him getting the manager's job at TimePad, instead of the white-collar post at HQ she'd been hoping for.

'That ain't the way it works. You saw them other candidates you were up against. Some of them had university degrees. The top dogs at EdeldiCo would never have appointed you, if they wasn't afraid I'd spill the beans about their goings-on.'

'What goings-on?'

'Stop pretending you don't know how I pay our debts, Chelsea. The fact is, some people at EdeldiCo are desperate to keep on the right side of me. You see, I know all their dirty little secrets!'

'Them big shots ain't scared of you. You're just a dance teacher. I got my job by myself.'

Hetty suppressed an urge to laugh. 'Don't kid yourself, son. I want to help you get ahead in life, I really do. But whatever Archy is mixed up in is new on me. I don't know how it works. You'd better keep clear.'

'That's all I ever hear off you! Keep clear, stay out of it, don't get involved!'

'Only because I want the best for you. Let me take the risks if you want to get to the top.'

'Have you seen who's at the top? There ain't a clean pair of hands among them. And look at yourself, trotting around with your little bags of cash! Your way don't work. It's time to play with the big boys!'

For almost thirty years Hetty had been listening to Chelsea's rants. She'd had enough of his laziness. If he wanted to get somewhere in life, he'd have to get off his arse and do something for himself.

'Since an old friend of mine died, I've had a hard time. Now I have a new contact at EdeldiCo and the work is starting to come through again. I can put some of it your way, if you like. You can help me out with the digital stuff.'

Chelsea shook his head. 'I don't want no part of what you're up to online.'

'What do you mean? I don't know nothing about computers.'

'Liar. You've been using my bank account to launder dirty money.'

Hetty tried to unlock the door of her studio, but Chelsea foiled her escape by leaning against it.

'You're going to listen to me, Mum, whether you like it or not. The other night, I went down the club. When I tried to buy a round there was a problem with my card, and I had to ask a mate to cover the damage. When I got back to TimePad, I switched on the laptop to check my account. It was three in the morning, and I wasn't expecting nothing but a headache. The balance was pretty much what I expected. After I found out I can't give the money back to my mate until payday, I went on staring at the screen. I was wondering if I'll ever have enough cash to throw

168

around without thinking about it, like those guys who work at EdeldiCo. That's when the figure on the bottom line changed. When I saw how much money had gone into my account, I could hardly believe it. I rubbed my eyes and looked again, but the total stayed the same. All of a sudden, there was thousands of pounds in my account. But you knew that, didn't you? Mum, just for a moment, I believed. I wasted a few minutes, dreaming about how I was going to spend my windfall. For starters, I was going to buy a top-of-the-range motor. Then I was going to pay Dad back what I owe him. And I was going on the holiday of a lifetime, maybe with a girl like like Sam Gumby for company. I was even going to bung you a few quid. Then I realised there was no time to lose. I had to spend, spend, spend before the bank discovered the mistake.'

'And did you?' Hetty shuddered, imagining thousands of pounds of card debt, never to be cleared.

'No, because when I looked at the screen again, every penny of it had gone! As if you didn't know!'

'What makes you think I had anything to do with it?'

'Because it was me who taught you how to transfer money online! And you stole my passwords!'

Cornered, Hetty knew she was not going to be able to talk her way out of this one. She racked her brains for a way to deflect Chelsea's rage. Hadn't he mentioned Sam? Didn't he say something about taking her on holiday, if he had the funds? It had never before occurred to Hetty that her son and Urban's widow could be a match. All at once it hit her that if they hit it off, it would solve everyone's problems at a stroke.

Sam must have got on the wrong side of Lucan. Otherwise she'd be enjoying the high life, instead of hiding in Coopers Hook. Whatever was going on in her life, Sam was obviously in need of protection, and Chelsea knew how to handle himself. In spite of her son's many faults, Hetty's maternal pride assured her that he was every young woman's dream. After all, he had his mother's looks, and like his father, he was a talented chef. True, his earning potential was low, but once the problems with Sam's inheritance were sorted out, she'd have more than enough money for both of them.

'I'm sorry, son, I really am. You weren't supposed to know anything about the transfer. It was just unlucky that you happened to be up at that hour. It must have been upsetting for you. I didn't mean no harm, truly I didn't. I promise, I'll make it up to you. Listen, I have news for you. I overheard Sam talking to her friends in the café. She was saying how much she likes you.'

The anger drained away from Chelsea's face. 'Yeah? Are you sure?'

'One hundred per cent sure. I won't tell you what she said about you, in case you get a big head.'

'I really like Sam, Mum. Tell me how to get on the right side of her. I'll do anything you say.'

'Next Salsa Night, just dress smart and try to behave like a gentleman. I'll do the rest.'

'Sure thing. You can rely on me, Mum. I won't let you down.'

Watching her son's broad back as he bowled away, Hetty hoped that this time, he meant it.

26

Plain Ease
Samvida

By the middle of May, my life was a constant struggle for survival. The sense of freedom I'd enjoyed since arriving in Coopers Hook was wearing off. There was recycled 'grey' water to be carried to the thirsty mobile gardens, pests to be picked from precious food crops and the constant game-changing of the weather. Soil was ingrained in my thumbs, and there was a permanent line of dirt under my broken nails. I wondered what the beauticians Urban had hired to attend to me would say if they could see me now. Back then, looking beautiful for my new husband had been my sole aim in life. Now I was losing sleep over how to keep slugs out of the curly kale. To make matters worse, Reed had spotted my talent for organisation. When he had to visit his other projects, he often left me in charge of the Plain Ease. This unwanted responsibility, combined with anxiety about the recent violent attack on Yessy, increased my stress levels.

Meanwhile, thousands of miles away in Costa Rica, Mum and Dad were beginning to suspect that something was wrong. They replied to my brief emails from an internet cafe with lists of awkward questions. What was wrong with my phone? When was I going to visit Gus at boarding school? Why had I not acknowledged the letters and gifts they sent to the Penthouse? I couldn't reply to this interrogation without revealing that I was living in poverty and surrounded by danger.

One afternoon I was in the Hub, piercing milk cartons to make planters for a children's workshop, when Bushra sneaked up behind me and put her arm around my waist.

'Hi! I brought biryani.'

Bushra and her Nan Puja had been very kind to me. It was Puja who gave me sheets and blankets for my bed at TimePad. Often Bushra would bring me a share of what Puja had cooked for her large family. But since our disastrous attempt to dye sheets, which had resulted in the launderette being closed for a week, my relationship with Bushra had been strained.

'No thanks,' I said, although both of us knew I was always hungry.

'But it's Nan's special recipe.'

She set one of Puja's treasured Tupperware containers on the potting table and opened it. The escaping steam blendes the scent of spices with the Hub's characteristic smell of tomato leaves, lavender and soil.

'I even brought a proper spoon, so you won't have to use one of Reed's nasty wooden ones.'

I couldn't resist the treat.

'Cheers, Bushra!'

'Enjoy!'

When I was scraping up the last few grains of rice Bushra

said, 'I dried out the notes we found at the laundrette. You can hardly see the green dye.'

'How much?' When Bushra told me the figure, I dropped my spoon.

'Grandad put it through the bank with the takings from his shop. You and I are going to share it.'

I shook my head. 'Whoever stashed that cash is going to come looking for it.'

'We can worry about that later. For now, will you at least let me treat you? Hetty gave me three tickets for Salsa Night, so you and Folu and I can go all together. Say you'll come! Pretty please!'

I'd been longing to go to Hetty's Salsa Night ever since my first day in Coopers Hook, so Bushra's invitation offer was irresistible. After I said I'd go, Bushra practised a dance step in her Doctor Martens on the bare earth floor of the poly-tunnel,

'I'll see you at six. And wear those fabulous boots!'

I looked down at the clumpy safety shoes Reed had lent me.

'Are you winding me up?'

'They're cool. And you'll need them. You'll see why.'

When I told Folu that Bushra had free tickets to Salsa Night and we were both invited, she was so happy she burst into tears. Since giving up her cleaning jobs, my room-mate had spent her days trying to get a job as a chef. She was badly in need of some fun.

Dressed in our cleanest jeans and shirts, Folu and I were ready to go when Bushra, stylish in yellow, met us on the steps of Time-Pad. We made it to Arlo's ten minutes before closing time. Bushra paid for three big slices of pizza and Arlo gave us the last of the day's salad. When I bought cans of pop they all laughed, remembering the day when Folu spilled her drink on my blue trench.

'You've not had it cleaned, Sam,' said Bushra. 'And after Folu gave you that fiver!'

'I'm keeping the fiver for luck. But Folu, you can borrow my coat any time.'

'Thank you, Sam! I'll wear it when I go job hunting.'

Bushra giggled. 'No, Folu! They'll think you've come to buy the restaurant.'

It was ten minutes walk from Arlo's to Hetty's dance studio. The mock-Tudor building with boarded up windows was known as the Wicker. From a hundred metres away we could hear Latin American music filtering through the sound of traffic. An arrow painted on the wall directed us to a side entrance, where Hetty was standing in the narrow doorway. She was greeting regulars, welcoming new faces and stowing cash in a bum bag slung across the front of her red dress.

When she saw us her thin lips contorted into an awkward smile. 'Hi, Bushra! Thanks for coming. And you've brought your mates! Good to see you, Folu, and you, lovely Sam.'

We weren't accustomed to such friendliness from Hetty. Alarmed, we glanced sideways at each other. Seeing us hesitate, Hetty hugged each of us in turn, then kissed me on both cheeks. 'I wanted to do something nice for you girls, to thank you for the work you do for at community garden. You can order any drink you like, no charge.'

The music switched to a dance rhythm. Hetty stood to one side, allowing us to glimpse the cheerful crowd behind her. I was the first to cast aside my suspicions and head for the dance floor. Folu and Bushra were close behind me. The lights were low and a battered sound system was turned up high. The large room, once the pub's saloon bar, had kept its air of refinement. The fixtures and fittings had been ripped out, but oak panelling and a parquet floor remained unscathed. Dusty red velour curtains, hanging alongside shuttered windows, added a seedy glamour to the atmosphere.

The studio was already half full. More people were pouring in, many of them in office clothes. Like Bushra and me, many of the women wore sturdy boots. At the far end of the room two professional dancers were posing on a dais. The man wore tight black trousers, with a frilled white shirt open to his waist, and the woman's knee-length white dress had layers of flounces. On their perch, they looked like exotic birds with fluffed feathers. When the studio was crammed to capacity, they began to demonstrate the steps, while Hetty sang out instructions. 'Start in neutral, like a car, feet together. Forward on left, return to neutral. Back on right, return to neutral. Beat four is a rest. One, two, three, four!'

'There are so many people here!' For once, Bushra sounded nervous.

Folu hung back. 'I can not do this!'

I took hold of my friends' hands, and led them to join one of several rows of women facing lines of men. Rows of swaying dancers snaked down the room, then up again, changing partners every few minutes. When Hetty called out 'Switch!' everyone moved along one place. Soon we relaxed into the Salsa rhythm. Bushra's steps were slick, but Folu's were more graceful. As for me, I hadn't felt so happy and free since before I met Urban. I danced as if my feet had wings. But an hour into the session I my momentum was halted. One of Hetty's arms was around my waist and the other held a cocktail.

'Hot, ain't it, Sam? Fancy a nice cold drink? Try a sip.'

It was the most natural thing in the world for me to swallow a mouthful of the delicious cocktail she invitingly held to my lips.

'The bar's through there. One, two, three, four!'

Without missing a beat Hetty sashayed back into the dance, calling out Salsa steps at the top of her voice. It was months since I'd last tasted alcohol and I craved more. Hetty had said the drinks were on the house, so there was no reason to deny myself this pleasure. Folu and Bushra were swaying in the midst of the dancers. I turned my back on them and went in search of a margarita.

In an upstairs room at the Wicker, Hetty had transformed what had once been a spit-and-sawdust beer hall into a breakout space. On the walls, posters for local dance and music gigs clung to the flaking plaster. People were chilling with drinks on upcycled chintz sofas. Along one wall, the original counter survived, held together by decorative wrought iron and decorated with jam-jars full of flowers. Behind it, Chel was lining up bottles of cider. I tried to retreat, but he'd already seen me.

'Hey there, Gumby! What's your poison? Mum said I was to give you whatever you want.'

It was unthinkable to me that Chel would pester me for sex, when I was there at his mother's invitation. 'I'd love a margarita,' I said, sinking into an armchair.

27

The Wicker
Samvida

Chel proved to be a talented mixologist. The cocktail he served up was citrusy and heavy on the tequila. I'd drunk margaritas with Urban in the world's most exclusive bars, but none of them tasted as good as this one. I enjoyed it so much I hardly noticed the armchair's broken springs. After savouring every drop, I coaxed Bushra and Folu into the bar to share the treat. I was disappointed when they'd only accept tumblers of bottled lemonade.

'What a waste! I'm sure Chel can fix a fabulous mocktail.'

Bushra raised her eyebrows. 'No way! He's the kind of man who'd spike your drink.'

'What's he going to do, right under his Mum's eye?'

Folu rubbed her ankles. 'I do not trust Chel, or Hetty. Anyway, I must leave soon. Every time the men in the row behind us step backwards, they hurt my heels.'

'Sam, did you tell her to wear boots?'

'I did. Did you forget, Folu?'

'I only have one pair of shoes,' said Folu. 'Thank you for inviting me. I have enjoyed the dancing very much. I have to go to the Arches. Then back to Timepad to sleep. Come with me, Sam!'

'I don't want to leave. Please stay. Whoever you wait for at ten every night never turns up.'

'After all the evenings we spent hiding from Chel, you are stupid to let him fill you with booze.'

'Chel is a fool, but his margaritas are to die for. Just for once, we have a chance to stay out late and have a drink. Snap out of it, Folu! What's the matter with you? All you do these days is sleep, and wait for some man who's never coming back. '

'I have a good reason to wait for him. The best. Think about it, Sam.'

Bushra hugged Folu. 'Be careful out there. I'm going to dance until my uncle comes to pick me up. Sam can walk home with us.'

I ordered another margarita. The rest of the evening melted away in a haze of alcohol and hypnotic Latin rhythms. I rotated between the dance floor and the bar, knocking back margaritas as fast as Chel could set them up. When Bushra's uncle arrived I refused their offer to see me back to TimePad. Instead, I asked Chel to mix her a mojito, just for a change, before joining a late-night Salsa session. When the studio was empty I danced alone, calling the steps even after Chel turned off the music and Hetty was sweeping the floor. 'Forward on left, back on right. One, two, three, four!'

Hetty leaned on her broom. 'Walk Sam home, Chelsea. And play nice.'

'Don't worry Mum,' he said, 'I know how to treat a lady.'

I was so drunk I believed him.

By the time we turned into a side street off the main road, it had dawned on me that Chel intended to walk me all the way to TimePad. Even after several cocktails I knew I was in danger. I shook his hand free of its grip on my elbow.

'Chel, let go! I can find my own way.'

'What's your problem? I won't hurt you.'

'Leave me alone. I need to clear my head.'

'Okay, if that's what you want. But don't forget, I can make your life easy if you're nice to me.'

I waited on the corner until my troublesome landlord had disappeared into the darkness, before following him along the quiet residential street. It was two in the morning. The ever-present sound of traffic had faded to a low rumble, and no noise or light came from the Victorian terraced houses ranked on either side of me. This street had been gentrified. Neat front gardens with evergreen hedges protected their occupants from the vibrant street life that attracted their occupants to Coopers Hook. After hours of dancing in a hot, crowded room, it was pleasant to be alone under the street lights, breathing in cool night air. For a while I forgot my problems. Then I caught a glimpse of someone dodging into the shadow of a gatepost a few metres ahead, and my happy dream was shattered.

Then the trickling sound of a man urinating reached me. It was only some guy relieving himself, but it reminded me that I also needed to empty my bladder. Sober, I'd never have pissed in someone's front garden, but the cocktails had addled my brain. I went into the nearest garden and, under the overhanging shade of a tree, lowered my jeans. Then someone grabbed me around the waist from behind.

'I knew you was a freak,' Chel mumbled into my hair.

'Let me go, Chel! I don't want to have sex with you!'

'Yes you do. Why else would your pants be round your knees? You knew I'd be waiting, didn't you? You made the right decision, Sam Gumby. I'm going to show you a good time.'

I opened my mouth to scream. But when I thought of how the family who lived in the house would react to finding me half naked in their front garden, I shut it again. Then Chel put his hand over my mouth and shoved me forwards until my stomach was flat against the tree trunk.

'Relax babe! You know you want to.'

There was only one way to stop him. I pushed hard against the tree, levering my lower body against him, and peed down his legs. Swearing under his breath, he jumped away from me. Blinds were being raised and door chains were rattling. I dragged on my jeans, surprised and pleased that they were dry. My aim had been accurate as well as effective.

Chel was running down the middle of the street while trying to do up his trousers. I hid in a nearby hedge until I was sure none of the residents had woken up. Then I also began to run. I raced through a maze of back streets, trying to put as much distance as possible between myself and Chel. I didn't stop running until it struck me that I had nowhere to go. Sleeping at TimePad was out of the question from now on. I'd have to ask Folu to bring my things to me. Meanwhile, I had nowhere to spend what was left of the night. A few hundred metres the Arches were looming up. At this time of the night they looked dark and mysterious. I was close to Arlo's Café and Plain Ease. If Yessy could sleep in the community garden, then so could I. I knew a place where the slats of the fence were loose. Once inside there was plenty of cover.

When I heard footsteps behind me, I began to walk faster. Behind me the footsteps also speeded up. I didn't dare turn around, for fear of what I might see. Before long I reached the gap in the fence. It was going to be easy to wriggle through it into the garden, but I was afraid whoever was behind me might follow. I didn't want to crawl through a fence with an unknown threat at my heels, so I turned and walked towards the footsteps. Outside Arlo's, something was moving in the shadows. Even in the dark I recognised the skinny, loose-limbed body with the mop of tangled hair.

'Is that you, Yessy?

Arlo's security light clicked on. Now that Yessy and I could see each other, I felt safer. I wasn't afraid of Yessy, who had always been gentle and protective towards me.

'I'm in trouble. I'll have to sleep at Plain Ease tonight. I promise I won't get in your way.'

'Yes.'

He was becoming more and more agitated. I became aware of an engine running nearby. A van was creeping along the kerb, closing in on us like a prowling cat. When Yessy clutched my hand and tried to pull me towards the café, I was astonished. He'd never done anything like that before.

'Yessy, what's the matter?'

'Yes! Yes! Yes!'

The van stopped and a man got out. Yessy let go of my hand and ducked behind a stack of tables. The stranger made a grab for him, but somehow Yessy managed to slide out of his reach and vanish into the night. The man swore and turned towards me.

'Who are you?' he said. 'Why are you out here with the dummy, at this time of night?'

'I could ask you the same,' I said, although I was shaking at the knees.

'I'm Dudu. And you are drunk.'

I was inches from the door of the café, with my hand poised above the bell.

'You don't want to do that,' the man said. 'Arlo needs his beauty sleep.'

I lowered my arm. 'You know Arlo?'

'I know he has to work all hours to pay off his debts.'

It sounded as if Dudu was the muscle for some loan shark. From the way Yessy had reacted to him, he must show up regularly to collect payments from Arlo. I relaxed. Whatever difficulty Arlo was in, it had nothing to do with me.

'I have something for Arlo. Will you give it to him?'

'Okay.'

Dudu reached into his pocket. I held out a hand and felt something sharp pierce my forefinger. Too late, I realised I was lost. My arms and legs felt like lead. Around me was total darkness. I tried to fight the drug that was closing my body down, but I only had time to let out one long moan before losing consciousness.

28

Coopers Hook
July 1952
Young Irene

Irene thought the blue dress was too good for a hanging. On the day it had been made Aunty Hester, Mum's sister, was allowed to use the sewing machine in exchange for minding Edie on her day off. Mum had taken the old pram to collect a load of dirty sheets from a rich lady. She got paid for laundering sheets at the Public Baths, where there were huge washing machines and driers, as well as a press with enormous rollers. Last time Edie went with Mum to the Baths she'd nearly got herself squashed flat along with the sheets. It took two people to mind Edie. That's why Irene was kept off school so often.

Aunty had borrowed a dress pattern from a friend at work and swapped the last of her clothes coupons for five yards of royal blue cotton. 'Forget make do and mend,' she said. 'The War's over.

Reen, please keep an eye on your sister while I make myself something pretty to wear.'

While Aunty was pinning paper shapes to the fabric spread out on the table, Edie screamed for the pincushion. Irene had to play this-little-piggy on her toes to calm her down. Then Aunty cut the fabric into pieces with Mum's pinking shears, and for once the house smelled like new cloth instead of reeking of wet laundry. When the pedal of the sewing machine began to rattle under Aunty's pumping foot, Edie made a grab for the flying needle and almost lost a finger. To keep her sister quiet, Reen took her into the back yard and made mud pies with marigold flowers for chimneys.

By the time Mum came home with the empty pram, Aunty's new blue dress was ready to try on. Although it was tacked together and bristled with loose threads, its wasp waist and full skirt flooded the narrow hallway with Parisian glamour. Mum knelt to pin up the hem.

'You look lovely sis,' said Mum. 'Like a film star.'

That was two years ago. Since then, everything in Irene's life had changed. Some of the changes were for the better. After Mum stopped keeping her at home, Irene's marks had improved. In September she was going to the new girls' grammar school. But she was confused by goings-on in the adult world. For a start, she didn't understand why Aunty Hester was heating water to fill the tin bath for her. She'd had a bath on Sunday, and nobody needed more than one a week.

Irene went upstairs to the bedroom she used to share with Edie and tried on the blue dress. She was tall for her age, so it was only a little bit too long. After she'd stuffed handfuls of newspaper down the front to make it look as if she had boobies, she looked at least thirteen. When Aunty came upstairs Irene asked her if she could wear the dress to visit Mum. Aunty shook her head and held up a gingham dress Irene had almost grown out of. Her school shoes were too tight for the long journey ahead of them, so Aunty made her put on Mum's old moccasins, which were a size too big.

Aunty herself was dressed as if she was going on a date, in a flowery summer dress, straw hat and sandals with heels. Together they wrapped the dress in brown paper and tied it with string. On the trolley bus to Holloway, Irene poked a hole in the parcel with her finger, so she could stroke the fabric. It felt like next door's kitten.

In the corridor outside the cell stood two women guards. One of them looked fierce, while the other one smiled in a way that scared Irene even more than her colleague's frown. The prison walls were green at the bottom and cream at the top, like the walls of the primary school she'd left for ever the week before. There was a long green curtain down one side of the cell. On the other side the sun was streaming through a window caked with dirt. The smiling guard said this window was special. You could peer out of it to watch the prisoners exercising, but they couldn't see you.

When Irene peered out of the window she saw two circular paths. One was inside the other. The women on the inner path walked fast, as if they had somewhere to go. Those on the outside shuffled along, as if they weren't going anywhere. It was like the song Here We Go Round The Mulberry Bush, except there were no trees in the prison yard.

On a plant stand in a corner of the cell stood a fish bowl. In it were two goldfish - the kind the rag-and-bone man gave you in jam jars in exchange for empty bottles. When she got tired of looking out of the special window, Irene sat down on a hard wooden chair, with the brown paper parcel on her lap, and watched the fish. Like the women in the yard, they went round in circles, Behind her, Mum and Aunty talked in the voices they usually kept for funerals.

Mum said, 'I never did like wearing your cast-offs. I sure as Hell don't want them now. Not after what you done to me.'

Aunty said, 'I thought you'd want to keep up appearances.'

'Since when have you cared what people say? I bet the whole street's talking about that rag on Reen's back. It's so short it's barely decent. And why did you make her wear my old shoes? Promise me you'll sell your blue dress and use the money to buy Reen a school uniform. I don't want her to go to the grammar looking like a scarecrow.'

'I'll try, but nobody down our way wants a cocktail dress. I took it down the pawn shop, but they wouldn't have it because of the cigarette burn. The uniform at the grammar school is the same colour. If I can't sell the dress, I'll cut it down to make her a tunic.'

It was stuffy in the cell, and Irene hadn't had a good night's sleep in weeks. With her eyes fixed on the circling fish, she dozed off. She woke up with a shock when Aunty pulled her to her feet. The fierce prison guard was standing between Irene and Mum.

Someone was crying.

'Keep your eyes on the floor,' said Aunty. 'You don't want to see this.'

Irene clung tightly to the dress in its parcel while Aunty and the smiling guard half dragged, half carried her into the corridor.

'Stop whingeing. You murdered your daughter for money, and now you've got to pay.'

For a second Irene thought the mean guard was talking to her, and she felt very afraid.

'There's a crowd out front,' the guard said. 'They're queuing up to read the notice of execution. I'll take you out the back way.'

The guard hurried Aunty and Irene down a wrought iron staircase and through the service areas, where there was a strange yellow fog in the air. Just like at home, Irene could smell boiled cabbage and wet clothes. And just like at home, there were no men. In most places she went to there was a man to boss the females around, but here she saw only women guards and women prisoners. They were sweeping floors, peeling potatoes and hanging up wet clothes to dry. She was surprised and pleased to learn that women could run a whole prison by themselves.

'Aunty,' she said as they ran, 'Where are all the men?'

In her high heeled sandals, Aunty was finding it hard to keep up with the booted guard's brisk trot. 'The men are hiding,' she panted. 'Tomorrow morning they'll crawl out from behind the green curtain. It's men what'll hang her.'

Irene pointed towards the prison laundry. 'Why can't those washerwomen do it?'

'Hanging people is a man's job,' said Aunty. 'Women ain't strong enough. Stop asking questions. My feet are killing me.'

Irene began to run in the loose moccasins. By the time they'd sneaked out of a back door and bolted to the bus stop, her feet were as sore too.

'Thank God that's over,' said Aunty Hetty. 'Give me the dress, you've ripped the paper half off. Here's your fare, don't lose it.'

'Aunty,' said Irene.

'I can't take no more questions!'

'Just one, Aunty.'

'All right, just one.'

'Has Mum got her bus fare?'

'What do you mean, her bus fare?'

'For when she comes home on the bus tomorrow. After she's been hanged, I mean.'

'Strewth,' said Aunty, 'You think she's going to be hung out like the washing! Your Mum ain't never coming home. Didn't you know?'

Irene's world began to go round and round.

Like the women in the prison yard.

Like the goldfish in the bowl.

Like the noose waiting for her mother's neck.

29

Arlo's Café
Arlo

Arlo was busily stacking plates, wiping tables and setting out the equipment he'd need to serve breakfasts the next morning. It was half past six in the afternoon, and he was preparing to lock up. By seven o'clock he hoped to be on the sofa in his flat with his feet up, watching the football. When he heard the door open he was relieved to see that it was only Yessy.

'Come in, mate,' he said. 'It's all right. We're on our own.'

Yessy held out his leather purse and loosened its neck. Arlo opened the till and counted out a few coins. Carefully he dropped them into the pouch. Then he put some of the previous day's sandwiches into a paper bag. Yessy took the bag gratefully and tucked it inside his ragged shirt.

'Next time, go round the back, like I told you. I don't want anybody to see me giving you the money. I can't feed every hungry kid in Coopers Hook.'

'Yes.'

Arlo turned around to find Jammy standing in the doorway. The policeman must have seen and heard what had just passed between himself and Yessy. It occurred to Arlo that anyone with a suspicious mind would think the transaction looked odd, to say the least. He made up his mind to share his best-kept secret.

'Off you go, Yessy. Jammy, sit down. Fancy a tea?'

Soon the policeman was seated at his usual corner table, with a mug of tea and a biscuit. Arlo wasn't sure what would be the best way to begin what might be a difficult conversation. In the end he came right out with it.

'I suppose you're wondering why I've been giving Yessy money?'

'Since you ask,' said Jammy, 'That's exactly what was going through my mind. Whatever's going on between the two of you, its unusual to say the least.'

'I know,' said Arlo. 'I can see why it might look suspicious. But there's no funny business going on, I swear. Yessy's been hanging around Coopers Hook ever since he was a little kid. Nobody knows where he came from, and as far as any of us can tell he's all alone in the world. It made me sad to see him going hungry and I wanted to help him out. But I couldn't let everyone see me giving away free food. There are so many sad cases around here, I'd end up feeding the whole neighbourhood. So I give Yessy some money on the quiet every evening, and he gives it back to me the next day in return for a plate of pasta. We'd kept it up for years without anyone finding out, until you walked in.'

'That's very generous of you, Arlo,'said Jammy.

'Not really. Yessy knows he can only have pasta, because it's the cheapest thing on the menu.'

'Fair enough.'

'Don't tell anyone, will you? I don't want it to get out that I'm giving away food. A queue would form at my door in no time.'

'I won't say a word. By the way, I'm planning to alert social services to Yessy's situation. Maybe they can do something for him.'

'Good luck with that. Puja's been trying to get help for Yessy for years. The trouble is, there's no record of him anywhere. Officially, he doesn't exist. When he was younger he used to hide when he saw the social workers coming, and now it's too late. I don't know exactly how old he is, but he must be over eighteen. He's an adult now, so he's on his own. Which is the way he likes it.'

Arlo carried on straightening up the tables and chairs. He was relieved that the policeman had given his blessing to his financial arrangement with Yessy. In spite of his dislike for having coppers on his premises, he'd formed the opinion that the community police officer was a decent guy and an asset to Coopers Hook. His best quality appeared to be his love of a quiet life. He wasn't the sort of policeman who went looking for trouble. When Jammy asked him what his accent was, Arlo answered honestly.

'I was born in Belfast. I moved to London when I was seventeen. You wouldn't think it to look at me now, but I was offered a football apprenticeship.'

'Wow, that's amazing,' said Jammy.

'At the time it was amazing,' said Arlo. 'But I only made semi-pro. After a few years I picked up an injury. And that was the end of my career.'

'Why didn't you go back to Ireland after you were injured?'

'By then I was going out with Hetty. I met her when she was in a pantomime in the church hall. She looked like a fairy off a Christmas tree.'

'Did Hetty give up her dancing career when she got pregnant with Chel?'

'She had to pack it in long before that. Like me, she had a knee injury. Hers is on the left, mine is on the right. We used to joke that we limped through life together, like a three-legged race. But the days when Hetty and I could share a joke are long gone. Have you had a good day, Jammy?'

'Not bad. There's been a lot of shoplifting in the mini-mart, so I popped in a few times.'

'Catch anybody?'

'I didn't want to catch them. Too much paperwork. It's better to put them off in the first place. When shoplifters are made aware of a police presence, they soon move on.'

'Good thinking, mate.'

'And I had a chat with some of the excluded kids.'

'You mean, like Yessy?'

'I'm talking about kids who are excluded from school. They hang about in the park together.'

'I wouldn't know. I never have time to go to the park.'

'I want them to get used to seeing me around. That way they've got some kind of protection. I get something out of it too. Those kids know everything that goes on in Coopers Hook.'

The conversation was moving on to dangerous ground. Arlo took off his apron and hung it up behind the counter. 'I bet they do. Sorry to rush you, but it's closing time.'

Jammy stood up, pushed his chair in and handed his empty mug to Arlo.

'Thanks for the tea,' he said. 'Speaking of information, I'm hoping to catch the brute who attacked Yessy at Plain Ease. I believe a grey transit van may have been involved. Have you seen a van of that description in the area?'

'If I see one,' Arlo said cautiously, 'I'll let you know right away.'

'Cheers. I've enjoyed our chat. Don't worry, I won't say a word about Yessy's dinner money.'

When he was safe in his flat at last, Arlo reflected on his encounter with the policeman. He'd been wrong to think the man was idle. Jammy looked as if he'd never done a day's work in his life, but between his ears, it was all going on. He'd have to be more careful what he said to the man in future.

Arlo switched on the sports channel and tried to focus on the game.

30

The Mansions
Irene

In Irene's dream butterflies were grumbling like pensioners when a bus is late. 'You wait and wait, then two come along together,' they moaned, dragging their rough wings across her eyelids. They'd infested the roots of her thinning hair and were gnawing at her scalp. All over her body giant versions of the bedbugs she remembered from childhood were sinking their pointed teeth into her flesh. She threw a chamber pot at them. It smashed against against the crooked sash window and burst like a bomb from the Blitz. The insects became fiery sparks. Shards of glass floated lighter than air above Irene's head. Water flooded in through the shattered window, forming a blood-red river that filled her mouth and nose and threatened to crush her.

It was the tapping that woke her. At first she thought the butterflies she'd been dreaming about were dancing inside her head. Then she remembered butterflies don't wear shoes. With a huge effort of will, Irene managed to free her mind from the nightmare and force herself to wake up. In the depths of a wintry Spring night, rain beat against her bedroom window. While she slept, perhaps the sound had led her to imagine someone was tapping on the flat's front door. But that was impossible, because she and Viv were the only people still living in The Mansions. Was her daughter unwell and signalling for help? Viv was making a good recovery from her minor stroke, but Irene lived in constant fear of her being taken ill again.

She slid her legs over the edge of the bed and sat there listening, with her feet flat on the floor and her head upright. This was no time to give way to vertigo. One by one, she rotated her ankles, to kick-start her joints. At first, her old bones refused to spring into action. When at last they lost their stiffness, she shuffled along the hall and looked in on Viv. She was relieved to find her daughter asleep in the single bed her Dad bought for her when she was a teenager.

Was someone waiting outside on the landing, or was this merely a hangover from her insect dream? Irene decided to find out, and shoved her feet into loose slippers before she put one eye to the spy-hole. The second-floor landing was deep in darkness. The light bulbs had not been replaced since last year, when the last of her neighbours had stopped resisting the will of the landlords and gone away. For sure, the tapping noise must be part of her nightmare. She was on the point of going back to bed when a voice she remembered, but could not at first put a name to, called her.

'Help me, Reen! I'm scared!'

It was the first time anyone had called her Reen in fifty years. No living person had ever used her childhood nickname. She must still be dreaming. But whose voice had the butterflies stolen?

'Reen, come and help me!'

Irene opened the door. Rainwater was dripping from the fractured panes of the big landing window. A bleak glow from the night sky revealed nothing but bare floorboards, stair rails and the old-fashioned cage lift. 'Who's there?'

There was silence for a long moment. Then the half-remembered voice spoke again.

'I'm so frightened, Reen.'

'Who are you?'

'Have you forgotten your own mother?'

Dark shadows and bright flashes pinballed inside Irene's head. She closed her eyes and leaned against the wall in an effort to regain her balance, scraping her knuckles on crumbling brickwork where plaster had fallen away. When she staggered to the other side of the landing, to lean on the rail and gaze into the empty stairwell, the floor felt solid under her feet. Was she dreaming, or awake?

'I'm locked in, Reen. Hurry!'

Irene had heard it said that a traumatic death binds a soul to earth, unable to escape this world's suffering. She had never taken the idea seriously, but suddenly she felt sure her long-dead mother was pleading to be released. But where was her spirit trapped? The only possible place was the lift.

'Mum?' The word, evocative as a flavour remembered from childhood, felt delicious on her tongue. 'How ever did you get stuck in the lift?'

There was a pause before her mother's ghost replied. 'When they come to get me, I tried to run away, but I fell and ended up in here. Please let me out, Reen!'

An icy chill froze Irene's heart. For the past six months, a notice saying 'Out of Order' had been taped to the lift door. She had no idea how to open it and set her mother free. Surely, after all this time, a disembodied spirit could wait one more night to be released? In the morning, she'd ask for Jammy's advice. 'I'll talk to the police. They'll know what to do.'

The voice, familiar, insistent and impossible to ignore, echoed in the stairwell as she began to retreat towards her flat. 'You don't want to do that, Reen! It's the police what's chasing me! They're going to hang me by the neck until I'm dead! I'm so scared! Hurry, before it's too late!'

Unable to resist her mother's desperate plea, she pushed the control button of the lift with all her strength and leaned her full weight against its outer doors. When they gave way and fell open, anger added itself to the mix of emotions rioting in Irene's heart. The landlords had been lying about the lift being out of order. All along, Viv could have been using it, instead of risking a fall on the stairs.

'The coppers are cuffing me, Reen!' Mum's voice seemed further away, and Irene was almost sure she could hear footsteps on the stairs. Overwhelmed by her confused emotions, her mind reeled. Was she awake, or asleep and dreaming? Perhaps, if she opened the lift and let the insects fly out of her dream, she could sleep in peace.

'I'll save you, Mum! Don't be scared!'

Irene leaned forward and stretched out her foot, meaning to step up on to the suspended floor of the old-fashioned lift. She didn't notice when her slipper tumbled down the empty shaft, because she was transfixed by what she saw beyond the latticed metal inner gates. Mum knelt there, dressed as she had been when Irene last saw her at Holloway Prison, when she was a child visiting the condemned cell with Aunty Hester. She seemed unaware of her daughter's presence, and was staring upwards at the ceiling of the dangling lift, her face contorted into a mask of horror. Although she dreaded seeing whatever was frightening her mother, Irene could not resist the urge to throw back her head and look.

A noose swung overhead, moving lower every second, carrying with it fear, pain and death.

Suddenly aware she was in danger, Irene tried to regain her footing and lost her balance. She could not prevent the full weight of her body swinging forwards, to hover on the edge of the void. For a second she clung to the metal cage, but gravity dragged her to the rim of the shaft, just as the lift's neglected mechanism creaked into motion. Within seconds, it had ground to a halt, blocked by Irene's bones and flesh, crushed between the inner metal cage and the shaft wall.

31

The Wickers Dance Studio
Hetty

Hetty lay on the floor of her studio, limbs spread out like a starfish, sobbing and gasping for breath. She'd run all the way from The Mansions to The Wicker Gate. Her lungs felt as if they were tied together in a knot, and her heart was pounding like a snare drum.

Never before had she reacted in this way after carrying out a scam. To an experienced petty criminal like herself, what she had just done at The Mansions was a minor offence, so why did thinking about it fill her mind with horror? Shudders raked her body top to toe.

She never dreamed Irene would come out of her flat to answer her ghostly calls from the floor below. Brill women were as superstitious as they were hardcore. Irene had believed her mother was communicating with her from beyond the grave and responded with heartfelt emotion. That was what had spooked

Hetty. Realising that her voice must be like that of her great-aunt, the condemned murderess, shook her to the core. Sometimes genes packed a punch.

Hetty had crept down the stairs and out of the front door of The Mansions just in time. Irene's shouts must have woken Viv. The two of them were probably sitting at their kitchen table trying to figure out, over a cup of tea, who was most likely to have played such a cruel prank on them. They were no fools, so it was only a matter of time before they remembered the spare key Irene had given Arlo years ago. Hetty made a mental note to replace that key on its hook in the café's kitchen before Irene came looking for it.

It was four o'clock in the morning. There was plenty of time to nip round to Arlo's, let herself in through the back door and cover her tracks, before Irene and Viv put two and two together and realised they added up to Hetty. She peeled herself off the parquet, took some deep breaths and did a few stretches. Quickly, she took off her track suit and pulled on jeans and a jumper. It would never do to be seen in the same clothes she had worn when creeping into The Mansions a few hours earlier.

Outside the Wicker, the street was deserted. There had been a flash storm while Hetty was at Irene's. It added to the other-worldly atmosphere of Coopers Hook at night. The pavements shone with moisture, but rain was no longer falling and the air smelled clean and fresh. Walking briskly towards sanctuary at her ex's place, Hetty's anxiety level sank and she regained her confidence. She remembered watching Chelsea and Sam walk along this same route after Salsa Night, a few hours earlier. The girl had pushed her son's hand away when he tried to hold hers, and they looked as if they were arguing about something. Hetty put the memory to one side. She had done everything she could to bring the pair together. Now, it was up to Chel to woo the wealthy widow.

Hetty was about to turn into a side street when a grey van drove past her, shining silver under the lights of the dual carriageway. When she caught sight of the driver she did a double take, because she'd seen him before. He was an Edeldico driver - the same man who'd left her alone on the derelict site by the river. She put it to the back of her mind, because she no longer had anything to fear from Lucan and his heavies. If Irene didn't haul her wrinkly backside out of the Mansions within a week, after the fright she'd given her, Hetty was prepared to eat her best handbag. Nevertheless, she walked as fast as she could until she got to Arlo's.

Yessy was lurking at the back of the café. This was unusual. After sleeping all night at Plain Ease, he generally fed the hens and did various odd jobs to prepare for the day's activities, before strolling around to Arlo's for lunch. Hetty waved a hand to shoo him away. 'Get out of here! Nobody wants you hanging around.'

'Yes.'

'Don't give me that! I know you ain't as stupid as you pretend to be.'

'Yes.' The young homeless man stood between Hetty and the kitchen door, showing no inclination to get out of her way.

'If you don't clear off, I'll tell Arlo not to serve you any more. Then, what will you do? No-one else will put up with you.'

Arlo appeared round the corner of the café. His face was the colour of milk. When he saw his ex, he reached out a shaking hand to touch hers. 'You'd better come in and sit down, love. Something terrible has happened.'

Hetty's hand flew to her heart. 'Not Chelsea?'

'No, poor old Irene. She's had a shocking accident. Viv found her, and she didn't know who else to call. She's in a terrible state.'

'Who's in a state? Irene or Viv?'

'Both of them. I asked Yessy to keep an eye on the back door. That's why he wouldn't let you in.'

Sitting in the café kitchen, surrounded by familiar objects, her hands clasped around a mug of hot tea, Hetty listened with growing horror while Arlo talked. He had taken a hysterical call from Viv, who had got up in the night and noticed the front door of the flat was open. On the landing, she had found her mother's mangled body, jammed between the lift and the wall. Somehow Viv had found the strength to call Arlo, who had alerted the emergency services, before returning to secure his premises.

'I have to go back and look after Viv. Chel's on his way. Hetty, as it's an emergency, will you help him out? We'll close to most customers for the day, of course, but we'll have to support Reed and the Champions. They'll be in an awful state.'

Hetty had been in too many tight places to give in to her emotions. In spite of the shock the news of her cousin's death had given her, at some level her brain went on ticking over, seeking a way to conceal her involvement.

'I can't face people. Not after what happened to Irene. I'll have to go upstairs and lie down.'

'Sorry love, I shouldn't have asked. Irene was family to you, wasn't she? Go and get your head down. I'll send Chel up with a cup of tea later on, after the ambulance and police have gone. I can hear them now.'

'Don't tell anyone where I am. Not even Chel. Nobody must know I'm here. If anyone asks, you ain't seen me.'

Arlo raised his eyebrows. 'I suppose shock affects people differently. You go straight to bed when you've drunk your tea. I won't tell a soul. Before I go, have you seen that spare key Irene asked us to keep for her? I thought I left it on the key rack, but I couldn't find it earlier. Viv had to throw me hers from the window, so I could let myself in.'

'Maybe it's been knocked off the hook.' Hetty pretended to look around on the floor, peering into corners, concealing Irene's key in the palm of her hand. 'Yes, here it is.'

Standing up, Hetty kissed Arlo full on the mouth, while she pressed the key into his hand. Surprised and pleased by this rare show of affection, her ex hugged her. When he opened the back door, the sound of sirens filled the kitchen. Quickly, Hetty locked it behind him before she went to gag over the sink, to ease her roiling stomach.

Irene was dead. She must have tried to open the lift, although it had been out of order for months. Had she imagined that the ghost of her mother was inside? A shudder of guilt passed across Hetty's heart, until she reminded herself that this was not her fault. The stupid old cow should have had the sense to know there's no such thing as ghosts, she thought, so I'm not to blame. Am I?

Whatever the rights and wrongs of the situation, there was a call that had to be made. Hetty reached into her bag and found the burner phone Lucan had given her after their conversation at his club. When he answered after one ring, she began to shake all over, and had trouble forcing her words out. 'Lucan? I did what you asked me to. I tried to scare Irene into leaving The Mansions. And now she's dead.'

There was a long silence. When Lucan finally spoke, there was a tremor in his voice. 'There was no need for violence. I only asked you to frighten her.'

'That's what I did, but then there was an accident….' Hetty could not bring herself to say more.

'What happened? No, wait, don't tell me. It's best if I don't know. This is going to cause endless trouble. Because EdeldiCo owns The Mansions, there's no way I can avoid being dragged into your mess. '

'There ain't going to be no trouble. Nobody saw me going into or coming out of The Mansions. I didn't even know what had happened to Irene. It was Arlo who told me. All we have to do is keep our heads down until it all blows over.'

'You're a fool, Hetty. I was crazy to give you a second chance.'

'I'm sorry, Lucan.'

For once in her long criminal career, Hetty was genuinely sorry for her actions. Irene had been judgmental, interfering and bossy, but nobody deserved to die like that. And now she was gone, only Hetty remained to remember her grandma Hester, and the other hardcore Brill women from her childhood. An unfamiliar feeling seeped into Hetty's cold heart, bringing tears to her eyes. Was it guilt, or loneliness? Not being in the habit of analysing her emotions, she couldn't tell the difference.

'Where's my missing money? Have you found Vida yet?'

Lucan's blunt questions woke Hetty up to the reality of her situation. It was madness to allow herself to become emotional when there were business matters to be dealt with. She hadn't been able to claw back the cash lost from the launderette and the compost toilet. She'd have to distract Lucan from the money she'd lost by offering a bigger prize.

There was no alternative. To save herself, Hetty was going to have to throw Sam to the wolves.

'Believe it or not, Lucan, of all places, Vida's been hiding right here, in Coopers Hook.'

32

Looker Hill
Samvida

I struggled back to consciousness from a long way down. My head was throbbing and my tongue was swollen. Lying on my back with my eyes closed against a whirling universe, I didn't care. I'd had my fun. Chel's delicious cocktails had been the first to pass my lips in months, so it wasn't surprising that I'd turned into a lightweight. The dancing and free drinks at Salsa Night had been well worth a hangover, even this one, so acute even my fingers and toes ached.

The thought of going to work made me feel nauseous, but I had no choice. I'd never yet missed a shift in the community garden. I was too afraid of getting sacked. The cover story I'd made up on my first day in Coopers Hook would be true. If I lost my job I'd really be homeless and unemployed. And to keep a roof under my head I'd be under pressure to sleep with Chel. Then I recalled how Chel had forced himself on me in the street after Salsa Night. I'd run away from him, all the way to Arlo's. I was never going to be able to go back to TimePad. But I'd ended up in my bunk. I had no idea how I got there. Perhaps my room-mate knew. I called out to her.

'Folu? Are you awake?'

There was no answer.

I opened my eyes to find myself surrounded by total darkness.

I felt for the blanket I slept under at TimePad and realised I was fully dressed, right down to my boots. When I tried to get out of bed my fingers scraped across grit. There was no bunk bed - only a dirt floor. I was beginning to be very afraid. Slowly my eyes adjusted to the faint daylight filtering through cracks in the walls. I was in some kind of cabin or shed, and I was not alone. Human shapes were sprawled all around me on the floor.

'Folu, are you there?'

There was an angry muttering. Curses and complaints in unfamiliar languages were thrown back at me. Then a man's deep voice rose above the tumult, and the voices died away.

'Is Folu here?' A shape loomed over me. 'Who are you?'

Images were flashing through my mind. Yessy trying to drag me out of danger. A sudden sharp pain in my finger. Lying on the floor of a moving van.

'My name's Sam. I don't know where Folu is. Who are you? What is this place? Why am I here?'

'I'm Zan. This is Looker Hill. You got here the same way we all did. Dudu caught you. How do you know my wife?'

'Folu is your wife?' I said, bewildered.

'Yes. We travelled from Africa to the UK together, because we wanted a better life. And look what happened to us. Have you seen her? Is she okay? And our baby?'

'Baby? What baby?'

Hinges creaked and daylight flooded in. A woman was standing in the doorway. She was very short but looked strong. The cropped hair sticking out from under her cap was grey and her face was marked with lines. Her age could have been anything from fifty to seventy. She wore heavy work boots. A leather apron protected her thick denim clothes. Under one arm she carried a short whip.

'Keep away from the new girl, Zan. You're on a warning.'

The woman whistled and the bodies on the floor came to life. Most of them were very young and all were pitifully thin. The skin visible through their rags was pitted with scars and open wounds. Some of them had weeping ulcers.

'Move yourselves! Show the new girl the latrines.'

Suddenly I was surrounded. A dozen pairs of hands clung to my clothes. I kicked out and screamed at the top of my voice for help. The old woman's whip bit into my thigh.

'Shut up! Nobody who cares can hear you. I'm Tia, your ganger. You must do as I say.'

The slaves dragged me out of the shed and along a path between shoulder-high brambles. A few metres from the cabin was a clear patch of ground. Trenches had been dug and planks laid across them. With the point of Tia's whip in my stomach, I had to watch while the other slaves crouched on the planks and voided their bodily waste into the trenches.

'Now you, new girl. Do it or I'll make them push you in.'

The slaves gathered behind Tia. Their eyes were dull from hunger and brainwashing. I knew they'd obey her without question, so I walked on to a quivering plank and did as I was told.

Tia held up her whip. 'Get in line!'

Tia walked along the line of slaves, placing a pill on each of their tongues. I was the last in line. When I saw what was in Tia's hand I shut my mouth tightly. She thrust my chin upward with her whip and forced the drug between my lips.

'You have a strong will in a strong body, new girl,' she said. 'But I am stronger than you.'

Behind Tia's back Zan stuck his tongue out at me. I knew what he meant. I hid the drug under my tongue and spat it out after the ganger had turned her back.

A rusty metal tank stood nearby. It was full almost to the brim with rainwater and partly covered with a piece of plywood. A dipper hung from a hook on one side. When the other slaves had taken their turn to drink greedily, Zan scooped up water in the dipper and offered it to me. Although the water in the dipper was the colour of mustard and dotted with dirt specks, I sipped a few drops. The alcohol I'd consumed at Salsa Night, combined with the sedative Dudu had pumped into me, had left me dehydrated.

Then the slaves, most of whom were barefoot, began to march. I was in the centre of the group, just behind Zan. It soon became clear I was a long way from London. Sheds like the one I'd woken up in were scattered across a wilderness of scrubby bushes and ponds laden with scum. Plastic bottles, empty tin cans and snack wrappers lay underfoot, half-concealed in tussocky grass. High above our heads green hillsides surrounded the camp, concealing it from the outside world.

A dozen gangers were leading their teams of slaves towards a dilapidated structure of wood and corrugated iron. The huge building might once have been a factory or an aircraft hangar. Around it, caged trailers loosely packed with many different types of waste were scattered at random across a wide expanse of concrete. Under Tia's watchful eyes, four of the slaves pulled open the Pit's high doors. The ganger prodded me with her whip.

'This is the Pit, new girl. Look inside and see the gold.'

So I stared into the Pit. I could see all the way to the far end, where a lorry was parked several metres above the level of the floor. From it a torrent of trash was falling on to heaps of rubbish. Zombie-like forms wrapped in rags were wading ankle deep in filth, picking out the best bits.

I'd often heard my father complain about the cost of disposing of commercial waste. He'd told me that some contractors paid unscrupulous landowners big bucks for the privilege of dumping rubbish on their property. Also, I'd spent the previous two months listening to Reed banging on about recycling. I recognised Looker Hill as a site where waste was dumped illegally. I knew somebody was making a fortune out of this operation. In a way, Tia was right. There was gold in the Pit - but not for the slaves suffering there.

I said, 'I can't see from here. Show me.'

Tia took a drawstring bag from the pocket of her apron and emptied it into her hand. Shiny stones clustered in the lines of her dirty palm.

'Look!' she said coaxingly. 'The Pit is full of gold.'

I said, 'That's not real gold. It's iron pyrite. When my brother was younger he bought some at a museum. He thought it was pirate treasure, but it's fake. They call it Fools Gold.'

The end of Tia's whip was digging into my chin. 'Are you calling me a liar?'

I was too exhausted and confused to lie. 'I'm saying that is not real gold.'

'Why, new girl?'

'Because it isn't. And saying it's real won't make it so.'

Tia whistled. Again I found myself surrounded. This time it was by muscular gangers.

'I cannot train this one. She does not love gold. Take her to Dudu,' said Tia.

33

Arlo's Café
Arlo

The café was closed, and disappointed regulars who had been expecting to collect their takeaway breakfast coffees were peering through the window. At first they were confused by the sight of Arlo and Chel standing at the counter as usual. The presence of Reed, Puja and Bushra gathered around the green table added to the appearance of normality. But when they saw Jammy standing to attention, they assumed there'd been an incident and went away. No-one inside the café was prepared to go outside and share the reason why no breakfasts would be served that day. Arlo hadn't even been able to bring himself to write out a notice explaining that Irene O'Callaghan, age seventy-two, local Champion and retired councillor, had suffered a violent death.

'I was first on the scene after Viv. It was horrible,' said Arlo.

'I was off duty when the call came in,' Jammy said, his voice full of regret. 'Otherwise I'd have been there to support you.'

'Viv rang me around three. She heard a noise on the landing and went to see what was going on. She found her Mum dead, trapped in a lift shaft.'

Chel, who was handing out cups of tea, said, 'Irene was good for her age, but who'd have thought she was strong enough to crack that lift open? Its been out of order for months. She must have lost her balance, fallen into the shaft and got caught up in the machinery. Then it started moving....'

Puja threw back her head and howled. Bushra glared at Chel. 'That's enough gory details. My Nan is distressed enough already.'

Arlo said, 'I wish I could unsee it. The social workers have taken Viv to hospital for observation. They're afraid the shock might bring on another stroke. I can't imagine what it was like for her, seeing her mother that way. And how's she going to cope, all alone?'

Jammy spooned sugar into his tea. 'Viv must have family and friends in Coopers Hook. She lived here all her life. Isn't - wasn't - Irene related to Hetty in some way?'

Arlo nodded. 'Hetty's Gran and Irene's Mum were sisters. There was a big age difference, though. By the time Hetty was born, Irene was married with two children.'

'Two? I assumed Irene was a single parent and Viv was her only child.'

'Viv's older brother Rob went into the Army. He was killed in Northern Ireland.'

'What happened to Irene's husband?'

'Jim died of a heart attack a few months before Viv had her stroke.'

'I'm sure it'll be a comfort to Viv to have Hetty nearby,' said Jammy. 'I know she and Irene clashed, but when tragedy strikes communities pull together.'

Chel said, 'Not always. Communities shut people out as often as they take them in. And communities are afraid of bad blood.'

Reed, whose head had been bowed ever since he heard the news of Irene's death, looked up. 'Irene didn't have bad blood. She was a model citizen. A local Champion.'

'That don't mean nothing. She was a Brill. So am I, through Mum. The Brills was a legend in Coopers Hook, back in the day. But most of them moved away out of shame.'

Arlo touched his son's arm. 'Don't talk about what happened. Not today.'

Curiosity took Bushra's mind off her grief. 'Go on, Chel, you have to tell us now. What was the Brill family ashamed of?'

Chel said, 'The old lady's gone, Dad. It can't hurt her. They may as well know.'

'But think of Viv….'

'Know what?' said Reed.

'Irene's mother was a child murderer. She poisoned her own daughter.'

The shocking words floated almost visible in the air. To his obvious satisfaction, Chel had everyone's attention. Even Puja had stopped crying to listen.

'Back in the day, there was two sisters, Hester and Eliza Brill. Eliza had two daughters, Irene and Edie. After her husband was killed in the War, Eliza had to take in washing. Lots of poor women like her worked as washerwomen back in the day, but Eliza had a sideline. She made medicines from weeds she dug up on the Marshes. They worked more often than not, so she built up a reputation as a wise woman. All the old dears used to go to her for cough mixture and ointments for their aches and pains. Word got around and the young wives turned up on Eliza's doorstep. They wanted pills to stop them having babies.'

'Back then abortion was illegal. Was Eliza convicted of being an abortionist?'

'No, Jammy. None of the women what bought Eliza's potions ever told on her. They'd have got in trouble themselves. What done for Eliza was being poor. Even with her laundry business and her sideline in herbal remedies, Eliza couldn't hardly afford to feed and clothe herself and her daughters. So she took out life insurance on Irene's sister Edie, then poisoned the poor kid to death. When she claimed on the policy, people asked questions and the police got involved. Eliza was tried for murder and found guilty.'

'How much was Edie's life insured for?' Bushra asked.

'Fifty pounds. It don't sound like much to us, but to Eliza it was life-changing. Remember, all of this happened over sixty years ago. The other thing to remember is - back then there was a death sentence for murder. Irene was only eleven when her Mum was hanged, and she was left alone in the world. Her Aunt Hester, that's my great-grandma, took her in, because there wasn't nowhere else for her to go. Mum told me Granny Hester always felt to blame for her sister's death, because she told the police about Eliza's herbal medicines. At her trial the prosecution used it to make Eliza look like an evil witch.'

Bushra had picked up every detail of Chel's story. 'So what happened was, Hetty's Nan accidentally grassed on her sister. That's why Eliza was put to death. And Irene held Hetty responsible for what her grandmother did, even though Hetty wasn't even born at the time. It's not surprising that Irene and Hetty didn't get along.'

'May I ask one more question, Chel?'

'Of course you can, Jammy.'

'Were forensic tests carried out on Edie's corpse?'

Chel shook his head. 'By the time the police got involved,

Edie'd been in the old graveyard beyond Plain Ease for months. She was buried in what they used to call a pauper's grave, with lots of other dead poor kids. It would have been like finding a needle in a haystack.'

The shocking story had changed the mood in the café from mourning to horror. When Folu knocked on the window, wearing the expensive blue trench coat Sam claimed to have bought from a charity shop, the group's dynamic shifted again.

Bushra hugged her friend close. 'Folu dear, have you heard the sad news?'

'What news? Is Sam okay? I want to show her how good I look in her coat and thank her for lending it to me. I will soon find a job wearing this.'

'Didn't she sleep in her bed last night?'

'I last saw her at the Wicker. She was dancing with a cocktail in her hand.'

'Chel, have you seen Sam?'

'I ain't touched Sam, Bushra. She blew me out after Salsa Night.'

'Then you saw her last!' said Folu.

'Folu, please sit down,' said Arlo. 'We have some very bad news for you.'

By the time Arlo had finished telling Folu the details of Irene's death, Chel had escaped to TimePad. Reed, Puja, Bushra and Folu were holding hands around the green table. When Yessy pressed his nose against the glass door, Folu let him in. She took the young homeless man's hand and led him to sit with the other Champions.

'Yessy, I know you do not understand, but I want to tell you that Irene is dead. And we cannot find Sam, who you like so much.'

'Yes.'

The homeless man was behaving oddly. Usually he was full of energy, but today he looked worn down and distressed. When Arlo offered him pasta, he took no interest.

Bushra looked closely into his face. 'Yessy, do you know where Sam is?'

'Yes.'

For the first time anyone could remember, Yessy took his purse from around his neck. When he turned it upside down on the table, a few coins and a handful of shiny stones fell out. Pushing the coins to one side, Yessy spread the stones on the table. Bushra rolled the stones around with her forefinger.

'My little nephew has stones like these. He calls them pirate gold, doesn't he, Nan?'

Arlo couldn't take his eyes off the fake gold.

'Everybody has to leave now,' he said. 'Except Reed and Yessy. I have a job for you two.'

34

Looker Hill
Yessy

'This is a waste of time,' said Reed, keeping his eyes on the road ahead. He'd been driving away from London for two hours. In the passenger seat Yessy sat bolt upright, looking out for landmarks and overhead signs. Arlo had bundled the two of them into the van with instructions not to return without Sam, but the project manager kept on talking. He was a people person, and Yessy, however uncommunicative, was the only person available.

'I don't know why the Champions are so worried about not being able to find Sam. She's an adult and she's only been missing for one day. Young people show up at TimePad from nowhere, stay for a few nights or a few weeks, then move on. That's probably what Sam's done - and why shouldn't she? She doesn't have to answer to anyone. But I must say I'll miss her help at events in the community garden. Sam is very intelligent and very reliable. I'm sure she'll be a big success, wherever she goes.'

They were approaching an exit. Yessy pointed to the signs. 'Yes.'

It was too much to hope for that his most hardworking volunteer was agreeing with his opinion of the cleverest. Yessy was giving him directions, in the only way he knew how. Reed would have felt much more relaxed if Yessy had shared the route, but when Reed offered him a satnav, he'd rejected it. When asked for a post code, he had replied by waving his arms around. In his own way, Yessy seemed to be saying, 'I know what I'm doing. Follow me.'

Reed swung the van into the slow lane in preparation for leaving the motorway. Following Yessy's hand signals, he circled a roundabout and took an exit that led even further into deep country. After a while he began to recognise the fields and woodlands lining the road, and realised that he'd often passed this way before. It was reassuring to know that when they reached the end of this wild goose chase, probably in the middle of a muddy field, he had a chance of finding his way home.

For several more miles Yessy remained alert. He was more nervous now. When a single car passed the van, going in the opposite direction, he ducked and hid in the well of the seat. Back in Coopers Hook he'd seemed confident and glad to help. Now he was tense and a little afraid, turning his head from side to side on the lookout for danger.

'You're fond of Sam, aren't you, Yessy? Don't worry, I'm sure she'll turn up safe and sound.'

Everyone in Coopers Hook knew Yessy worshipped Sam. At first, Reed had seen this as a possible threat to the stability of his team. He'd worried about what to do if Yessy made advances, which would inevitably be unwelcome. Fortunately this had never happened. Yessy's behaviour towards Sam was respectful and admiring. Sometimes, Reed had seen him gazing at her with a glowing look of gratitude, even though she rarely acknowledged his existence. Obviously Sam reminded Yessy of someone who had treated him kindly or been his friend.

Their surroundings were becoming more and more familiar to Reed. When he began to see woods and hillsides he could name, questions came into his mind. What did Yessy think he was doing? Was this some kind of prank? And why was there a smell of smoke in the air? It was too early in the year for burning stubble.

'What's going on? Yessy, have you been this way before?'

A skinny arm shot out, indicating a right turn. 'Yes.'

'Where are we? My family lives a couple of miles away and I didn't know this road existed. Yessy, there's no way you could know about it unless someone showed you.'

'Yes.'

A left turn took them along a road narrowed by hedges which had been allowed to grow wild. The smell of burning grew stronger and black flakes of ash began to hit the windscreen.

'This is ridiculous,' Reed said. 'As soon as the road widens I'm going to turn around.'

But Yessy was pointing with both hands in the direction of travel. When at last the lane opened out they found themselves on a stretch of concrete hemmed in by woodland. In an industrial grade fence a tall gate stood open. Smoke drifting in the air made Reed cough, but through streaming eyes he saw enough to realise where he was.

'What's going on, Yessy? How did you find your way to Looker Hill?' Reed propelled the van into a three-point turn. 'I knew this was a waste of time. We're going back to London.'

One by one four men emerged from the bushes and lined up

in front of the van. Reed didn't like the look of them. Against a single aggressor, maybe two on a good day, he was well able to defend himself. Against these rough-looking characters he had no chance. One of the men approached the van and wrenched open the driver's door.

'You! Out.'

Reed jumped down on to the concrete. Yessy tried to follow, but was prevented when a well-built Black man opened the passenger door.

'Well, well! It's the guy who only says yes. You're coming with us, friend.'

One of his companions said. 'We got enough trouble, Zan. We don't need him.'

'Oh, yeah?' said Zan. 'Do you know the way back to Coopers Hook? No? Well, I expect this guy does. He has a freak memory.'

'I have no idea how you know Yessy,' said Reed. 'But you're right. He does have a freak memory. Now, if you don't mind, I'd appreciate it if you took your hands off my van.'

'Sorry friend, but our need is greater than yours,' said Zan. 'We have escaped from sla. Yessy knows how it is. He has been with us in captivity.'

Pointing at Zan, Reed turned to Yessy. 'Is it true? Do you know him?'

'Yes.'

The three men with Zan were waving their arms about and grumbling. 'Why go carwash? Now we have van we go anywhere.'

'You can go where you like,' said Zan. 'But I'm going back to my wife and baby. And there's no better place than London to hide yourselves. You just have to keep clear of Dudu.'

Reed watched helplessly while Zan climbed into the

passenger seat and the rest of his gang piled into the back. He was horrified to see Yessy in the driving seat.

'You can't do this, Yessy!' he shouted. 'You haven't got a licence! I only taught you to drive so you could move stuff around Plain Ease!'

It was too late. The van was out of sight. Reed pulled his jumper over his head against the smoke and began to run.

35

Looker Hill
Samvida

Tia's henchman dumped me on my hands and knees on the concrete outside the Pit. I closed my eyes against dust blowing up from the trash and kept them closed while he tied me by my wrists and ankles to a wire cage and fastened a gag around my mouth. When I heard his boots crunching over scattered waste, I waited until the sound had died away before opening my eyes. At my feet the ground sloped away to the horizon. At the most distant point a copse of trees crested a hill. To me the landscape looked festive at first, with spots of bright colour and flags moving in the wind. In my confused state I imagined I was looking at a festival, but I could hear no voices or music. Then I thought it was a patchwork of fields with a diverse range of crops. It was a few seconds before my brain accepted what my eyes were telling me. I wasn't looking at fertile fields or a cele-bration, but at acres of land covered in layers of unsorted trash.

What I had thought were flags were rags and tatters, torn paper and ripped plastic bags. Acre upon acre of land was piled high with rubbish. The landscape spread out in front of me was formed from rotting waste.

In the shadows by the Pit someone with a cap pulled down over his face was aiming a rifle at me. Until I saw him guns had always made me feel safe. When I was a child in the country, my friends were the children of farmers who warned us away from locked gun cupboards. Travelling abroad as Urban's wife I became used to bodyguards with concealed handguns. It only hit me that this man had intended to kill me when he put down his weapon. Something about me had attracted his attention. He walked across the trash towards me, tore off my gag and gazed into my eyes. To my surprise, although he was a big man his facial features were small and dainty.

'Good morning, Mrs. Edeldi. Fancy meeting you here. I had you in the back of my cab in Lisbon and in London, didn't I? And I picked you up in Coopers Hook last night. I guess your ride in my van was not as comfortable as the back of the limo. At Looker Hill I am known as Dudu, the chief ganger. But you may remember me as Raul, your chauffeur.'

The situation was bizarre. As Raul, this man had helped me when Urban was taken ill in Cascais. He'd rushed us to hospital in an attempt to save my husband's life. Then as Dudu he'd drugged me and made me a slave in a place that resembled the suburbs of Hell. I couldn't make sense of it all, so I kept on talking.

'Who are you working for?'

'Sometimes I work for Edeldico. Mr. Lucan Edeldi likes me to drive him. A few weeks ago I collected you from the Pent-house to take you to a meeting with him. Then I took you back again. You did not look as calm on the return journey as you did on the way there. I wonder why?'

'What are you doing here?'

'Looker Hill is my family business,' Dudu said proudly. 'Your late husband lent me Edeldico money to set it up. I have been looking for you all over East London. If the dummy had not put himself in my way I would have found you much sooner. Mr. Lucan will be very pleased with me. I can ask him to write off my debt to Edeldico as my reward.'

I said. 'I won't let you take me to Lucan. He's a bully and a blackmailer.'

Dudu shrugged. 'I will deliver you alive or dead. The choice is yours. The only way to the top of the hill is through the trash. Long before you get there I will put a bullet through your head.'

I didn't believe Dudu's threat to shoot me. He'd be taking too much of a risk. I thought the worst that could happen to me was being delivered up to Lucan. And if I made it to the top of the hill of rubbish, I'd be free. I decided to call his bluff.

'I'll take my chances. Untie me.'

To my astonishment, Dudu undid my bonds.

I turned my back on the slaver and began to climb. The boots Bushra had made me wear to dance in protected me from the worst of the horrors under my feet, but they couldn't protect me from the smell. I gagged repeatedly while I struggled upwards. The sights around me were horrendous, but I tried to keep my eyes trained on the trees at the top of the hill. The morass I was walking over was unstable. I constantly slipped and stumbled, but miraculously I was able to stay on my feet. I knew I was disturbing rats because I heard them squealing and scuttering. I was more concerned about the biggest rat of all, Dudu, who was yelling at me. He called me foul names and told me what he was going to do to me before he gave me to Lucan, but somehow I kept on going.

I'd climbed so far I was almost out of earshot of Dudu when he began to shoot at me.

I was halfway up the slope when a bullet hit an empty oildrum on my right. I wasn't sure if it was aimed at me or an attempt to scare me. Either way, I didn't know what Dudu wanted me to do. I couldn't go back the way I came, because I'd be walking into the line of fire. I froze, hoping my tormentor would yell an instruction. On my right, a bullet hit a rat. I couldn't help looking. The creature, which was the size of a small dog, bared its teeth in a scream. As it limped away I threw up, while more bullets whizzed around me. I didn't know whether to stay still until Dudu got bored, or make myself a moving target. Then I realised he couldn't pick me out from the patchwork of colours and textures surrounding me. He was aiming at random. I crouched among the rubbish and did my best to look small.

That's when I smelled burning.

The bullets fired into the trash had sparked off several small fires which were growing bigger by the minute. I tried to drag myself further up the slope, but I only sank deeper into the shifting waste. Something was whirling around my head, stinging my eyes and making me cough. I hoped against hope it was dust and not smoke. I was terrified, but I pulled the collar of my shirt up over my mouth and pushed on.

Suddenly Dudu stopped firing. I turned around and looked back towards the Pit. From where I was I could see the whole of Looker Hill. Flames had spread from lower parts of the slope to the old building and tongues of fire were climbing the walls. I watched them reach the roof, and the fire was still spreading. Soon the Pit and the rough cabins surrounding it were alight.

Dudu was nowhere to be seen, but dozens of people were trying to escape the conflagration. I knew they must be screaming, but I couldn't hear them over the sounds of the fire. Several gates were open in the high fence that ran around the boundary, and vehicles were driving away. I hoped all the slaves would escape safely, especially Folu's husband Zan. Luckily for me, the fire had started towards the bottom of the slope and moved down. Now it was beginning to creep upwards. I could no longer kid myself that the suffocating mist rising from my footprints was dust. A spasm of terror shot through me when I realised it was smoke. When flames began to flicker around me I was filled with panic, but I fought the impulse to scream for help. I knew it was a waste of energy, because no-one could hear me.

I was going to have to save myself.

When I tried to drag myself out of the hot spot I sank deeper. It was like walking on burning quicksand. I was losing hope when I saw the wardrobe. It was the kind of narrow flat-pack wardrobe you see in a kid's bedroom. Lying on its side on a heap of bulging kitchen waste bags with the broken door hanging loose, it was my salvation. When I tried to pull the door away, a stream of rats poured out. They left behind bones and a skull in a stinking mass of rags and decayed flesh. I had no time to process what I saw, but instantly I made a connection. In the sex film which Urban made and Lucan used to blackmail me a slave had died. Until then I'd assumed it was faked. Now I wasn't so sure.

I've always been physically strong, and the weeks of manual work I'd done at Plain Ease had built up my muscles. I wrenched off the wardrobe door and laid it down on the smoking trash. I walked along it then stepped briefly on to the refuse. I threw the door so it landed ahead of me, stood on it and walked a few more steps. In this way I made a walkway out of danger for myself. While I was moving forward I shouted and swore at everyone who'd done me harm. I kept my spirits up by cursing Dudu, Tia, Chel, Hetty and the tribe of Edeldi. By the time I reached the woods, the wardrobe door was blackened and its edges were marked by flames. My hands were covered in blisters and my jeans were in rags. Through the holes I could see the livid burns on my ankles and lower legs.

I staggered away from the fire until my legs gave out in a meadow on the other side of the woods. There I lay on the grass and looked at the sky while I was coughing the smoke and dust out of my lungs. I was thirsty, hungry and in great pain. Then I heard the sound of a horse's hooves.

So it's true, I thought as I passed out. Death does travel on horseback.

36

Coopers Hook Carwash
Archy

The working day was almost over, and Archy was looking forward to a cold cider in the Rising Star. Now that his friendship with Nina was back on track and they were planning a trip together, he was feeling positive about life. As well as enjoying catch-ups with his old mates, he was receiving invitations from colleagues who'd never spoken to him before. Archy knew they were sucking up to him because he was close to the CEO's cousin, but it didn't bother him. He had stag nights lined up until Christmas. He was about to leave when Lucan appeared, looking disgruntled. A visit from his boss at this time of day usually meant he could look forward to a couple of hours of massaging financial data. Archy groaned inwardly and put his plans on hold.

For once, making money was not at the forefront of Lucan's mind. 'I have a lead on Vida's whereabouts. She's in Coopers

Hook. I'm going to look for her, and I want you to drive me there.'

Ever since the day he escorted Urban's widowed bride to the meeting pod on Floor Six Archy had been suspicious of Lucan's motives. He had no idea what the MD was going to do with his prey when he pinned her down, but he felt a growing reluctance to get involved. Whatever the nature of the conflict between Lucan and Samvida, it was unlikely to end well.

'I don't know what I can do to help, Lucan.'

'In situations like this it's essential to have a driver waiting. And I think Vida likes you. When she and I met to discuss her legacy, she seemed to find your presence reassuring. Arrange a car, will you?'

Archy drove from the City to Coopers Hook in an inconspicuous family hatchback. Lucan had been tipped off that Vida was staying at a hostel which, by coincidence, Edelico sponsored. They drove straight to TimePad, only to be told by the manager, who turned out to be Archy's stalker Chel, that Vida had checked out without leaving a forwarding address. At the community garden where Lucan said Vida had been working the gates were locked. At the café where she used to hang out the blinds were down. Across the street bouquets of flowers were piled outside The Mansions. Lucan said an accidental death there had been due to a faulty lift. He was unwilling to share more details and urged Archy to put his foot down. Archy wasn't surprised Lucan didn't want to be seen in the vicinity of The Mansions. If the amount of flowers placed in her memory was anything to go by, the old lady had been popular. The flats were part of Edeldico's property portfolio and due for redevelopment. Archy tried not to think about the methods some landlords used to nudge unwanted tenants out of their homes.

They cruised the streets until after nightfall, hoping to catch a glimpse of Vida. At ten o'clock they were driving past a line of railway arches when Lucan ordered Moe to pull over and turn off the car's headlights. Through the darkness, Moe peered at the tall, thin young woman who had attracted Lucan's attention. At first glance, her body shape was very much like Vida's. She was walking away from them, wearing a light-coloured trench coat that gleamed blue under the street lights.

'There she is! I know that coat. Wait here.'

Lucan got out and ran down the street. Archy locked the car down and watched the woman in the blue trench, who had paused by an arch once used as a carwash. She seemed to be waiting for someone. Suddenly a man ran out from under the arch and embraced her. They looked like a loving couple, wife and husband perhaps, reunited after a long time apart. He was appalled when he saw Lucan trying to force the woman to take off her coat. The CEO had a reputation for being insensitive, but Archy had never dreamed he was capable of doing anything so crass. The man and woman, who Archy could now see were Black, tried to push Lucan aside, but he wouldn't let go. Three White men appeared and dragged Lucan into the carwash. The couple ran away, holding hands.

Ten minutes later Lucan had not returned. Archy didn't know what to do. He wasn't sure the men had intended to do Lucan actual physical harm. Their body language had been menacing, but that was to be expected when he'd been aggressive towards their friends. It was possible they only wanted to frighten him. Playing the hero by going to the rescue of his boss wasn't an option. He could hardly take on three men by himself, and Lucan was unlikely to be much use in a fight. Recalling that he'd been brought along as a getaway driver, Archy decided to wait in the car. Ten minutes later, he was about to call the police when the men reappeared. They were dragging something behind them.

Archy ducked out of sight and lay prone across the front seats. When he peered out of the car window he saw Lucan's attackers disappearing into the night. He got out of the car and ran to the crumpled figure lying on the tarmac. Lucan's face was turned to one side, facing Archy. His cheek was pressed to the pavement. Blood streamed from a deep wound to his head.

37

Rankhorn Towers
Samvida

A scent of lavender was the first thing I noticed when I woke up in a four-poster bed. Then I became aware of the soft sheets under my naked body and the warmth of the quilt. A man was asleep beside me. He had broad shoulders and strands of his glossy brown hair were spread across the pillows. When I tried to move agonising pains shot up my legs from my ankles. I screamed.

'Are you okay, Sam?' said Reed, sitting up. 'I hope you're not upset. I'm very sorry about what happened last night. Honestly, I thought it was consensual. I mean, I had to give you a bath. You were unconscious and covered in all kinds of muck when I found you. And I held you in front of me on the horse all the way here, so I got covered in muck as well. It made sense for me to get in the bath with you. Maybe it was wrong of me to give you so much gin, but you were in pain. And then you….'

'Stop right there,' I said. 'I remember what I did next. And you're right. It was consensual.'

'When you feel better,' said Reed, 'Would you mind signing something to that effect?'

'Maybe later,' I said wearily. 'Can I have a cup of tea first?'

'Of course,' said Reed. 'You know where the bathroom is.'

He'd dug out some old clothes for me to wear. The long paisley patterned dress, hand knitted cardigan and granny knickers smelled of mothballs. He'd also cleaned my safety boots and left a pair of hiking socks next to them. By the time he came back with a tray containing a china teacup and saucer, a pot of Earl Grey and slices of lemon, I was fully dressed - except for the shoes and socks. I couldn't put those on because my shins were covered with livid burns. Sitting on an antique chair which wouldn't have been out of place at the Penthouse, I sipped the tea while Reed massaged my legs with ointment which smelled funky. It might have been horse medicine.

'I've been watching the reports of the conflagration,' said Reed. 'The whole of Looker Hill was in flames and all the emergency services were there. They don't know what started the fire, but the site was being used for an illegal recycling operation using slave labour. Fortunately all the slaves appear to have escaped in the confusion. Apparently Yessy was once a slave there. It's a miracle he was able to alert the Champions after you were kidnapped. But how did he know where you'd gone?'

'He saw a guy called Dudu kidnapping me,' I said. 'I was drugged. The next thing I knew I was waking up in a cabin. While I was escaping Dudu shot a rifle into the rubbish and sparked off a fire. I managed to climb to the top of the trash mountain. On the way I saw….'

I was going to tell Reed I thought I'd seen a dead body among the trash, but I stopped. It would mean telling him about

Urban's sex film, and I wasn't ready for that. Anyway, what I suffered at Looker Hill was already beginning to seem unreal. I'd have written it off as a bad dream, if my legs hadn't been so painful.

'Then you showed up on your horse and brought me here. What is this place?'

'It's my uncle's house,' Reed said. 'He's abroad at present. I call in occasionally to keep an eye on his dogs and horses. He and my late aunt - whose clothes you're wearing - had no children, so I'm his only heir. When he passes away I'm going to inherit the house and one hundred and forty-seven acres of land. You're probably thinking this doesn't fit in with my lifestyle as a project manager running regeneration sites.'

'That did cross my mind,' I said.

'That's why I'd be grateful if you didn't tell anyone how you got your injuries. Uncle Rollo would get into awful trouble.'

'Nonsense. It had nothing to do with your uncle.'

'Unfortunately it has everything to do with him, because he owns Looker Hill. But he had nothing do with the recycling scam. You see, the scammers were renting it from him. When I called him last night he was terribly upset. He swears he had no idea what kind of people he was dealing with.'

'So that's why you didn't take me to hospital. You were afraid your uncle would get into trouble.'

At that moment we heard voices and the sound of a horse's hooves on cobbles. I stood up and hobbled over to the window. I was looking down on the stable yard of a large country house. I could see a kitchen garden and, in the distance, the woods around the top of Looker Hill. In the yard below me a young woman wearing jodhpurs was handing her horse over to the care of a stable boy. A pair of black labradors were welcoming her enthusiastically.

'Ah,' said Reed. 'India's early.'

'Who is India, Reed?'

'She's my fiancée. I promised to go riding with her.'

Until Reed told me he was engaged, it hadn't crossed my mind that our relationship would be different now we'd slept together. I was in shock after my experiences at Looker Hill and my burns needed attention, My head was full of more urgent problems, but when I saw India sauntering around the stable yard I felt sick to my stomach.

I said, 'You could have said you were engaged before you got into the bath with me!'

Reed looked embarrassed. 'Yes, Sam, I should have told you first. To be honest, I wish I hadn't got into that bath at all. But it's too late now, so please don't make a fuss. I'd be lost without India. The house and land is worth millions, but my uncle has debts. By the time I inherit he won't have much cash left. India's an events manager. She knows how to make money out of minor stately homes. With her help, I can turn Rankhorn Towers into a sustainable business.'

I couldn't hold back my tears. 'That's all very fine, Reed, but what am I going to do right now? My legs hurt and I have nowhere to go.'

Reed put his arm around my shoulders. 'Don't worry, you can stay here for a few days. I'll introduce you to India as a friend who's been involved in an accident. Then we'll email your parents. I'm sure they'll come home and look after you.'

38

Plain Ease
Arlo

The circumstances surrounding Irene's death were suspicious, in Arlo's opinion. He couldn't imagine why she had left her flat in the middle of the night to wrestle with machinery she knew was in a dangerous condition. Such foolish behaviour was out of character for the former councillor. Also, Hetty had been behaving strangely. She'd closed the Wicker until further notice and was hiding in the flat above the café. Her excuse was that she'd been overwhelmed by her grief for Irene. Arlo, who remembered the harsh names the cousins had called each other, found this hard to believe. Also, Sam had vanished on the night Irene died, without saying a word to her friends. She'd not even told her room-mate Folu she was leaving. Arlo was sure the clever, hard-working young Champion had no reason to harm Irene. However, since he'd sent Yessy and Reed to search for her, neither man had returned to Coopers Hook. Arlo was beginning to think of Sam as a magnet for trouble.

Arlo had many questions about Irene's death, and the answers were eluding him. In the end he left Chel to mind the café and sat down at an outside table to think things through. At that moment Puja and Bushra appeared in the street. They were laden with cleaning materials, as if they were on their way to do some cleaning at Plain Ease. Suddenly the women stopped in their tracks. They exchanged looks, then turned around and walked back the way they had come.

It occurred to Arlo that he might find clues about what happened to Irene in the community garden. The gates of the track leading to Plain Ease stood open, so he set off along the Corridor of Eyes. Not being a fan of graffiti, Arlo had always found the wall paintings unnerving. When he reached the Yard he realised the painted eyeballs were not the only ones trained on him. Jammy was right behind him. Puja and Bushra must have seen the policeman approaching and cleared off.

'I thought I'd take a look around the garden,' Arlo said. 'For Irene's sake.'

'Great minds think alike,' said the community policeman.

'Fools seldom differ.'

Then they saw the van.

Jammy said, 'What on earth has Reed been doing to his wheels?'

Arlo didn't answer. He knew where the van had been, and was shocked to see it back so soon.

The transit with the green logo was Reed's pride and joy. Designed to transport volunteers and equipment, it belonged to the charity he worked for. Because Reed spent so much time in it, he treated it as a second home. Its rear was usually packed with spades, forks, pruners and other gardening gear. The front seats normally contained bottled water, snacks, plants and Reed's filing system. Although the project manager kept the outside clean and took care to maintain the working parts, the inside of the van had always been chaotic.

Jammy and Arlo circled the van. Instead of being parked in its usual spot it was dumped at an angle in the middle of the yard. Whoever returned it to Plain Ease had been in a hurry to get away. They'd left the van unlocked with the doors open and the key in the ignition. There was a strong smell of burning. The exterior was thick with dust and the hub caps were coated with motorway grime. It was empty apart from a layer of dirt full of gleaming particles. It wasn't unusual for the van's floor to be covered in soil, but it had never before been seen to glisten. When Jammy scooped up a handful of the loose dirt and allowed it to run between his fingers, a few shining stones remained in his hand. He checked the gauge and found the van was running on empty. Then he examined the tyres. More glittering stones were lodged in the treads.

'These are the same as the stones Yessy carries in his purse,' said Jammy.

Arlo avoided the policeman's eyes.

A pile of gardening tools had been left unsorted in a pile inside the Hub. Hessian bags, receipts, cereal bars and seed packets had been thrown into the poly-tunnel. It looked as if the van had been hurriedly emptied of its contents before being taken on a journey. And Yessy was nowhere to be found. After they'd searched Plain Ease and the abandoned graveyard without success, Jammy said he was going to ask forensics to check the van for signs of illegal activity. Arlo agreed that with poor Irene dead and Sam missing, it was best not to take chances.

When they got back to the Yard the van had disappeared into thin air.

'Good lad, Yessy,' Arlo muttered under his breath. He knew the van would be parked outside Puja's house, getting the best valeting of its life.

Jammy followed Arlo back to the café. By the time they were sitting down outside and the policeman was getting out his notebook, Arlo had given up all hope of escape. For years he'd concealed his suspicions about Urban and his links with dirty money. At first it was for Hetty's sake that he'd kept his mouth shut. She thought she'd hidden her financial ducking and diving from him, but he wasn't stupid. As soon as he found out Edeldico was sponsoring TimePad, he knew Urban must be involved. Then Chel was made manager of the hostel, and Arlo had to worry about both his ex-wife and his son. Like an ostrich he'd buried his head in the sand and hoped Edeldico's corrupt empire would disappear.

'Well,' said Jammy. 'Let's see what we've got. Yessy was missing from Coopers Hook for several weeks. Then he walked into your café as if he'd never been away.'

'I'm not Yessy's keeper,' said Arlo.

'But the money you give him for food is his only visible means of support. So why did he disappear for so long? And where did he go? Have you seen the news today?'

Arlo shook his head. 'I only watch the sports channel.'

Jammy said, 'Last night there was a conflagration in the Midlands. Derelict land known as Looker Hill was being used as an illegal dumping site for unprocessed waste. Tonnes of rubbish was lying around, and no attempt was being made to manage it properly. When some idiot fired a gun the whole lot went up in flames. After the fire was put out, pyrite was found scattered all over Looker Hill. Pyrite is also known as Fool's Gold.'

Although he already knew the answer Arlo said, 'What's this got to do with Yessy?'

'Those shiny stones Yessy keeps in his purse are pyrite. It looks as if the scammers were using slave labour. Fortunately the slaves seem to have escaped the fire and scattered in all directions. The scammers fled too. No living person was found at the site, but the fire exposed a corpse. They haven't yet established the cause of death, but it's the body of a young woman. She'd been dead for months.'

'That's awful,' said Arlo.

'Arlo, is it possible Yessy was forced to work at Looker Hill? Maybe the guy who beat him up at the foraging event was his slaver.'

The game was up at last. Arlo knew what he had to do.

'It's not my problem. I'm about to retire and move to Ireland.'

As Arlo had intended, his statement distracted the policeman from the matter of the van.

'This is sudden. Congratulations! When's the party?'

'I can't think about celebrating so soon after Irene was killed,' said Arlo.

'Killed? Do you suspect it wasn't an accident?'

'You know what I mean,' Arlo said quickly.

'Are you going to Ireland alone?'

'Who'd go with me?'

'I thought Hetty....'

'Hetty? Not likely. Surely you've noticed how things are between us?'

'You need a fresh start,' said Jammy.

'There's no such thing as a fresh start. Somebody always ties a tin can to your backside.'

'Perhaps if you met someone else....'

'Hetty's the only woman I could ever love,' said Arlo.

After a short silence Jammy said, 'You'll miss your café.'

'Maybe. Maybe not. It's been a struggle. When I set up in business there were parts of Coopers Hook where the police only went in pairs. I put down a deposit on a greasy spoon which had been empty for years. For years my whole life was cleaning, decorating and fry-ups. Chel used to bunk off school to help me. Hetty got bored and started going up West on business. But I stuck with it. And look at me now. Up to my ears in debt.'

Jammy put away his notebook. 'Regeneration hasn't worked for Coopers Hook, has it?'

'What do you mean?'

'Dreadful things are happening here. Homeless people have disappeared. The last tenant in a block scheduled for a redevelopment worth millions has been killed. The CEO of a financial firm showed up at a disused carwash and got mugged. A van that may be linked to modern slavery and murder appears and disappears. What's going on, Arlo?'

Arlo stood up. 'That's a lot of questions.'

'I need a lot of answers,' said Jammy.

'Well, you won't get them from me,' said Arlo. 'I'm retired.'

'I'll leave it for now,' Jammy said, 'But I'll be back tomorrow. Think about it, Arlo. I know you want to do the right thing.'

As soon as the policeman was out of sight, Arlo got on the phone to his brother in Belfast.

39

The Penthouse
Samvida

I hid the real reason why Reed had to rescue me from a burning landfill site from my Mum and Dad. I tried to spin them a story about losing my way during an environmental protest, but they didn't believe me. Bad things had happened and they couldn't understand why I was refusing to go to the police. I could hardly tell them I was afraid to get involved with the law because I'd unknowingly taken a starring role in a deviant sex movie.

Reed had to turn his charm on full to appease my parents. He was as keen as I was to keep the police out of it, because his uncle owns the land Dudu and Tia were renting. I suspect Reed's uncle was involved in the scam, but I can't prove it. He told Reed he never asked what kind of business they were running, so when fire broke out and exposed their scam, he was as shocked as everyone else.

Our family house was rented out, so Dad had borrowed his mate's caravan at the seaside. He and Mum cared for me there, literally waiting on me hand and foot. My brother was on study leave from Sixth Form so he joined us, even though he had to sleep in a tent. While I was recovering we talked a lot. It had never occurred to me that Gus had an opinion about my marriage, other than hating the suit I made him wear for the wedding. I couldn't believe what he said when he saw my burned legs.

'Urban is to blame for this. You shouldn't have married him. I knew he was trouble when he cleared Mum and Dad's mortgage and paid my school fees. Everyone said he was generous, but you don't become a billionaire by being giving away cash. He was buying you to be his robotic wifey. While you were married your brain was switched off. Now I want my cool sister back.'

'Oh, Gus! Why didn't you warn me?'

'Everybody was saying how great it was that you'd found a wealthy husband. I didn't think you'd listen to me.'

'I'm listening now,' I said.

When I wasn't hanging out with my family I spent hours gazing at the stormy North Sea, trying to make sense of my life. I thought about my reaction to Lucan's blackmail attempt and realised I should have taken time to think before running away. After I remembered how casually I gave Katya things that once belonged to Urban and Frankie, I began to feel guilty about my fall-out with Nina. In theory the property was mine, but I should have asked her first. I wanted to find out how Nina was and talk things through with her, but I was afraid to contact her after our fight.

Then I remembered the young guy who offered to help me after my nightmare meeting with Lucan at Edeldico HQ. Getting in touch with Archy Brise was a risk I had to take. Not only did I want to make it up with Nina - it was also vital for me to have a friendly contact at Edeldico. How else was I going to get hold of that flash drive? So I rang Archy on my new pay-as-you-go phone. I was blown away when Nina immediately called me back. I learned that after I left the Penthouse Lucan ordered Archy to find me. He found Nina instead. They've become close.

Nina and sobbed at each other over the phone for about an hour while we were making up. She apologised for getting high and beating me up, and I said I was sorry for giving away things she valued without consulting her. When we'd both stopped crying, she told me Lucan had been mugged at a disused car wash in Coopers Hook. Somehow he'd found out I was hiding there and was looking for me. As a result, he'd spent three days in a coma and might have brain damage. I saw no need to pretend I was sorry. He'd tried to blackmail me, and what goes around comes around. And with Lucan out of the way and Archy and Nina on my side, I had a chance to destroy the flash drive.

Clever Archy took advantage of Lucan's absence to carry out a power grab at Edeldico. As a result, he'd been able to arrange for the firm to pay my expenses. As soon as I began to feel better I made Dad drive me to a small hotel near Coopers Hook. He and Mum were uneasy about letting me out of their sight, but we'd begun to get on each other's nerves in the caravan, and they were longing to get back to their turtles. The next morning I returned to Coopers Hook for the first time since that awful night when Chel tried to rape me and Dudu kidnapped me to Looker Hill. Nina went along to support me and Archy drove one of the Edeldico limos.

Yessy happened to be coming out of Time Pad as we were parking outside. Now that Looker Hill has gone up in smoke he knows the slavers won't come after him, so he must think it's safe to sleep in the same place every night. He was so clean I didn't recognise him at first. Then he gave me one of those weird but wonderful smiles he's kept especially for me, ever since I walked into Arlo's.

I'll always be grateful to Yessy for helping to save my life. I'd love to know who he thinks I am. Maybe I remind him of a slave he knew at Looker Hill. The poor things had all made headscarves and masks from rags to keep the dust out of their faces. It was difficult to tell one from the other.

Arlo has retired and gone to live in Ireland, so Chel's running the café. I despise Chel, but I have to admit the atmosphere in the café is livelier with him in charge. Hetty broke Arlo's heart, and broken-hearted people don't make cheerful hosts. Chel is going all out to build up the business. He even tried to network with Nina and Archy. I almost laughed out loud when Nina looked Chel up and down, taking in his chain store jeans and his tacky goldy-looking chain. She clearly wasn't impressed, but it didn't bother Chel.

'Let me know when you next run a corporate event, Archy,' he said. 'I can supply sandwiches, salads, drinks - whatever you need.'

Chel's attitude was so arrogant I couldn't ignore it. I called him away from the others and said, 'I haven't forgotten what you tried to do to me after Salsa Night, you low-life.'

He actually looked offended. 'You're calling me a low-life? Take a look in the mirror, babe. I never touched you, except for trying to get you out of trouble. I mean, you was using somebody's front garden as a toilet!'

'So were you!'

'I'm a man. I can piss wherever I want. Women can't.'

'But you tried to rape me!'

'It's your word against mine, Sam Gumby. See you in court.'

I was so angry I almost exposed the scars on my legs and told Chel what I went through after I ran away from him. Fortunately, at that moment Reed and the Champions rolled up and distracted me. It's just as well. The fewer people who know what happened at Looker Hill, the safer I feel.

I was happy to see my lovely friends from Plain Ease again. Viv's mobility had improved since I last saw her. She was pushing her wheelchair, for support and to shift the vegetables they were already selling to local restaurants. Puja and Bushra were carrying bags of freshly harvested salads. Puja gave me a big hug and a massive bag of rocket.

Bushra said, 'Nan and I picked up your suitcase of clothes from TimePad after you left. We knew you'd come back for it. Shall I fetch it?'

'Thank you for doing that,' I said. 'But they're winter clothes and now it's summer, I don't need them. Do you mind taking them to a charity shop for me?'

'Sure,' said Bushra. 'But I'll keep the suitcase. I can use it for moving fabrics around.'

Reed and I air-kissed as if we'd never even thought about sleeping together. Then he got into a huddle with Nina and Archy. Like the public school types they are, the three of them spent ages making small-talk at the tops of their voices. I used the time to catch up with the Champions.

Bushra had passed her exams with distinction. She was back in touch with Folu, who now has a job in a restaurant and is expecting a baby any minute. Folu and her husband Zan, who is a skilled bricklayer, have applied for the right to live in the UK. Folu told Bushra to let me know she was taking good care of my blue trench coat. I asked Bushra to tell her she can keep it, and to make sure she rips open the lining. Folu gave me her last five pounds to get my coat cleaned. And it's not as if the money I found in the compost toilet belongs to me.

Viv was well on her way to making a full recovery and returning to her job in a bank. The council had re-homed her in an adapted ground floor flat. She was happy because it was close to Plain Ease, Arlo's Café and Puja's house.

'How did you talk Irene into moving?' I said. 'She always said she'd rather die.'

The Champions looked at each other as if they didn't know what to say. Then Viv told me what had happened to Irene. I sobbed on her shoulder while Bushra and Puja stroked my back. After I'd dried my eyes I asked Viv if she'd ever found out who her landlords were. I was shocked, but not surprised, by her answer.

'Edeldico owns The Mansions. It's the same firm that used to sponsor TimePad. They withdrew their sponsorship recently and Chel lost his job. That's why he's putting in so much time at the café.'

Bushra took a flyer from among the spring greens and fabric samples in her tote bag, and pressed it into my hand. 'You'll come to our summer festival, won't you, Sam?'

I told her I wouldn't miss it for the world. Just then I saw Jammy, the community policeman, appearing around the corner of the street. When he caught sight of me he got out his note-book. I didn't want to answer any of his nosy questions, so I told Archy and Nina it was time to leave.

While we drove back to the hotel my friends told me about the trip they were planning. Nina had never been to Brazil, although her mother Frankie grew up there. After Frankie's brother and his family disappeared in mysterious circumstances, she developed a mental block about the country and wouldn't allow anyone to talk about it in her presence. When Nina learned that Archy was born in Brazil but knew nothing about his family, she decided to help him trace his roots. Apparently he was once a refugee child in Coopers Hook.

Archy went to the same junior school as Chel, but luckily for me he turned out much better.

40

Plain Ease
Samvida

The summer festival was drawing to a close when I stepped out of a cab outside Arlo's. Walking gingerly so as not to chafe my scars, I passed through the Corridor of Eyes and entered Plain Ease. Herbal cosmetics had been brewed, stones painted and giant Jenga castles built. Now the sun was sinking and the kids from the drum school were packing away their bongos. Over by the Hub, Puja was serving the last few dollops of vegetarian chilli and Yessy was tending to the fire pit. Neither of them noticed me following the perimeter of the Yard into the woods.

At the bottom of the community garden a plane sapling was being used as a Wish Tree. Yessy had hung fairy lights in its upper branches and scattered logs around as seats. The hopes and dreams of children who had taken part in the Festival were written on brightly coloured labels tied to the tree's lower branches. When the Champions saw me they waved. Bushra had rigged up some of the fabric we dyed in the launderette to make a bower. She was sitting cross-legged under it with her hand-made blankets and rugs scattered around. Viv was sitting on an old kitchen chair, with a walking stick and her wheelchair close at hand. I was astonished to see Hetty ensconced on a folding chair opposite Viv. I sat down between them on a log to complete the circle.

When the rough bark brushed against my sore calves I winced. Viv looked down at me with concern. 'Sam, are you okay? Those red marks on your ankles look painful.'

'It's nothing.' Quickly I pulled one of Bushra's rugs over my legs and feet. 'Viv, I'm so sorry you lost your Mum. If I'd known I'd have gone to her funeral.'

'You didn't miss much. I couldn't afford a proper do. If it hadn't been for Puja and Arlo I'd have been all on my own.'

'And me,' said Hetty. 'I was there too.'

'Oh yes,' said Viv. 'So you were. I thought my eyes were deceiving me when I saw you sitting right at the back. You and Mum weren't exactly close. But I'm sure she would have been glad you came. When all's said and done, we're blood, and that's what counts.'

Hetty made a strange noise in her throat. She must have been embarrassed. So she should be, because she was horrible to Irene when she was alive. At least she showed some respect in the end.

Viv patted a large envelope she was holding in her lap. 'I haven't been back to the Mansions since Mum died. The social workers found these old cards and papers in her room. I can't bring myself to look through them, but I'd like to tie one or two to the Wish Tree in Mum's honour. The rest can go up in flames. Sam, you have a good strong voice. Please will you read them aloud?'

I sifted delicately through the fragile contents of the folder, as if they were clues at a crime scene, and took out a yellowing document.

'This is Irene's original tenancy agreement from the sixties,' I said. 'It's the kind of tenancy that's handed down in the family. So long as you pay your rent, you can't be evicted.'

'That's what Mum used to say, but it didn't seem possible.'

'It's possible all right,' I said. 'I used to work for a solicitor who dealt with these. Don't burn it whatever you do. It's worth a lot of money.'

I handed the agreement back to Viv, who placed it carefully in her handbag. Then I reached into the folder again. This time sheets of paper covered in childish handwriting attracted my attention.

'These pages were torn from an exercise book. Irene's name is written on them. I think it's a story she wrote when she was a child.'

'Sounds interesting. Go on, Sam, read it out.'

Bushra said, 'Are you sure it won't upset you, Auntie?'

'I couldn't be any more upset, love.'

'Okay,' I said. 'If you're sure. The date is March 1953. How old would Irene have been then?'

'Twelve,' said Hetty. 'She was living with my Nan at the time.'

As I started to read aloud, a breeze wafted odours of chilli and smoke across the garden.

'Once upon a time there was a poor widow with two daughters. The older sister was called Edie and the younger one was Reen. Hitler killed their Daddy, so the widow had to launder rich people's dirty clothes. One day she was up to her elbows in the washtub when a fairy appeared.

"I am your Fairy Godmother," said the fairy. "I have come to give you the magic power of making food and medicine from leaves and flowers. Take your daughters to the Marshes and the bomb sites and teach them everything you know. With plant magic they'll never go hungry."

The widow was very happy because the fairy had given her a magic gift. Every evening, she walked with her daughters along the hedges and taught them everything she knew about plants and flowers. But it all went wrong because the older sister, whose name was Edie, was simple-minded. She couldn't wash rich people's dirty clothes, but if a boy winked at her she winked back. The younger sister had to watch Edie all the time, in case a boy stole her away

While her Mum was foraging for food, Reen watched and learned. She knew the names of all the plants: comfrey, fennel, purslane, plantain, dandelion. Sometimes Mum crushed herbs into a powder, twisted it up in paper and sold it to a neighbour for sixpence. Whenever that happened there was meat on the table. Edie ate more than her fair share but Mum and Reen did the work. All Edie did was eat and try to sneak out of the house when a boy knocked at her window.

One day Reen heard Mum say to Aunty Hetty, "I'm at my wits' end with Edie. She'll be fifteen next month, but she ain't got no more sense than a three-year-old. She's forever running into the road. It's a miracle she ain't been hit by a tram. I've taken out insurance on her, because if she got herself killed, I couldn't afford to give the poor child a decent funeral."

Then Aunty Hetty said, "The way Edie is with them boys, the next thing you know she'll be in the club. Then you'll have another mouth to feed. To be honest, it would be better for you and Reen if she did fall under a tram."

I stopped reading. 'This is about Irene's sister. Viv, are you sure you want me to go on?'

'It isn't news to me. We all know their mother poisoned poor

Edie for the insurance money.'

It was almost dark. I switched on my phone torch and went on reading.

'One night the Fairy Godmother appeared to Reen in a dream. She said, "If Edie has a baby, she won't know how to look after it. You'll have to watch it while Mum does the laundry. Then you won't be able to go to the Grammar School. Get rid of your sister before she ruins your life." '

Hetty said, 'Stop right there.' Her face looked ghastly in the torchlight.

'No, carry on,' said Viv, who looked equally pale. 'I want to know the truth.'

I read on.

'Reen thought about what the Fairy Godmother had said. Mum had not only taught her about healing plants and the plants that tasted good. Reen also knew which plants held poisons: fool's parsley, deadly nightshade, water hemlock. She knew where they grew and how to pick them so the juice didn't stain her fingers. After school one day, Reen went to the marshes and harvested all the poison plants Mum had told her never to touch. She crushed them together and gave them to Edie in a cup of tea with seven spoons of sugar. Edie sucked it up greedily. Soon she became very very sick.

While Edie was ill, Reen was sent to Aunty Hester's house to be out of the way. When she came home there was no more Edie. For a while, life was good. Mum stopped taking in laundry, Reen got a new yellow dress and they ate meat every day. Then one night men in uniforms knocked on their door. Mum's face went as white as a rich lady's sheet. She said, "Reen, go round to your Aunty's while I sort this out."

Someone reported Mum to the police because she claimed fifty pounds life insurance to pay for Edie's funeral. The police took Mum away to answer a few questions. Reen is waiting at Aunty Hetty's for her. She's been gone a long time. Maybe she lost her bus fare. Miss, I'm sorry this story doesn't have a happy ending.'

Viv hid her face in her hands. The wind shook the Wish Tree, and the fairy lights flickered.

Bushra broke the silence. 'What a sad story. Edie was older than Irene, but she had special needs. Irene poisoned her and let her mother be hanged for the crime.'

I took Viv's hand. 'Irene was only a child. She didn't know what she was doing.'

When Hetty spoke, our three horrified faces, ghostly in the torchlight, gaped at her from the darkness. 'Irene knew what she was doing all right. What she didn't understand was that her Mum was going to be blamed for it, because she'd taken out insurance on Edie.'

Viv pointed her walking stick at Hetty. 'What do you know about this?'

'My Nan told me the truth when she was dying. Irene told her what she'd done, years later. Nan always felt guilty about it, because she'd put the idea of getting rid of Edie into Irene's head. In a way, Nan was as guilty of her own sister's death as Irene was of Edie's. But she never told nobody, because she didn't want to bring any more shame on the family. I bet it was my Nan who tore them pages out of Irene's school book.'

Thinking of the lifelong guilt Irene must have suffered, I wiped away a tear. 'Then why did she keep them?'

'My Nan believed in having dirt on your relations, in case they got out of hand.'

'A child murder is hardcore dirt,' I said.

'Irene looked like a nice old lady, but inside she was hard-core, like all of us Brills.'

'Do you think we ought to tell the police?' said Bushra nervously.

'What for?' said Hetty. 'It happened sixty years ago. Everyone involved is dead.'

Viv touched Bushra's sleeve. 'Help me into my chair. I don't feel steady enough to walk.'

Viv got into her wheelchair and Bushra pushed her back to the Yard. Hetty stumbled behind them, her dancer's strut abandoned for once. The beam of my torch woke birds from their nests. When we passed the Hen-House, the chickens cackled like gossiping neighbours.

By the time we arrived in the Yard, all the guests had left and the fire in the pit was almost out. Reed emerged from the Hub, excited by the success of his summer festival.

'Hi guys! Puja and Yessy are clearing up. We kept enough chilli for all of you. What have you been up to?'

I pulled myself together. 'We've been sitting under the Wish Tree, reading a child's story and remembering Irene. Now Viv's going to burn some personal papers, as closure for her Mum's life.'

'Perfect,' said Reed, 'I'll leave you to it. I have to keep an eye on Yessy.'

The four of us stood around the dying fire pit. Bushra and I supported Viv between us while Hetty looked on. Viv threw Irene's story on to the embers and followed it up with a cascade of old cards and letters. The dry paper spat and fizzled in the flames, sending sparks spinning like angry demons. When the evidence of Irene's guilt had been consumed, Bushra raked the cinders until there was nothing left but ash. Reed came over with a bucket of water to douse the pit.

'I love those Wish Tree stories,' he said. 'Kids write the cutest things. They're so innocent!'

41

Arlo's Café
Archy

Hetty Brill waited in the corner booth with an untouched latte in front of her. As she'd expected, Reed and the Champions were busy clearing up after the festival. Hetty didn't want anyone to listen in when she confessed to the crimes she'd committed in the name of Edeldi. That was why, while they were walking away from the smouldering fire pit at Plain Ease, she'd asked Sam to meet her in Arlo's the next morning.

Before she left Coopers Hook forever, Hetty wanted to clear her conscience.

She was deeply grateful to the authorities for writing off Irene's death as an accident. They had no way of knowing that the respected financier Lucan Edeldi, who wanted to evict the old woman and her stroke survivor daughter, had bullied Hetty into scaring them away. Under cover of darkness she had taken Irene's spare key from its hook in Arlo's kitchen and crept into

The Mansions. Hetty shuddered when she remembered how her voice echoed in the stairwell when she pretended to be Irene's mother, waiting in the condemned cell for her executioner. When she heard Irene emerging from her flat she'd lost her nerve and run away. Although she hadn't seen her elderly cousin die, the old woman's last moments would haunt her for the rest of her life.

Before she found out Irene was dead, Hetty had called Lucan and told him what she'd done. She was so shaken up she didn't check her secret bank account until a few days later. When she did she was both thrilled and shocked by what she found. The amount was beyond her wildest dreams. For Hetty's services in freeing up The Mansions for development, Lucan had paid her enough money to start a new life. But she didn't trust Lucan to leave her alone - and Arlo was no longer around to protect her. She'd made up her mind to join her estranged husband in exile. After she settled down in Ireland she could afford to set up a dance studio even better than the Wicker.

Today she was going to make her escape. There were many people she'd be glad to see the back of, and Yessy was top of the list. At that moment the young homeless man was standing at the counter, being given a hard time by Chelsea.

'My Dad was too soft with you, mate. I'm in charge now. I don't want you hanging around, making the place look untidy.'

'Yes.'

In spite of her inner turmoil, Hetty smiled. Things had changed for the better since Chelsea took over the family business. Arlo's sudden departure had sparked off an entrepreneurial streak she'd always known their son possessed. As for Chelsea's mean remarks about Yessy's appearance, he was only speaking the truth. The toffs who were buying up property in Coopers Hook wouldn't come into the café if they saw a pikey like him on the premises. When Chelsea reached across the counter, it looked as if he intended to pick the kid up by the scruff of his neck and chuck him into the street. Instead he slipped his hand into the leather purse hanging from Yessy's neck.

The purse was empty.

When a group of tech entrepreneurs entered the café, Chelsea's threatening expression changed to a tense grin. Between gritted teeth he said, 'Just this once, you can have your pasta for free. But don't show your face here again.'

'Yes.'

Chelsea dumped some penne on a plate. When Yessy didn't move he splashed a spoonful of salsa sauce over it.

'That's your lot.'

The techies looked sympathetically at Yessy. Not wanting to look ungenerous, Chel chucked a handful of grated Cheddar over Yessy's pasta. Yessy stood his ground with his eyes on a tray of baked beans. Just then a young man wearing a tailored blue mohair suit walked in. Hetty had not seen him for almost twenty years, but in spite of his expensive clothes and well groomed appearance, she recognised the skinny refugee child who used to play football in the street with her son.

'Chel, give Yessy whatever he wants,' said the newcomer. 'It's on me.'

Chelsea jumped to attention. 'Will do, Archy. Very generous of you.'

He served Yessy with a generous portion of beans. When Archy paid for the food and dropped a few coins into Yessy's purse, the techies nodded their approval. Hetty was astonished to see the homeless man's lips contort, as if he was trying to spit something out.

'Fanks,' said Yessy.

'You're welcome, mate. Did you hear that, Chel? Yessy said "thanks". Sam told me "yes" was the only word he knew.'

'Yeah, I heard him,' said Chel. 'Yessy's smarter than people think, and his memory is unbelievable. He's been hanging around here ever since he was a little kid. He showed up at our junior school a few times, remember? I don't think they knew what to do with him. Well, you can't tell how old he is, can you? But someone used to look out for him. There was always exactly enough money for pasta in his purse, until a few weeks ago.'

Archy approached the blue table. 'Good morning, Miss Brill. I'm Archy Brise.'

'I know,' said Hetty. 'Where's Sam?'

'I'm here to represent her,' said Archy, taking a seat. 'Do you have a message for Sam?'

'Yes. I'm leaving London and I won't be back. And there's something she has to know.' Hetty glanced around the café and lowered her voice. 'It's a matter of life and death.'

Archy's brow furrowed. 'Then you should go to the police.'

'Not bloody likely. But I've got to tell someone. You see, her husband Urban was an old friend of mine. So whenever I saw pictures of her, in mags or online, I took a real good look. I knew who she was the minute she walked in, wearing a flash coat and a black eye and calling herself Sam.'

'Can we make this brief? I have to catch a flight to Brazil.'

Hetty leaned over the table between them. 'Once upon a time, Urban and I had a fling. Two flings, to be honest. The first time was before he married Frankie. It didn't end well. A few years later, after Frankie passed, we bumped into each other again. That's when I started working for Edeldico, on the dark side, if you know what I mean. I used to courier goods, pass on cash and so on. It was small stuff, under the radar, but I made a living.'

Again she stopped to make sure no-one could hear her. The café was rocking with the chatter of the young crowd brought in by Chelsea, so she went on talking.

'Early last year an old friend of mine asked me to source a drug. At first I thought they meant the usual thing, cocaine or heroin. I could have got those easy, but they wanted something new.'

Archy's handsome face was impassive. 'Who is this friend?'

'You don't need to know. They asked me to source a poison. It had to be something you could slip in a drink, untraceable and unknown to the police. They was willing to pay silly money for it, so I talked to Irene.'

'The old lady who was killed in an accident with a lift? What did she know about poisons?'

'Irene learned foraging from her mother, who was hanged as a poisoner. It never come out at the time, but my Nan told me years later that Irene made a poison what killed her sister.'

'Really?' said Archy. 'That's shocking.'

Hetty drained her cup. 'All her life Irene lived with the guilt, even though she was only a kid when she done it. The first time I asked her to brew up a potion for me, she didn't want to know. But then her daughter had a stroke. They needed money to pay for physio and a decent wheelchair. Irene was half out of her mind with worry, and I kept on nagging until I wore her down. In the end she collected the same plants what killed her sister, done her magic with them and popped the poison into one of them little travel jars. I passed it on to my friend and we shared the payout.'

'When your friend asked for a poison, did you ask them what they were going to do with it?'

'Of course not. There are some questions you don't ask.'

'Do you know what use they made of the poison?'

This was getting heavy. Hetty looked at her watch. Her cab was due any minute and she'd stashed her overnight bag behind the counter. Chelsea was going to send the rest of her belongings when she had an address. She was all set for a quick getaway.

It was time to let the cat out of the bag.

'Urban's death was an accident. My friend didn't mean to kill him. And if I'd known what was going down I'd have warned him, for old times' sake.'

Archy's dark eyes widened. 'Do you mean to say Urban was poisoned?'

Hetty was unprepared for such aggressive questioning. For a moment she lost the plot. Sensing her weakness Archy leaned closer, ready to go in for the kill. Noticing the tension between them, Chelsea paused in the middle of clearing tables.

'You've gone white as a sheet, Mum. Is everything all right?'

With a shaking hand Hetty refreshed her lipstick. 'Keep an eye on my case, will you?'

Her mobile rang, but she couldn't answer it. The cab was waiting, but she was frozen by icy panic. Chelsea's voice brought her back to her senses.

'I've given your bag to the cabbie. Get a move on, Mum!'

When Archy stood up to block Hetty's way she slid past him. Her escape route was clear until he moved quickly to position himself between her and the door. She was going to have to talk her way out, and all she had to offer was information.

'I like Sam, I really do. She's a mover and shaper. I swear I'm on her side. And for her own safety, she's got to know why Urban died. Make her go to the Champagne Bar at St Pancras any Friday at eight and find someone wearing a blue fedora. Tell her not to mention me. She can use my old code name, which is "salsa". And she's got to go alone. Whatever you do, don't play the hero and go in her place. You have no idea what a can of worms that would open up.'

Archy made his move. It was only a touch on Hetty's shoulder, but she knew a citizen's arrest when she saw one. She ducked under his arm and made a run for it. Taken by surprise, Archy was a split second too slow. Broken crockery crashed to the floor. By the time he'd found his feet, Hetty was in the back of the cab.

When Archy tried to run after her Chel knelt at his feet to pick up debris from the tray he'd just dropped. 'Sorry mate, my bad.'

A sausage rolled across Archy's suede shoes, leaving a trail of ketchup. From the back seat of the moving cab, Hetty Brill blew him a kiss.

42

Estancia Arcanjo
Archy

The dirt track ran out on a bare hillside overlooking the forest. When Nina and Archy stepped out of the air-conditioned jeep, humidity wound itself around them like a living creature. The guide, a thin man who wore his long hair in a pony tail and spoke good English with a nervous drawl, lifted down their backpacks before taking a cigarette from behind his ear. When he struck a match, the flame trembled in his hand. 'This is as far as I go. Walk North to find the place. Make sure you are back here one hour before sundown.

Nina slung her bag over her shoulder. 'What if we get lost? We're five hours from the city, and it's been miles since we had a phone signal.'

Archy said, 'If you come with us to show us the way, we'll pay you double when we get back to the city.'

The guide took a last drag of his cigarette and threw it down. 'I have four children. Three boys, one girl.'

'Okay, so you need the money. We'll pay whatever you ask.'

'Not everything is about money. I want to see my kids grow up.' He slid into the driving seat and put his foot on the ignition. Minutes later, the jeep was out of sight.

Nina said, 'I wonder what that guy's afraid of?'

'Whatever it is, it's not our problem. This looks like a logging camp. Maybe we can find a lumberjack and pay him to guide us.'

Beyond the broken gate a wooden sign was propped against a rusting tractor. In faded letters it read, 'Estancia Arcanjo'. Further on, dismantled engines and broken pulleys lay at random across several hectares of bare earth. While Nina and Archy made their way across the cratered site they realised it was a long time since the ranch had been a going concern.

'Come on, we can do this by ourselves,' said Archy. 'How hard can it be to walk North?'

He led the way down a steep path into the forest. At the bottom of the hill they found themselves blinking in the dim light of a cathedral-sized space. Swollen tree trunks disappeared a hundred feet above their heads into a dense canopy of leaves. Drips of water fell from unseen heights to the forest floor.

'What's that noise, Archy?'

'Parrots. Macaws. Maybe monkeys too, way up in the trees.'

'How do you know? Do you remember them from when you were little?'

'I have vague memories from back then, but I can never hold on to them. Have you ever seen fish coming up to feed at the edge of a lake? Their mouths gape as if they're trying to tell you something, but they dive back into deep water before you find out what it is. That's what it's like with my memories.'

The path became narrower and more overgrown, but there were traces of human use. From a white stone here, a plank lying flat there, somewhere a stake driven into the ground, Archy made out the traces of a broken track. Following an imaginary line across the forest floor, he constantly checked his compass. Nina followed close behind. Thinking their own they lost all sense of time, until Nina broke the silence.

'The sounds have changed,' she said.

Archy stopped to listen. Above the shrieks of unseen birds a dull roar was welling up out of the forest.

'It sounds like heavy traffic,'he said, 'But there's no motorway around here.'

The roaring became louder three hundred metres further on, where the forest thinned out. A low carpet of vegetation ran up to the top of a steep slope. Above the ridge was only sky.

Nina pointed at the ground. 'I'm sure people once lived here. Look, there are paths criss-crossing in all directions. Does this place look familiar to you?'

For a second, Archy imagined he saw human shadows against the skyline. He blinked, and they were gone. 'In my recurring dream there's a wooden cabin. The door's open. Someone wraps a yellow blanket around me. A dark-skinned woman holds out a piece of fruit. A man laughs and a child giggles. I think the child is me.'

Archy hunkered down, took a knife from his backpack and dug in the damp mulch on the forest floor. When the compacted earth beneath it resisted his blade, his eyes welled up. 'No wonder our guide chooses to live in the city. There, he has a chance of surviving and educating his children. What must it have been like for my Mum and Dad, trying to make a living from this barren soil? They had to struggle in the heat to fertilise and hydrate it. When the killers came, they can't have had any fight left in them.'

Sweat and tears dripped from Archy's chin. Nina gently wiped his face and handed him a water bottle. He drank deeply. 'We've taken enough risks for today. By the sound of it, there's a busy road beyond that bank. We might catch a phone signal. Maybe I can text the guide to pick us up.'

Quickly they took photographs of the deserted settlement. Now that their quest had reached some sort of resolution, they were conscious of the shadows cast by the sinking sun. While they checked the equipment in their backpacks and sprayed themselves with insect repellent, the heavy tree canopy above them seemed to sink closer.

'There's something over there that looks like the remains of a log hut,' said Nina.

'You stay here with the bags. I'll go and have a look.'

Archy strode up the slope to a level patch of ground. Along its boundaries rotting logs stood upright, as if they had once formed part of the walls of a cabin. If this was his childhood home it must have been abandoned over twenty years before, but it was as bare of vegetation as if it was trodden on every day. However, he could see no proof that anyone had ever lived there. He decided it was time to leave this place of uncertain memories and certain danger. Onwards and upwards, he told himself.

At the summit of the earth bank mud and engine oil were deposited in thick layers. In the same moment when Archy saw the raging torrent below, his foot slipped. When he crashed into the flood and sank below the surface he thought he was about to die. Then he stopped thinking and allowed his strong and well-trained muscles to take over. A strong swimmer, he was compelled by instinct and training to power upwards. When at last he reached the surface and could see again, he tried to grasp one of the huge exposed tree roots dangling over him. He opened his mouth to shout to Nina for help, and a rough-coated dead thing washed into his throat. While he gagged and spat, a current dragged him back into the heart of the river.

Archy was being pulled under. Water crashed into his mouth and nose and unseen objects struck him on his head and body. Some were hard like wood or plastic. Others were soft like the bodies of animals. A snake ten feet long swam past him underwater. Live creatures trapped with him in the flood clawed at his skin, as if begging him to save them. In his mind's eye he stood at the open door of a hut. His mother was sitting on the floor, offering him a slice of papaya. His father was laughing at something she said. They were strong young people with happy faces, his mother's dark, his father's fair. He had something very important to tell them. Then he heard his own voice screaming above the roar of the water.

'Mum! Dad!'

When he regained his senses Archy was splashing in a backwater. From the bank Nina was holding out a broken branch. He seized it and his feet touched bottom. He did his best to haul himself back on to firm ground, but the bank crumbled under his clutching hands and feet. Without warning a heavy section of soil slid down the bank and into the water.

Nina screamed.

When the earth and stones stopped falling the landslide had exposed layers of rock. Archy, an experienced climber, ascended them like steps, using his free hand to grab any ridge that offered him leverage. Safe on the bank, he threw himself on his stomach and vomited. Sobbing, Nina lay down beside him.

'Archy, are you okay?'

'I will be in a minute.'

'Why isn't this river on the map?'

'The map is wrong. The guy we bought it from cheated us.'

After he had caught his breath Archy crawled as near as he dared to the flood. He found himself staring down at what looked like a disturbed graveyard. Not only had the landslide dug a crevice in the bank, but the fallen earth had exposed several metres of subsoil. Nina crept up behind him.

'Look, Archy,' she said.

Two long-buried human skulls had been washed out of the bank by the flash flood.

'Quick,' said Archy. 'Get a camera from the bags.'

It was too late. The river had pounded into the gap, hiding what it had once exposed. When the water drained away it took with it the skulls, a few bones and more of the subsoil. A large piece of ragged fabric was trapped in the wall of the bank, half in and half out of the earth. Cleansed by the raging water, the blanket was pale in colour. Once upon a time, it might have been yellow.

'Archy, it's a yellow blanket, like the one in your dream. What shall we do?'

'Get out of here. fast. It's getting dark.'

The route back to the abandoned logging station seemed twice as long as it had on the way out. Nina developed a blister and began to limp. In spite of his own weariness, Archy carried her the last hundred metres on his back.

'There's the jeep.' Archy's voice was shaky with relief. 'Can you walk?'

Nina slid to the ground. 'I'll catch up. You go ahead. Don't let the guide leave without us.'

After he had stumbled half-way across the abandoned Estancia, Archy realised that although the jeep waiting on the track was the same one that had brought them from the city, the man coming to meet him was a stranger. His head was shaved, the leather jacket stretched across his powerful shoulders was slashed with knife cuts, and his jeans were stained with what looked like engine oil. In contrast to the rest of his appearance, he had a baby face with small features.

'Welcome back,' said the new guide as soon as Archy was within earshot.

'Where's the other guy?'

'You look like shit. What happened?'

'I fell into a river that wasn't on the map.'

'Around here, new rivers appear overnight.'

'How is that possible?'

'Developers cut down rain forests to plant beans. The water has to go somewhere.'

Nina hobbled up to join them. When she saw the new guide she frowned.

'Where's the other guy?'

The stranger took their backpacks and tossed them on to the front seat of the jeep.

'He went for a walk.'

The cicadas were droning. Night was about to fall. Archy weighed the unknown risks of getting into a car with this sinister stranger against the known risks of a night in the forest, and made his choice.

'We'll wait for him to come back.'

'I'm Dudu,' said the new guide. 'Allow me to drive you. É o meu trabalho. It's my job.'

43

The Champagne Bar
Samvida

I was shocked to learn that Hetty Brill had recognised me immediately when I arrived in Coopers Hook. She told Archy she'd
been following me in the media because she and Urban once had
a fling. That was a mental image I could live without. She also
told him that if I wanted to know why Urban died, I should go to
a certain bar in central London and talk to someone wearing a
fedora. Archy advised me not to go alone. He said he'd go with
me after he and Nina returned from their heritage trip to Brazil. I
agreed - but I was lying. I couldn't wait to find out who'd killed
my husband.

I wouldn't have been in such a hurry if I'd known what I was
about to find out.

One afternoon I took a cab to St Pancras. Some of the crowd
in the champagne bar were having pre-drinks before a night out.
Others were celebrating with office colleagues. Many of them

had just got off a Eurostar train or were about to board one. You look at crowds differently after you realise how many people are up to something nefarious. Everyone looked suspicious to me, but I saw no-one rocking gangster headgear. I bought a glass of champagne and took a seat where I could see the entrance. An elderly woman was sitting in the armchair next to mine. Her hair was tucked under a jaunty hat with a leather trim. A white linen suit flattered her light brown complexion. She looked like someone's grandmother waiting to be treated to a musical. After a few minutes of watching the door I took a closer look at her hat.

The old woman was wearing a styled-up blue fedora, and I recognised the face under it. This scrubbed-up granny was Tia, the ganger from Looker Hill. I was so surprised my champagne went down the wrong way and returned up my nose. When Tia heard me splutter and cough she looked up from her iPad and snorted in disgust.

'Girl, if you don't know how to treat the good things of life, leave them alone.'

The ice was broken. Now all I had to do was strike up a conversation. Archy had given me the code name Hetty used in her dealings with Edeldico. I picked up a menu.

'I should eat before I drink,' I said loudly. 'Perhaps I'll order....salsa.'

Tia put down her iPad. 'Who sent you?'

Archy had promised Hetty he'd keep her name out of it. I didn't care what happened to Hetty, but I had to protect Archy. I decided to blame my presence on Lucan.

'I have a message for you from the CEO of Edeldico.'

Tia gasped. 'I thought Lucan was murdered on the night of the conflagration.'

'The reports were exaggerated, but someone has put him out of action for a while.'

Her eyes brightened. 'Then maybe my old friend Irene is also alive? I heard she died the same night.'

I was astonished to learn that Tia had known Irene. I could think of no connection between the two women, except that they were around the same age.

'Irene did die. I'm sorry.'

Tia looked genuinely saddened.

I said, 'Lucan is recovering in hospital. He asked me to let you know he's taken care of business.'

'So the recycling scam at Looker Hill has been closed down?'

Somehow I managed to keep my voice calm. 'Yes.'

'And the operation at Coopers Hook is secure?'

It was news to me that Lucan's corrupt dealings had affected the London backwater where I'd taken shelter.

'Safe as houses,' I said.

Tia chuckled. It was an upleasant sound.

'Your colleagues at Edeldico are very clever. They have passed TimePad, The Mansions and Looker Inc around the companies register like a spliff at a wedding. It will be impossible for the authorities to follow the money.'

I was shocked by Tia's revelations. It sounded as if Edeldico had been laundering money through several small businesses. This had happened both at Looker Hill and in Coopers Hook. Hetty had something to do with it, which meant Arlo's Café was in the mix. And because the illegal operation had been going on for some time, Urban must have been involved. I tried not to let the shock and disappentment I felt show on my face.

Tia drained her glass, refilled it from the bottle beside her and leaned over to top up my glass. That's when I realised she was tipsy. If she'd been expecting to meet a business contact, I'm sure she'd have been sober, but I'd taken her by surprise.

'I think I've seen you before somewhere. Are you Lucan's personal assistant?'

'I'm on his team.'

'Do you know Archy Brise?'

So far I'd had no difficulty in making up answers to her questions, but this one floored me. Fortunately Tia, who was turning out to be a chatty drunk, didn't wait for me to respond.

'Archy's mother Ana was my favourite niece. After she and her husband died he came to live with me in Coopers Hook. At the time I was married to an Englishman by the name of Brise. So Archy became Archy Brise. Back then I was a child-minder and poor Irene worked as a dinner lady. Archy made friends with a little boy who had a girl's name. The boy's mother was called Hetty. At the school gate Irene, Hetty and I got to know each other. It was a happy time, until Archy was taken from me and sent to boarding school. I believe after he got his degree he went to work for Edeldico.'

'Sorry,' I said, 'I haven't met him.'

I'm close to my family, so I found it strange when Tia spoke carelessly about a nephew she hadn't seen since he was eight. I asked her if she'd ever tried to get in touch with Archy.

'No,' she said. The idea seemed to surprise her. 'I had no reason to contact him.'

'It's sad that he lost both his parents. What happened to them?'

Tia took a big mouthful of champagne. 'Ana and her husband Teddy were environmentalists. They tried to prevent the destruction of the rain forest, but the developers cut them down along with the trees they were trying to save. We looked everywhere for their bodies but we never found them.'

'That's awful,' I said. 'Who was responsible?'

'The man I blame for their deaths was Urban Edeldi.'

Up until then I'd believed every word Tia said. This was a step too far.

'That's impossible. Urban never went to Brazil.'

'There was no need. It was all done through lawyers. Teddy was the brother of Urban's first wife, Frankie. After Ana and Teddy were killed, money changed hands and ownership documents were forged. By legal means Edeldico stole the ranch my family had owned for a hundred and fifty years. Then they leased it to illegal loggers who stripped the land bare and left it derelict. We were broken, but we hoped all might yet be well. You see, we had faith in Urban's wife Frankie. Frankie and Teddy grew up in Brazil and they spoke perfect Portuguese. Frankie was kind and generous. We were sure she would give us back our land.'

'Ah,' I said. 'But Frankie….'

'Frankie died. We were still hopeful, because we thought Estancia Arcanjo would go to her daughter Nina. It was only after Urban married the gold-digger that action became necessary. A girl half his age, with no connection to Brazil! We could not allow her or her spawn to inherit the land of our ancestors.'

My heart missed a beat. Tia could only be talking about me.

Her cold eyes sparkled above the rim of her glass when she asked me if I knew how Urban Edeldi died. I wetted my dry lips with champagne.

'Remind me,' I said.

'My old friends from the school gate helped me to procure a quick-acting poison,' said Tia, leaning closer to me and lowering her voice. 'I travelled from London to Lisbon with the brew in my handbag. My nephew was working at the office of EdeldiCo Portugal. Urban and the gold-digger were due to eat lunch there. A jealous receptionist had promised to help us. Everything was in place for us to carry out our plan, but at the last minute it all fell apart.'

Tia paused. She was waiting for me to say something, but I couldn't speak. At last she continued her story.

'The gold-digger threw a tantrum. She begged her husband to take her by train to the seaside, and he agreed. My nephew had to drive me at top speed from Lisbon to Cascais. We soon tracked Urban and Vida down to a restaurant. At the next table to them some people my age were celebrating a birthday. I joined the party-goers. They were having such a good time they didn't notice the stranger among them. At the right moment I knocked over a tray to distract everyone's attention. While no-one was looking I slipped the drug into her drink.'

'Did you say her?' I stammered. 'Then why did Urban die?'

'He died because he was greedy. He swallowed his wife's drink as well as his own and died in her place. Now Samvida Edeldi controls Estancia Arcanjo. But her luck cannot not last forever. One day we will kill her.'

I thought I was going to pass out. My husband had died because he drank poison intended for me. I lifted my glass with shaking hands and drained it in one. Tia chose that moment to order another bottle and make a fuss about the vintage. It gave me time to recover myself and come up with a plan. When our glasses were full again I proposed a toast to Estancia Arcanjo.

Tia clinked her glass against mine. 'When Lucan has recovered, will you ask him to give us back our land?'

'Miss Arcanjo,' I said, 'There's no need to involve the CEO. I work in Edeldico's legal department. It's my job to process land ownership documents for our Brazilian projects. I can easily change the deeds of Estancia Arcanjo in order to return the ranch to the possession of your family. No-one will notice. I doubt if anyone at Edeldico remembers the place exists.'

I didn't know how I was going to make this happen. All I was thinking about was how to stay alive.

'But we cannot afford to pay you,' said Tia with a frown. 'The Arcanjos are poor.'

'There's no charge,' I said. 'But some day I might ask you to do me a favour.'

Tia said, 'If you can pull this off it will make Dudu very happy. He sold his soul to Urban Edeldi to try to get our estancia back. He did everything for that man from driving a limousine in Lisbon to making porno films.'

Dudu had made porn for Urban. Here was my chance to find out who secretly made the film that implicated me in sexual homicide and murder. It was because of this fake film that Lucan had been able to blackmail me. I was on the edge of my seat, hoping Tia would say more, when her phone rang.

'My sister is calling. I have to tell her what you have promised to do for us. Yo! Tenho boas noticias sobre a Estancia Arcanjo!'

I got out while the going was good. Halfway down her second bottle, Tia didn't notice me leaving.

44

Estancia Arcanjo
Dudu

Nina slapped at a bug. 'We can't stay the night in this godforsaken place. Pay him whatever he asks. What difference does it make? We've already paid out a fortune in bribes.'

'Shut up, woman,' said Dudu. 'And stay there. Men are talking.'

Grasping Archy by the arm, Dudu propelled him along the dust track. They stopped when they were almost out of Nina's earshot. From where Archy stood, close behind the jeep, he could see a piece of cloth dangling from the trunk. It was soaked with a dark liquid. A heavy drop fell and was absorbed into the dry earth.

Dudu released Archy and looked him up and down. 'Don't you remember your old friend Dudu, city boy?''

Archy was sure the man meant no good, but his name evoked long-forgotten tastes and smells. A clash of emotions threw him off balance. The withered landscape of Estancia Arcanjo seemed to vibrate around him. Dumb mouths gaped at the edge of a lake of memories.

'Sorry mate,' he said. 'We haven't met.'

'How can you deny me after we went through so much together?'

Archy was at a loss to understand why the stranger was behaving like a rejected lover. 'My friend is wealthy. We'll pay whatever you ask if you take us back to our hotel.'

'I don't want your money.'

'Then what's the deal?'

'I am not the deal maker. It was you who travelled from London to view Estancia Arcanjo.'

This made sense to Archy. His contacts had told him there was a long-standing dispute over the ownership of the ranch. It was possible Dudu had been hired to scare off prospective buyers.

'If you think I'm planning to develop the site, you're wrong. We're on holiday.'

'You don't fool me,' said Dudu with a sneer. 'Businessmen never stop working, even on vacation. They are always looking for new ways to grow their profits.'

'This isn't a business trip. My friend and I are environmentalists. We're exploring the rain forest.'

Nearby a young brazilwood was struggling to survive. Pointing at it, Dudu shouted to Nina at the top of his voice. 'Woman, what is the name of this tree?'

Nina yelled back. 'How should I know?'

'You see?' said Dudu. 'Her father tore down our rain forests and killed our fish to make her rich, but she cannot name one tree.'

Out of the corner of his eye Archy was watching the dark

liquid dripping from the boot of the jeep. The drops followed each other faster and faster. They looked like blood.

'Urban Edeldi stole the land from the Arcanjos,' said Dudu. 'I want it back. Help me or take your punishment.'

For a second, Archy was very afraid. Then his business brain kicked in. Edeldico owned many abandoned chunks of land in hidden corners of the world. Most of them had been purchased by Urban. They had been run down and were waiting to be picked up by speculators. Estancia Arcanjo must be one of them.

'If you want to buy this property from Edeldico, there's no problem. You can have it dirt cheap. As soon as we get back to the city I'll start work on the deal.'

Dudu's face was a mask of scorn. 'I will not pay for what was stolen from me.'

Archy tried a different approach. 'The truth is, Nina and I came here to research my family roots.'

'You have no roots. Your parents are dead and the forest is dying. There is nothing left but this miserable piece of land. Give it to me.'

'Okay,' said Archy. 'But there will have to be due process.'

Without another word Dudu punched him to the ground.

Although Dudu was strong, he was at least forty. Archy knew he could hold him off for long enough to give Nina a chance to escape. He braced himself before head-butting Dudu in the belly. The two men overbalanced and fell together. Archy wrapped his legs around Dudu's and hung on for dear life. Rolling together across the uneven ground, they gouged at each other's eyes and landed punches and kicks where they could. Archy was young and strong, but the older man was a hardened fighter. When Archy managed to free one arm and reach for his pocket knife, Dudu moved fast.

Archy was pinned down with the point of his own blade at

his throat. With what he feared might be his last breath, he called out, 'Nina! Run!'

Suddenly the jeep's engine roared into life. It was moving towards the struggling men. Archy rolled out of its path, but Dudu's reactions were too slow. By the time he realised the vehicle was headed straight for him it was too late. A tyre had crushed his legs and was embedded in his abdomen.

Archy hauled himself to his feet and stumbled to the rear of the jeep. His hands shook as he released the catch of the trunk. The dead body of the pony-tailed guide who had driven them from the city that morning was curled up inside. His throat had been cut.

Nina was at Archy's side with her phone in her hand.

'There's no signal. What are we going to do?'

'How did you start the jeep?'

'I didn't. He must have left the engine running and the brake off.'

'Keep well clear of it while I see to Dudu.'

When Archy spoke his attacker's name for the first time, a memory he'd been suppressing for most of his life hit him like a bullet.

Eyelids flickering, breath shallow and gasping, Dudu was moving in and out of consciousness. At boarding school Archy had trained in a cadet troop. When he looked down at the injured man, everything he knew about how to deal with an emergency flashed in front of his eyes. He was incapable of allowing another human being, even a murderer, to die without trying to help. They were many miles from the nearest hospital and there was no phone signal. Archy decided to search the jeep for drugs to ease Dudu's inevitable death.

In the jeep under the dead guide was a blood-drenched first aid kit packed full of cocaine. As Archy laid his body at the foot of the tree Nina had been unable to name, he thought of the man's children waiting for him to come home. Then he took a bag of cocaine and a bottle of water and went to kneel beside Dudu. He poured some of the water on the dying man's lips.

'Dudu, you stole me from my parents and smuggled me into England. Why?'

The reply came in gasps. 'Land developers shot Ana and Teddy. I buried them. You watched from the forest. I took you to Aunt Tia to be looked after. Then Urban took over.'

Ana and Teddy. His parents. Now only one piece of the puzzle was missing.

'Who am I, Dudu? What's my name?'

'You are an Arcanjo, like me. Your given name is Marcelo.'

Marcelo Arcanjo. The name rang in Archy's ears like a bell.

'You're lying. The land developers paid you to kill my parents. That's why you buried them in secret. You kidnapped me in case I told people what I'd seen.'

Dudu's eyes were full of tears. 'I need a priest.'

Archy held the cocaine under his nose. 'You want absolution? Breathe deep.'

When Dudu was dead Archy scattered the rest of the cocaine on and around Dudu's body. Then he went to look for Nina. He found her crouching a few metres away from the jeep.

'Put your hands up and turn around,' she whispered.

Archy raised both arms above his head, swivelled around and froze. A tall, thin young woman was threatening him with a machete. Her features were scarred and her bare limbs were marked by untended injuries. She wore a green dress with a black leather jacket and high-heeled sandals. Her wrists and ankles were weighted with chains hung with open padlocks. A jewelled choker shone through her long dark hair.

'We won't hurt you,' said Nina. 'What's your name?'

'I am Quila.'

She threw down the machete and Archy kicked it into the undergrowth.

'I'm Nina. He's Archy. Why are you here?'

'Dudu give me drugs like always. He don't lock chains, first time ever. I wake up. Keys there. Engine start. I drive over him.'

'Take off your chains,' said Archy. 'Dudu is dead.'

'Dead? No more rape? No more pimp out? No more porn film?'

Nina said, 'Never again.'

With a lithe movement Quila shucked her chains. Then she crawled into the back seat of the jeep and passed out. Archy and Nina looked at each other.

'What do we do now?' said Nina.

Archy said, 'Drive like hell.'

He took the wheel and Nina climbed in beside him. They both tried not to think about the two dead bodies they were leaving behind at Estancia Arcanjo. When Archy reversed over what was left of Dudu, Nina covered her eyes with her hands.

By the time they stopped on the outskirts of the city, night had fallen. Nina waited in the jeep while Moe bought petrol and food. When he was back in the driver's seat, Quila's ashen face appeared between them.

'Junk in porta-luvas. Give.'

Nina took a bag from the glove compartment and passed it to her. When her craving was satisfied Quila accepted some water and a cracker. Nibbling, she peered at Nina. 'Girl, you look like Dudu boss. Old man have white hair, scar here.' She drew a line across her forehead with her finger.

'Maybe. No big deal. My father employed hundreds of people, all over the world.'

'You rich. How much you pay for necklace?'

When the choker Quila had been wearing fell into Nina's lap, she cried out and held it to her heart.

'Where did you find this, Quila?'

'Dudu give me. At Looker Hill he make me wear it in porno film. My friend in porno too. Something happen and my friend die. Dudu say accident. He take me away, say necklace makes him horny, gives it me. How much you pay?'

'These are the finest Brazilian emeralds,' said Nina, caressing the choker.

When Archy saw tears rolling down her face he assumed it was a reaction to trauma. As a result of their attempt to find out where he was born two men had died violent deaths - one of them in front of their eyes. He himself had almost died when he fell into the flash flood. Nina must have been terrified when she saw him go under the water. If he'd been lost she'd have been left alone in the forest. It was no wonder she was freaking out.

He parked up and put his arms around Nina. While she was weeping on his shoulder he recalled the story of Lucan's quarrel with Vida, when pearls fell from the sky on to Canary Wharf. To keep the peace Urban had given each of them a present. Vida's gift was an emerald choker.

'Don't cry,' he said. 'The emeralds are yours now.'

'They were always mine.'

Archy didn't question her. He was having enough trouble coping with his own traumas.

After they reached the city they stopped at every cashpoint from the outlying suburbs to the centre. When Quila woke up she demanded to be dropped at a bus station. Nina and Moe handed over a thick wad of cash and watched her disappear into the night.

Nina fastened the choker around her neck. 'We left two bodies behind. The police will be looking for us.'

Archy shook his head. 'Estancia Arcanjo is in the back of beyond. Dudu and the guide won't be found for days. And the police will assume they died in a gang battle. We'll dump this jeep and call Edeldico's local agent. He'll have us on a plane before dawn.'

'I'm glad I'm rich,' said Nina. 'You can get out of any kind of trouble if you have money.'

On the way back to their hotel, Nina fell asleep. When rain began to fall Archy turned on the windscreen wipers. Marcello Arcanjo, they sang. Marcello Arcanjo. Marcello Arcanjo. As Archy had predicted, he and Nina watched the dawn from business class in a plane bound for London.

45

Edeldico HQ
Samvida

For the time being I felt safe. I'd rented a flat close to Nina's and Gus was staying with me while he waited for his A-level results. Archy had almost finished sorting out the financial mess created by Urban's sudden death. But I wasn't out of danger yet. Urban had made a faked sex film, hoping to intimidate me into giving up my inheritance. This film was in the possession of Lucan, who was still the CEO of Edeldico. And as long as Tia and her extended family believed I owned Estancia Arcanjo, they had a motive to murder me.

My future safety depended on Lucan and Tia, both of whom hated me. There was only one way to take back control of my life. I had to become the CEO of Edeldico.

Because Urban had failed to make a will, as his legal wife I automatically inherited all his property. This meant I owned a big chunk of the firm he founded. If I was brave enough, nothing could stop me taking control. I knew I had the ability to achieve my target. I chose not to go to university, but I did well at school. And before I took a temporary post at Edeldico I'd worked short-term contracts with high-flying finance firms. Along the way I'd learned that having testosterone, a wealthy family and letters after your name doesn't make you a whizz at business. Lucan was the living proof of this.

In order to succeed in my takeover bid I needed the support of my friends - and Lucan. That's why I enlisted Archy's help before I called a meeting. Archy was my secret weapon. While I was researching Edeldico I'd discovered he was a financial genius - the kind of guy who makes a million every day before breakfast. In spite of this he hadn't been headhunted for top jobs. Maybe this was because he didn't go to Oxford or Cambridge and his family background was a mystery. Or it might have been because he was a stickler for following the rules. Whatever the reason, I was fortunate to have Archy by my side.

The shareholder I was most worried about was Nina. Since she and Archy returned from South America she'd been quieter and less flamboyant than usual. Both of them had a secretive air. They seemed to be very close, but I was sure they weren't sleeping together. The vibe I was getting from them was tender, but not romantic. I was curious about their relationship, but I had to wait until they were ready to share.

Lucan was recovering from being mugged at the carwash in Coopers Hook. After being in a coma for three days, his mobility was poor and he'd lost his short-term memory. He even appeared to have forgotten he'd tried to blackmail me. Out of consideration for his condition Nina, Archy and I agreed to meet in his office. When he hobbled in on crutches I almost felt sorry for him - but this didn't change my plan to take advantage of his weakness.

To support my bid to head up Edeldico I'd created a stunning report. The content was down to Archy, but if I say so myself, I'd done a superb job on the presentation. While Nina and Moe were studying their copies and Lucan was trying to find his glasses, I began my pitch.

'As you know, when Urban and I married his previous will was automatically revoked. Because he owned property in several countries, there were all kinds of difficulties with making a new will. Unfortunately he died before it was ready to sign. As Urban's widow I inherited fifty percent of Edeldico. Nina and Lucan, you each own twenty per cent. The remaining ten per cent is shared between overseas investors. Because I own the largest share, I intend to head up the firm myself.'

Nina, Archy and I had a long conversation after they returned from Brazil. We'd shared some, but not all, of the information we held. They knew about my plans for Edeldico, so they nodded in agreement. Lucan was struggling to read the tiny font I'd deliber-ately chosen for the hard copies. He'd only read a few para-graphs when he threw down his glasses.

'Your report is competent but dull,' said Lucan. 'You have no vision for the firm's future.'

This was the moment I'd been waiting for. I said, 'My vision is for us to become Angels.'

Lucan groaned. 'I refuse to go down the route of Angel Investment. It's impossible to evaluate the potential of start-ups. Hardly any of them can write an acceptable business plan. And there's no guarantee of a decent return on our money.'

'True. But on the positive side, nobody dies,' I said.

Somewhere in his addled brain Lucan must have recalled that Urban, Irene and the nameless slave at Looker Hill had all been killed because of corrupt business practices. When he didn't respond, I pressed on.

'I've made a list of start-up entrepreneurs I intend to fund. It's all in Section….'

Archy was ready to support me. 'Section 3.6. The first entrepreneur's name is Bushra. Her proposal is to create and market fashionable but modest clothes for women.'

'How is that different from all the other fashion startups?' said Lucan.

I said, 'Bushra grows dye plants in a community garden. She uses them to make natural dyes for outfits she designs herself. She hopes to rent a small shop and invest in developing a range of organic fabrics.'

Archy moved on fast. 'Next up is Folu, who proposes to start a food enterprise.'

'Who is this person? What does he know about running a restaurant?' said Lucan, opening his eyes.

I said, 'Folu is a talented fusion cook. She only wants to borrow enough money to set up a food stall.'

I hadn't yet tasted any of the dishes Folu enthused about. However, I was willing to risk a few hundred pounds of the firm's money to give her a better chance in life.

Lucan managed to stay awake while Archy read out the rest of my report. He looked so exasperated I expected to see steam coming out of his ears.

'This list is pure fantasy,' he said. 'Why should Edeldico offer more than the market price to buy somebody called Viv O'Callaghan out of a protected tenancy? Or write off a loan taken out in the name of Arlo Greer? We won't make any money this way.'

It was time to lay my cards on the table.

'This isn't about profit, Lucan. Hideous crimes have been

committed in the name of Edeldico, and I want to make amends.'

I waited for Lucan to try to prove me wrong, but he said nothing. That's how I knew my suspicions were correct. The knowledge gave me the confidence to make my final, crucial moves.

'Archy, I want you to take possession of Estancia Arcanjo.'

Lucan's eyelids had been drooping again, but this woke him up. 'Why are you making Brise a present of one of Edeldico's overseas properties?'

I hadn't expected such a direct question. My mind was racing. What answer could I give? That the Arcanjos were prepared to kill for a barren tranch of earth? That they'd accidentally murdered Urban in a botched attempt to do away with me? That I'd promised Tia Arcanjo to return the land to its true owners, and if I wanted to stay alive I had to make it happen?

Fortunately Nina spoke up. 'Archy and I visited Estancia Arcanjo while we were in Brazil. The ownership of the ranch is disputed. In view of the low value of the land, it will be more cost-effective to abandon our claim than to fight it through the courts.'

Nina's words struck Lucan as funny. He burst out laughing and went on guffawing until it hurt. He asked Nina to pour him a glass of water, so that he could take a painkiller. When he could speak again he said, 'As CEO of Edeldico, I oppose the gifting of Estancia Arcanjo to Archy Brise. And you know you can't do it without my approval.' Then he lay back in his chair, folded his hands and closed his eyes.

It looked as if my endeavours were doomed to fail - until Nina spoke up. She'd told me a lot about what happened when she and Archy were in Brazil, but I was sure she was keeping something back. What she said next surprised and delighted me.

'As Luc won't agree to return the land freely, I'm willing to buy Estancia Arcanjo from Edeldico and gift it to my cousin Marcelo.'

Lucan opened his eyes a crack. 'What did you say?'

'She means me,' said Archy. 'I am Marcelo Arcanjo.'

Suddenly Lucan was wide awake. 'So that's why Urban gave you the internship. He probably paid for your education too. He must have been carrying out poor Frankie's last wishes. After Ana and Teddy disappeared, she was so distressed she couldn't bear to hear their names mentioned.'

'Tell me more about Ana and Teddy,' said Archy.

Maybe Lucan realised he'd said too much. Or perhaps he was genuinely suffering the after-effects of his injuries. His eyes had closed again and he was snoring.

At that moment I was too excited to worry about the ups and downs of the dysfunctional Edeldico family. All I could think of was that Nina supported my plans, and she was prepared to put her own money up front to implement them. But Archy had other ideas.

'I can't let you do this for me, coz. Anyway, your wealth is tied up in property. It would take a very long time for you to raise the cash.'

'Not as long as it will take you to prove your identity and claim whatever you're entitled to inherit from my Uncle Teddy.' Nina took a jewellery box from her bag. 'We have to move fast to get Edeldico back on its feet. And I have portable goods whose value will more than cover the price of Estancia Arcanjo.'

She opened the box. Nestled inside it were my own wedding and engagement rings. I hadn't seen them since I slipped them on to Nina's unresponsive fingers after our fight at the Penthouse. I gasped when I saw the glittering neck-piece curled up beside them. It was the missing emerald choker.

'Nina,' I said, 'Where did you find my emeralds?'

'They're not yours, Samvida. They used to belong to my mother, so they're mine now. A slave girl called Quila was forced to wear the choker in porn films. She sold it to us while we were in Brazil. Now I know where Mum's emeralds have been, I can never wear them again. I want to sell them to help repay Marcelo for the injustice my family inflicted on his.'

'Let's take a vote,' said Archy. 'All those in favour of Samvida becoming CEO of Edeldico and Estancia Arcanjo being gifted to me, please raise your hands.'

Nina and Archy put their hands up. Lucan went on snoring.

'Three in favour and one abstention,' said Archy. 'Congratulations boss.'

My plan depended on one final step. I had to get hold of the flash drive and destroy it. However, I wasn't sure if the new damaged Lucan remembered that he'd tried to blackmail me. And I had to get Nina out of the room. I didn't want her to find out that her beloved father had taken the leading role in a murderous sex film.

I said the first thing that came into my head. 'This calls for a celebration. It's almost lunchtime. Nina, please will you go to the dining room and order something delicious?'

She frowned. 'Why don't you ask one of the PAs?'

'Because you'll order the good stuff,' said Archy. 'Nobody has better taste than you. And while you're gone I'll make sure your jewels are locked away in the safe.'

When the door had closed behind Nina, Archy said, 'What's going on, Samvida?'

It was Archy who led me to the meeting pod on Floor Six, so he knew there was unfinished business between Lucan and me.

I said, 'My future with EdeldiCo depends on a flash drive. I think it's in Lucan's safe.'

Lucan looked puzzled. 'Have I got a safe?'

'Yes, you have,' I said. 'This office used to be Urban's. There's a safe behind that ugly oil painting.'

'If there is a safe,' said Lucan, 'There's probably nothing in it.'

'Let's have a look,' said Archy. 'Our new CEO is obviously not going to discuss terms with you until the matter of the flash drive has been resolved.'

'I've forgotten the combination,' said Lucan. 'My memory is in pieces.'

At that point I was ready to give up hope. While Lucan had the flash drive I remained under his control. He could destroy my reputation whenever it suited him. Then what would become of my dream of transforming Edeldico into an ethical investment firm?

Archy saved the day. He strode over to where the safe was located, lifted down the painting and propped it against a wall. 'It's okay, Lucan. I've often watched you entering the combination. You should be more careful with your personal data.'

Minutes later the flash drive lay on the table. The handbag I'd left in the pod was there too, with my passport and phone inside. Lucan's hand shot out to retrieve the tiny but powerful piece of tech, but Archy was too fast for him. He grabbed the flash drive and dropped it into the glass of water.

Just then we heard Nina talking to the PAs in the outer office. By the time she entered the room, her jewellery was in the safe, the flash drive was hidden in my bra and Lucan was glaring in outraged silence at Archy, who was changing the safe's combination.

'Gosh,' Nina said. 'I haven't seen that bag since....'

'What's for lunch?' said Archy.

While we were enjoying the delicious food and wine Nina had selected, Archy asked me for the title of Vice-President. I said yes. As long as he helped me to create a socially responsible Edeldico, I didn't care what he called himself. Lucan reluctantly agreed to be a sleeping partner, on condition that his status would be renegotiated when he'd fully recovered from his accident.

As I write, that time has not yet come. If I have my way, it never will.

Printed in Great Britain
by Amazon

17990604R00169